No Good Deed...

THE ADVENTURES OF ELSABETH SOESTEN

NO GOOD DEED...

FORTHCOMING

BAIT AND SWITCH

PRIZE PLAY

THE GONNES OF NAVARRE

THE CONFESSION AT GODRA

THE ADVENTURES OF ELSABETH SOESTEN

NO GOOD DEED...

D. E. WYATT

Wyrmfyr Press
St. Louis, Missouri
2020

This is a work of fiction. Some characters, settings, and events have been inspired by historical record, but any direct depiction of historical events and individuals both living and dead is unintentional.

The Adventures of Elsabeth Soesten: No Good Deed...

Copyediting by Debbie Manber Kupfer
Cover Art by Rebecca Frank, Bewitching Book Covers, LLC
(bewitchingbookcovers.com)
Heraldry image resources sourced from HeraldicArt.org

Second Edition

ISBN-13: 978-0-578-75673-8

For my father, who put Tolkien in my hand and helped
start me on this journey.

A NOTE FROM THE AUTHOR

A number of terms contained within this work may be unfamiliar to you, the reader. As such, I have provided a glossary at the end of the book for your convenience, along with a quick guide on how to read the blazons for the coats of arms described herein.

NO GOOD DEED...

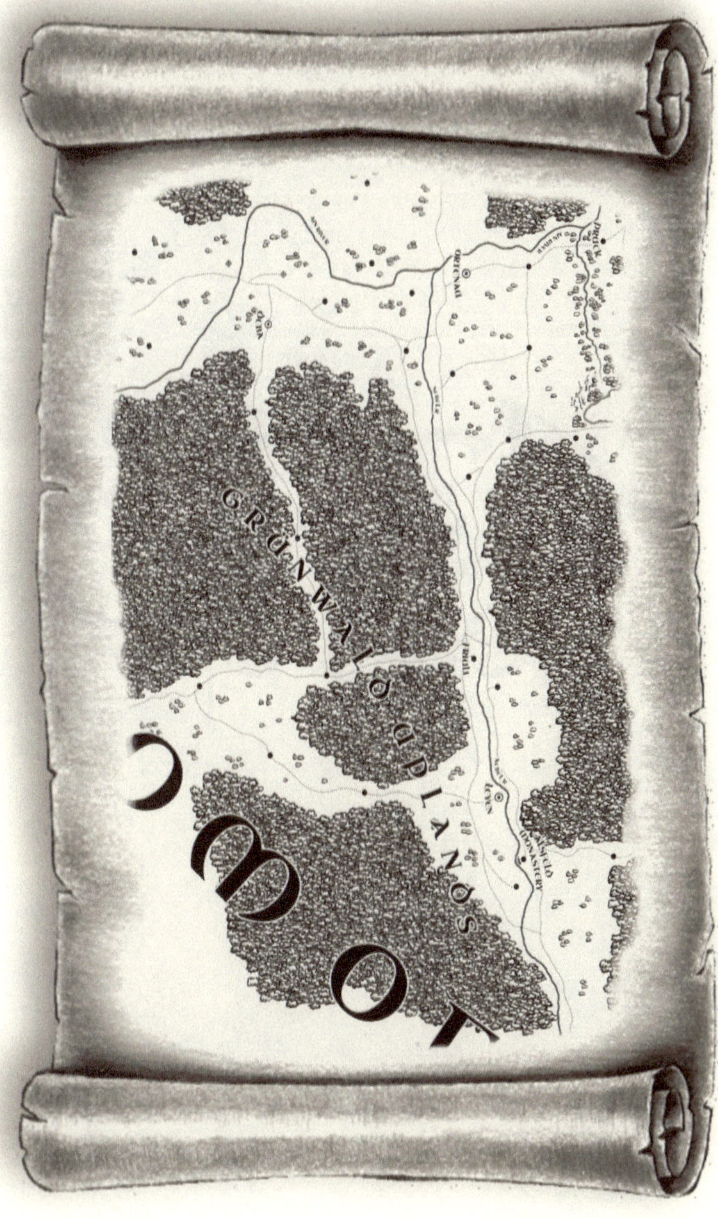

GRÜNWALD UPLANDS
ORTENAU
DRECK
LÖWEN
MONASTERY
MAISFIELD
OBRA

HE SLAP ACROSS THE SERVING GIRL'S backside cut through the din of many voices all talking over one another, and she nearly leapt out of her shoes at the sudden and unexpected blow.

Howls of laughter filled the common room of the inn, and drowned out the clatter of tankards, bowls, and cutlery. By some miracle she managed to maintain control of the tower of dirty dishes stacked high upon the tray she carried, though they swayed and rattled quite precariously. Heinrich's companions only laughed harder when she speared him with an indignant glare on her way back to the kitchens, which he avoided with a look of feigned innocence.

The inn was full that evening, though not quite bursting at its seams, and loud and boisterous enough that one's voice would not carry far from one's table. Heinrich rather enjoyed that aspect of such rustic establishments; the background rumble of so many voices speaking at once offered a measure of privacy often lacking in the more exclusive drinking halls popular amongst those of his station. Nor did he need guard himself against anyone listening in; such folk were much more earnest than his peers, who were wont to extend one hand in friendship while concealing daggers behind their backs with the other.

Heinrich leaned back at ease in his chair, and cupped his tankard in both hands.

"…'tis a two day ride west of here, Peyr," Ÿtel was saying, resuming the quarrel Heinrich interrupted with his swat at the serving girl's backside. "We ought to be gone by first light if we want to make it in time."

"And that is only because you know your own poor prospects," Peyr retorted with an amused smile tugging at the corners of his lips. "Every woman in the town watched you fall off your horse and land on your fat arse in the mud. The best you can hope for now is some pitiable glances."

Ÿtel's face heated. He was certainly a rather heavyset fellow, though his features were not unpleasant to the eye. "My damned foot caught in the stirrup!"

"Because you are a lousy horseman, and no more graceful on your own two feet. A woman — even provincial rustics such as these — admires a man who can dance without stomping all over them, or tripping over himself."

Heinrich snorted into his tankard. "And what would you know of it, Peyr? I have seen you cross yourself up strutting across a tavern floor, much less a dance floor. Even Ulrich, here, is more sure-footed, and he has been lame since his horse collapsed on him at tournament."

"Well, I have certainly had no complaints," Peyr said, his lip twisting petulantly.

"That, my friend, is merely charity," Ulrich said. "And with a face like yours, you are certainly in need of it!"

"At least I need not ride on Heinrich's coattails, and pick up the ones he leaves in his wake."

Ulrich merely shrugged. "Given his leavings would ordinarily be well beyond my mark, I have no place to complain."

Heinrich laughed. "Too true! Remember the daughter of the Count of Pfirt? I can just imagine her surprise the morning after when she discovered you were the fourth son of a lowly Ritter!"

"'Tis because you dress me so pretty when I ride in your company," Ulrich said, and blew him a mocking kiss.

"And why would I not? Anyone riding in my company ought to look the part. And fourth son or not, when one has friends in high places, one ought to avail oneself of the benefits."

"Speaking of high places," Ÿtel interjected with a roll of his eyes. "Are you not forgetting that you have business to attend to? I don't think it reflects well on you if you should be late."

"'Tis my father's business," Heinrich said. "I am only here because he cannot be troubled with it, so someone must see it done or 'twill not be done at all. Especially given the dotards he employs for menial tasks such as this."

Ÿtel opened his mouth to speak, but was interrupted when the door to the inn creaked open, and everything fell silent. A lone figure, silhouetted by sunlight spearing into the dim lamp-lit common room stepped inside. The awkward silence hanging like a pall over the inn was broken only by the distinct *clack* of pattens on the wooden floor as the stranger doffed a pair of gauntlets and approached the innkeeper. Then the tongues of those seated nearest to the door began to wag, and curious whispers became almost deafening while the patrons speculated about the newcomer.

Heinrich frowned at the sudden commotion, and peered intently at the stranger. Ÿtel twisted round in his chair for a better look, and Peyr and Ulrich craned their necks.

At first little could be made of the newcomer beyond her sex, for the stranger was, much to Heinrich's surprise, a woman. Her long coat of brown leather could not quite obscure the telltale swelling of her hips, but her face was shadowed by a black felt hat with a low, rounded crown, and broad brim pinned up at one side. Everyone, however, noted the slender longsword in the red leather scabbard slung rakishly low at her hip.

The woman disappeared upstairs after a word with the innkeeper and an exchange of coin, and the inn went back to its business.

"What was all of that about," Ÿtel said as he turned back in his seat. "You would think his Grace the Prince-Bishop himself just strolled through those doors with the way they carried on."

"I have not the slightest idea," Heinrich said.

"'Twas a woman, or so it seemed to me," Peyr said, and the others nodded their agreement. His features twisted in distaste. "'Tis an unnatural sight to see a woman so armed. Someone ought to go and take that blade away from her before she cuts herself."

"'Tis probably all for show; something to keep outlaws and the like at bay upon the road at a glance. She will be down here shortly plying her trade among these ruffians soon enough."

"Peyr may actually have a chance for some company tonight after all," Ulrich said.

"Bah! The common whores who would work in places such as this are not worth a *pfennig*."

Ulrich smirked at him over the rim of his tankard. "You know what they say of beggars and choosers. It seems you are headed for another cold and lonely night."

A creak on the stairs just audible over the din in the common room announced the strange woman's return, and the sight of her knocked the breath from Heinrich's lungs, for this was indeed no common whore.

Hidden beneath that long jacket and hat (which she had left in her room along with her sword, gauntlets, and pattens) was an exquisite woman perhaps two or three years older than his nineteen. She was tall, and possessed a slender athleticism and fluid grace of movement. Her features were set in a fair heart-shaped face framed by hair the color of burnished copper, worn scandalously free and without cover, and trailing to just below her shoulder blades. She wore a sleeveless red velvet doublet over a blouse of linen, and a pair of woolen hose that fit so closely to her lower extremities that they left nothing of the shapely curve of her backside or legs to the imagination. The slightly belled sleeves of her blouse — pulled close to her upper arms by ribbons running from her bicep to elbows, and with cuffs short enough they would not interfere with her hands — were the only real concession to femininity in her dress. When she turned at the stairs he spied a rondel in a red leather sheath matching her sword stuffed into her belt at the small of her back.

The vision scandalized most of the locals and tantalized the rest as she made for a table in a back corner, where she could put her back to the wall and watch the door. She kicked her feet up on the table, retrieved her rondel, and laid it on the table.

"What do you think of that, Heinrich?" Ÿtel said.

Heinrich took a long draught from his tankard of ale, and watched her closely from his table. He was not alone; almost every man in the inn was transfixed. An amused grin spread across Ulrich's features. One of the serving girls placed a tankard of ale and a platter of food on the table for her, and the woman nursed her drink while watching the door.

"'Tis like something out of a fairy story, is what I think," he said. "I think I am bewitched!"

"Still think she is not worth a *pfennig*?" Ulrich said.

Peyr only gawked in silence.

"I think I should go introduce myself," Heinrich finally said. He drained his tankard and thumped it down on the table. "Don't wait up for me, my friends!"

And with that, he levered himself from the table onto unsteady legs, and wove past the serving girls bearing trays laden with drinks to the waiting guests and locals. He snatched a pair of cups from a tray on his way past one of the girls, and strutted up to the woman's table.

"Good evening," he said, flashing her his most charming smile. The woman looked up from her drink, but said nothing. "Do my eyes deceive me, or has the Lord of All sent an angel among us?"

She heaved an impatient sigh and rolled her eyes. "Love, I have not had nearly enough to drink for that to do you any good."

Heinrich pouted. "Tch, I see you here alone, and could not bear the thought of leaving you unaccompanied among such rabble."

She quirked a grin, and studied him closely with narrowed eyes. Were he sober he might have recognized the mocking twist of her lip.

"Ah, so 'tis a gallant knight to my rescue, then?"

Heinrich sketched a bow. He forgot the drinks in his hand, and ale sloshed out and spilled onto the floor.

"Heinrich von Goslar, son of Burkart, Landgrave of Goslar, at your service."

"Quite a long way from home for someone so young."

Heinrich puffed out his chest. "Don't let my youthful beauty deceive you; I am a man of nineteen, and more than capable of handling myself. And you, for that matter."

"I am sure you are," she said, and took a draught from her tankard. "Now do run along and pester your nursemaid, love. I am here to meet someone."

"A fortuitous coincidence, then, for you have indeed met someone!"

Heinrich circled the table and dropped onto the bench beside her without waiting for an invitation. The woman let her feet fall to the floor, and shifted in her seat to slide away from him. Heinrich scooted closer. He offered her one of his drinks, but she made a show of the one already clasped in her hands.

"And 'tis a good thing too," he said, and leaned in conspiratorially. "A woman of your beauty, alone among such ruffians as these? 'Tis scandalous what thoughts they would entertain."

"Oh, I am certain I could imagine. Your concern and gallantry is misplaced, love. I am more than capable of handling myself."

"And do you often? Handle yourself, that is?" A self-satisfied grin pulled at one corner of his lips over the innuendo.

"More often than you realize," she said. Had he not been so deep into his cups, he might have recognized the growing irritation in her tone.

"Truly? May I say I had many a thought of handling you myself when I first saw you. I promise, I am good for it."

"You seem to have mistaken me for some common alehouse bawd. I suggest you go back to your companions before you make any bigger fool of yourself."

He clicked his tongue in rebuke, "I don't mistake you at all. You are anything but common!"

"On that we can agree, but I shall reiterate as you seem to be missing my point: I am not for sale, now be off with you, and leave me be!"

Heinrich's face heated in indignation.

"Now see here! Do you know whom you are addressing?"

"You made it quite clear, love, and I am not the least bit impressed."

He reached out with one hand and laid it upon her knee. The woman flinched under his touch, and her jaw tightened.

"You will be, come the morning."

Her eyes narrowed, and the lethal threat in her glare set the finer hairs on his neck on end.

"I warn you fairly: Remove your hand now and go back to your friends, and I'll forget the impropriety."

But he did not remove his hand. Instead, he slipped it further along the length of her thigh, and leaned towards her.

"I have been nothing if not polite thus far," he said. "The least you could offer is some appreciation!"

The woman seized him by the hair and slammed his head down onto the table. Stars exploded across his vision and the inn spun around him. Then he was flying across the table, scattering tankards and platters in all directions, before he struck the floor on the far side and lay there for a moment in a daze.

Heinrich staggered to his feet again with an effort, and felt every eye in the deathly silent common room on him. His head swam — whether from the blow or the drink he was not quite certain — and blood trickled from his nose. He now wore the woman's supper down the front of his doublet, and he was wet from head to toe from the tankards of ale he had scattered on his flight across the table.

Howling laughter erupted among the patrons, and even his own companions mirthfully beat their fists on the table. Heinrich spun around on the woman. She leaned over her table, and her green eyes watched him with a mixture of pity and no small measure of annoyance. His face heated.

"Insolent quim!" he snarled, and stormed back to her table. He pressed his hands against the table, leaned over it, and put his face in hers. "If you were not a woman I..."

His worlds trailed off in an impotent growl. But she only narrowed her eyes dangerously.

"If I were not a woman you would what?"

"I would teach you some respect, is what!"

"My sword is right upstairs, love," she said evenly, and Heinrich was taken aback by the coolness of her tone. "Don't let what I have 'twixt my thighs hold you back."

At first he could only stare at her in disbelief. And then he laughed incredulously. "Me? Fight a woman? You are not only impudent, you are mad!"

"So I see you are not only a disgusting pig, you are also a craven one."

Heinrich slammed his fist down on the table. The woman's rondel bounced into the air and landed again with a *thud*.

"No one accuses Heinrich von Goslar of cowardice! Ÿtel! My sword!"

"Your pardon?" Ÿtel said, his voice bewildered by the unexpected demand.

Heinrich spun on him and speared him with a glare. "My sword! Bring it here at once! This harpy needs a lesson in manners. Go!"

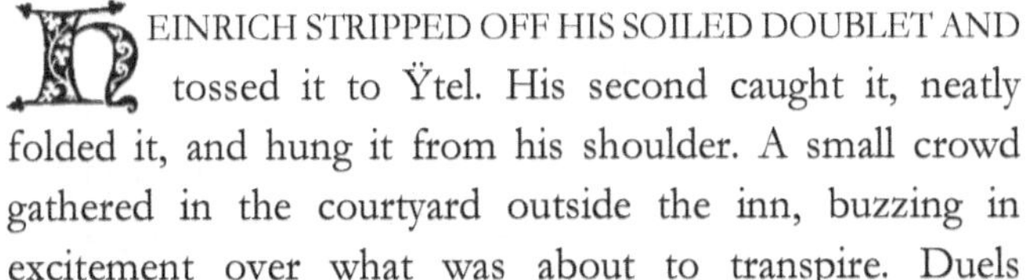

HEINRICH STRIPPED OFF HIS SOILED DOUBLET AND tossed it to Ÿtel. His second caught it, neatly folded it, and hung it from his shoulder. A small crowd gathered in the courtyard outside the inn, buzzing in excitement over what was about to transpire. Duels happened, even in such a rustic corner of the Empire as this, but no one had ever seen a *woman* fight.

He paced anxiously, like an animal trammeled within a cage. It ought to have been a pleasant evening; it was a warm summer's eve but not too hot. The sun was bright enough to give plenty of light to see by, but there was no glare to distract the combatants. The shadows stretched out with long and searching fingers as the afternoon waned, and the sky darkened in the east.

The dulling of his wits from the day's drinking had passed, and Heinrich's belly churned. He felt the eyes of the rough peasants crowding the courtyard on him, and he suddenly became aware of the ignominy that awaited him if, however unlikely, he should by some cruel stroke of fate *fall* to the sword of a woman. His father would certainly denounce him on the spot, and his friends would surely find great amusement at his expense. Heinrich tightened his jaw. He could not withdraw from the fight now, either. Too many had witnessed the challenge, and worse than the prospect of dying at her hands was the thought of being labeled craven.

If she ever showed herself.

Heinrich paced. He flexed his hands around the hilt of his sword, and sketched the occasional flourish to loosen the muscles in his back and arms. At least the crowd appreciated the deft spinning of his blade through his fingers. But whenever he looked to the door of the inn, it did not so much as budge, and the woman did not appear.

The crowd grew restless. A low murmur worked from one end to the other as they questioned whether all of this would be for nothing. Heinrich mused that perhaps he had worried himself for nothing; she was a woman, after all, and there was no face for her to lose by slipping out the back door while they watched the front.

However, the creaking of the door roused him from his private thoughts as she stepped out into the dying sunlight.

Lovely as she was under the lamps of the inn, he admitted with some chagrin that she was even more striking in the light of day, and Heinrich lamented at separating her pretty head from her slender neck. The cause for her delay was soon evident; she had taken the time to plait her long copper tresses, and pile them neatly atop her head to keep her hair from her face and prevent it from being used as a ready hand-hold by her adversary. Heinrich twisted his lip in consternation, for his hair fell into his eyes throughout his flourishing. She tugged on her gauntlets, and in this light he could see that her black leather boots were soft and supple, with thin and flexible soles well-suited to the frenetic footwork of the duel.

The woman cradled her naked longsword in her arms, and upon the sight of it, Heinrich recognized the work of a true master of his craft. The slender blade was a good four and a half spans from its hilt to the tip. Its convex profile tapered to a formidable awl-like point, and the sun glinted along the prominent rib of its hollowed diamond flats. The guard was straight and made of steel, and a matching scent-stopper pommel at the end of the waisted, red leather grip counterbalanced the blade. It made up for in the lethal elegance of its lines what it lacked in ornamentation. His own sword, with its fittings of bronze and gold and enamel, seemed suddenly gaudy by comparison, and he blushed in furious envy that she should carry so fine a blade.

The woman stepped out into the courtyard dressed in her doublet, and Heinrich scowled.

"Your doublet," he said.

"Pardon?" she said innocently.

"Off with it!"

The woman clicked her tongue.

"Really, now. Here we are on the field of battle and you still think to sneak a peek?"

Heinrich clenched his jaw at her cheek.

"If I am fighting naked in my undershirt, so do you. Now off with it!"

"Tch. Fine then," she muttered.

The woman undid the silver hooks fastening her doublet closed, and casually shrugged out of it. She tossed it aside without further complaint. When it struck the ground, the distinct rattle of metal plates echoed across the courtyard. Heinrich glared, and his face heated indignantly. A low murmur broke the silence.

"Better?" she said, with a teasing lilt to her voice, and made a show of turning in a circle so he might inspect her garb.

Heinrich fought not to think of the close fit of her hose around her bottom when she turned her back to him.

"Are you quite finished?" he said instead. "I don't relish the thought of slaughtering a woman, so I would rather get it done!"

"Well, if it weighs that heavily on your conscience, you can still back out by offering your apology for your boorishness."

He raised his sword above his head into *vom tag* and tightened his hands. "I'll not be taken for a coward!"

She sighed in annoyance and rolled her eyes. "Of course you shan't, instead you would rather die needlessly over your fool honor."

Heinrich smiled maliciously. "I don't intend to die here. My father taught me to fence from the day I took my first steps, and he was personally taught by Russdorffer himself."

The sardonic click of her tongue echoed across the square as she dropped into *alber*, her sword loose in her hands with the hilts at her hips and the blade pointed at the ground. "That base showman. Well, at least you will offer the spectators a mildly entertaining show."

"Enough talk!" he snarled, his temper flaring at the show of disrespect. "Lay on!"

Tense silence filled the courtyard while they circled one another, and shifted from guard to guard as they sought an opening. The woman moved lightly and smoothly, and trepidation tempered his wrath. She stepped with precision and without wasted motion. Through all his bluster, Heinrich never considered she might *actually* know what she was doing, and his palms grew cold as he tightened his hands round his sword hilt. If his adversary noted his new disquiet, it did not tell upon her features.

Heinrich found an opening to his liking first, and struck a powerful falling blow at her left shoulder. His adversary casually stepped into the strike and snapped her sword up into *ochs* to deflect, then followed with a stiff thrust at his face. He wound around her blade into *ochs* himself to displace her counter, and thrust down towards her hip. She hung her point to divert his strike, then snapped her sword around for a short-edged cut at the top of his head. The movement came so quickly Heinrich could not cover in time. And yet rather than the expected bite of her steel into his scalp, she instead tapped him upon the head with the flat of her sword, and lightly darted back out of range again, with her sword held in *pflug*.

He stumbled back a pace, astonished, and touched his fingertips to his head. They came away without blood, and when he caught the playful smirk tugging at her lips he realized the strike was meant only to humiliate him.

His blood boiled at her insolence, and he attacked again with renewed determination. And again she responded with quick precision, her sword dancing through her slender hands without a single wasted motion. She stepped lightly around him, toying with him like a cat playing with a hapless mouse. She was good. Very good. Heinrich did not know if she was truly *better*, but her speed and directness quickly took advantage of the showmanship that dazzled his audiences on the tournament field. Every strike he threw was met by her sword. Yet she did not press her advantage, no matter how many times she opened him for a fatal counter.

Heinrich's breath came in ragged gasps. Sweat poured down his face and slickened his palms. His chest burned; he had not fought such a prolonged bout since drilling in the yard in Goslar. Yet still she did not make a move to end the fight. If she was winded by her exertion it did not tell upon her features, and not a hair was disturbed from the plaits piled atop her head. Her expression did not slip once from that confident smirk while she played with him. And the longer the fight dragged on, the louder and more exuberant the crowd became. Shouts of encouragement mingled with the ringing of steel, and echoed across the square.

Finally, she bored of the game. He struck another falling blow at her shoulder, and she countered with a wrathful strike from above. As their blades met she exploded towards him and snaked a leg behind his. One hand jumped out onto her blade, and she hooked him round the neck with her pommel. A quick twist of her hips and shifting of her weight was all it took to throw him backwards over her hip.

Heinrich landed hard on his back, striking with enough force to drive the air from his lungs. His sword clattered from his hand, and a collective groan erupted in the square. His head bounced off the ground and his vision blurred. When it finally cleared again he found the woman's sword-point leveled at his throat.

He did not move. He dared not even scramble back from her. Instead, he rose up on his elbows and met her eyes with resignation. The playful sparkle was gone now, replaced with cold and deadly intent. His heart hammered against his breastbone, and ice formed a ball in his gut. An expectant hush settled over the crowd surrounding the square in anticipation for the final, fatal stroke to decide the contest.

And yet it did not come.

Heinrich twisted his lip impatiently. "What are you waiting for?" he said, his voice ragged from his exertion, and the prospect of death staring him in the face. "Finish it!"

"Had I wanted to kill you, love, I would have in the first exchange," she said coldly. And though she had yet to strike, there was no mistaking the lethal threat in her voice. "I offer you one last chance to apologize."

The gathering watched him expectantly. The woman's sword-point hovered so close to his throat he could nearly feel its awl-like point pricking his vulnerable flesh. Self-preservation and pride warred with one another in his head.

"Well?" she said.

"All right! All right!" he pleaded.

"You were a pig."

"Yes, I was a pig!" he said, not quite able to keep the irritation at being so coerced out of his voice.

"Tch. Apologize like you mean it, love."

Heinrich closed his eyes. He gritted his teeth and tightened his hands into fists. In the darkness shutting out the woman, her sword, and the crowd around him he drew a deep, steadying breath. Then he opened them again, and looked up solemnly upon his adversary.

"My behavior was unacceptable, and I most humbly offer you my sincerest apologies for my assaults upon your person."

He let the words hang between them. The audience watched and waited, and the woman's green eyes peered deeply into his, as if searching him down to his very soul.

And then she lifted her point away from him, and that smirk — and now he admitted it was every bit as alluring as it was aggravating — returned to her lips.

"Apology accepted," she said, and started back towards the inn.

"Wait!" he called from his back, still unable to find his legs as the relief of his life being returned washed over him. She paused and turned back. "May I at least have your name?"

She tilted her head back pridefully, and she curled a corner of her lips into a smile.

"The name is Elsabeth Soesten, love. I suggest you remember it."

LSABETH SUPPORTED HER SWORD IN ONE hand and peered along its length. She lay on her bed with her back propped up against the wall and her ankles crossed in front of her, and ran the whetstone along the edge to work out every notch and burr from her duel with von Goslar. The distinct rasp of stone on steel filled her room and drowned out the distant rumble of activity from the common room below.

The fight put her out of any desire for the company of the common room and, once it became apparent her expected companion would not be arriving that night, she had retreated to the privacy of her room to resume her interrupted supper.

She paused to take a drink from the mug of beer on the table next to her empty supper plate. The room was not particularly spacious and only meagerly appointed, with only the bed and table in the way of furniture. She hung her jacket and hat from a wall hook next to the door, and her pack occupied a corner nearby with her boots, pattens, and doublet. It was not the worst room she had ever stayed in. At least the mattress was comfortable and the drink was good, even if the company left something to be desired.

The hour grew late, and slowly the sounds of mirth and laughter — much, she suspected, at the expense of her adversary — died away until the inn was still and silent. Elsabeth ran a thumb along the edge of her sword to test it for any places she might have missed. Once satisfied with her work, she set her stone aside and picked up a cloth and little bottle of oil from her kit, and wiped down the blade and fittings. Once finished, she returned her sword to its scabbard, and she gazed for a long moment at the badge of silver, gold, and enamel fixed between the belt straps.

The badge was fashioned into a shield bearing a coat of arms — *Quarterly 1st and 4th Azure, on a bend Or three bears statant erect Sable Quarterly 2nd and 3rd Gules, two longswords in saltire proper in chief a gauntlet Or* — and a hollow, empty feeling filled her belly as she lovingly brushed her fingertips across it. Tears welled up in her eyes she quickly blinked away, and hard memories threatened to break free from the deep recesses of her mind whence she had banished them.

A knock at her door broke the peace of her room and shook her from her reverie.

She did not answer at first, hoping the intruder would go away. However the knock came again rather insistently. She sighed and slid off the bed with her sheathed sword still in hand.

"Half a moment," she grumbled. "'Tis the middle of the bloody night, so this best be important."

Elsabeth reached the door and swung it open. She found one of von Goslar's companions standing in the doorway with his hand raised to knock again. He was a heavyset fellow, though his features were still pleasant enough. She could not recall to mind his name, for she only heard it in passing when von Goslar called for his sword. She rolled her eyes and leaned her shoulder against the door jam, with her sword cradled in front of her.

"Oh this had best be good."

He stood flummoxed for a moment, but quickly composed himself. He folded his hands at his back in that official-looking manner noblemen affected when delivering matters of import, but from his fidgeting she guessed it was as much from uncertainty over what else to do with them.

"Forgive the interruption, Frau Soesten, but I was bidden by Herr von Goslar to deliver a message."

She quirked an eyebrow. "Did he, now?"

"Yes, Gnädige Frau." He reached inside his doublet and produced an envelope sealed with wax. Elsabeth let a quiet laugh escape over the thought of von Goslar lugging a full writing set around the country. "I am to read it to you, if that is necessary."

"Quite presumptuous to assume I can't read it for myself, is it not?"

His face paled, and his eyes darted to the sword cradled in her arms. "Forgive me, Gnädige Frau! I meant no offense. But 'tis not a common thing to find a woman of any station who can read."

Elsabeth clicked her tongue and held out her hand. "And I thought we had already established that I am hardly a common woman. My letters are but one of a number of things my father had the good sense to have me taught." She twitched one corner of her mouth into a meaningful smile. "Your Lord has already seen another."

"Yes, Gnädige Frau," he said, and handed her the letter. Then he bowed politely — Elsabeth raised an eyebrow again, for that was hardly the behavior one expected of a man of his station when addressing someone he presumed of hers — and made to leave her door. "Good night, Frau Soesten."

"Are you not to deliver my response? Is that not how this works?"

"Forgive me, Gnädige Frau, but Herr von Goslar bid me only to deliver the message, not await an answer, because he expects none."

Elsabeth turned the envelope in her hand, and considered the seal with some amusement. "Well, if I did not have an interest in what he had to say before, I am certainly curious now. Thank you."

He inclined his head again, then turned on his heel and departed. Elsabeth leaned around the door frame and watched him disappear into a suite of rooms at the end of the hall. She shook her head and rolled her eyes, then retreated back into her room and closed the door behind her.

Alone again, she returned to her bed once more and propped her sword upright beside the bed where it would be near at hand. Elsabeth turned the envelope in her hands again, and for a moment she considered discarding it. But von Goslar's decision to have it hand-delivered by one of his companions rather than through the innkeeper — and that he did not even anticipate a response — piqued her interest. She broke the seal with her thumb, removed the note from the envelope, and opened it.

ELSABETH LEANED OVER HIM, CUPPED HIS FACE IN one hand, and kissed him deeply. She savored the warmth of his breath and the movement of his mouth against hers. Heinrich's hand reached up to her cheek and brushed the stray hairs back from her face. The other slid down between her shoulder blades and along her back until it came to rest on her backside with a gentle squeeze. She moaned softly against his mouth, then drew away with a lingering, sucking nibble on his lower lip and settled down into the bend of his arm.

"Well," he said, breathlessly, "I can safely say this is the strangest end I have had to any duel I have fought."

She pillowed her head against his shoulder and reached her arm across his chest.

"Fought many women, have you?" she said, and a smile tugged at her lips.

"You are actually the first. I think. There was this one fellow at Wismar of whom I had suspicions."

"Well, at the very least let this serve as a lesson to you in how you treat women from now on."

He offered an embarrassed grunt and hugged her closer.

For a long moment they lay silently in his bed at the inn with the covers in disarray, flung without care towards the far end. Moonlight streamed in through the window and faintly touched everything within with silver. Heinrich's black, shoulder-length hair was plastered against his face by a light sheen of sweat from his exertions, and the moonlight glittered in his blue eyes. Though only four years her junior, his clean-shaven features made him seem even younger and lent him a beauty that by its own merits ought to make her heart flutter. The rest of him was certainly well-built enough; she traced a finger along his chest, slid her leg along his thigh, and felt the firm muscle beneath his skin.

"Far be it for me to question such a turn of fortune," he finally ventured, "but I can't help but wonder why you decided to bed me after all."

Elsabeth rested her chin on his chest, craning her neck so she could look at him. He gazed up at the ceiling, his expression somewhat wistful, and with a hint of his earlier arrogance tugging at his features.

She grinned. "'Twas quite the letter of apology you wrote. Perhaps had you approached me in that fashion, I might have been more agreeable simply as a matter of practicality."

Heinrich looked at her quizzically. "Practicality?"

"As you yourself quite aptly demonstrated earlier, when a woman enters an inn alone there are certain assumptions made about her character. And when a man thinks a woman is of a certain character, he is wont to act upon it."

He blushed fiercely at her pointedness.

"So," she continued, "I have learned 'tis best to find a suitable companion for myself, so I need not fend off the advances of every cock in the room. Tonight was only different because I was expecting to meet a friend. But he was late, and I was unexpectedly left to my own devices."

"Well, if my experience is anything to go by, that is quite the lucky friend."

Elsabeth barked a laugh.

"He is not that sort of friend! Not in the least. And don't be giving him any ideas. He has enough of them bouncing around his head.

"But at any rate, he never arrived."

"I must admit to being quite wounded that I was nothing more than a convenience for you," he said with a pout.

Elsabeth clicked her tongue and rolled her eyes.

"Don't devalue yourself too much, love. You would have been a lovely enough man were it not for your utter boorishness at our introduction. In fact 'twas your humility after you finally had the good sense to apologize for your behavior that convinced me I might have been rather harsh in my reaction."

"No, I think your reaction was perfectly justified," he said. He shifted in bed to roll over her, supporting himself on his elbow. One hand reached up to brush the hair back from her face and caress her cheek. "My earlier behavior was quite unacceptable."

Elsabeth smiled up at him. The hand on her cheek wandered down the front of her throat, and glided along her collar bones. Heinrich leaned down and kissed her again; at first a feather touch of his lips against hers as his fingers explored her chest, until he neatly filled his hand with one of her breasts. He drew her in once more into a deep, full kiss that heated her entire body from head to toe. Their tongues met and intertwined, and it seemed that Heinrich would draw the breath clean out of her lungs. She snaked her arms around his neck and drew him down on top of her.

Heinrich again broke contact with her mouth and trailed a light series of kisses from the point of her chin to the corner of her jaw. Elsabeth's heart hammered against her breastbone. Her breaths came in deep gasps at the sensation of his lips on her neck and the hand gently kneading her breast.

"As I see it, love, you still have a bit of apologizing left to do before the night is through," she gasped.

"Am I ever to be completely forgiven?" he asked, between nibbles at the base of her neck and shoulder.

"I hold a long grudge, so time will tell."

"Then best I get at it."

Heinrich slid down the length of her body, trailing kisses along her collarbones and the center of her chest, tending to each breast and nipple in turn. Elsabeth's whole body was on fire. She moaned and licked her lips, and her head rolled back as she relaxed under his lips working down the length of her belly and towards the space between her legs.

***

THE COMMON ROOM WAS MOSTLY EMPTY WHEN she and Heinrich emerged from the stairwell from the private rooms above. A small knot of men gathered round one of the tables conversing privately over breakfast. Elsabeth recognized the messenger and the rest of Heinrich's companions from the night before. The former's jaw slackened in surprise at the sight of them walking arm-in-arm, and a smug grin tugged at her companion's features.

"Well, it seems we have an audience for our grand entrance," he said.

Elsabeth leaned in close, tapping him pointedly on the arm.

"Remember what we talked about, love. 'Tis not enough to be a man of noble blood but a gentleman, as well."

He chuckled quietly. "Somehow I think you shan't let me forget. From here to the end of my days, I shall have your nagging tongue in my ear, and shall never have a moment's peace!"

"And I thought you quite enjoyed my tongue in your ear."

Heinrich colored abruptly.

"Among other things. 'Tis a shame we must part here, but I must be moving on. I have an appointment to keep out west, though I am loathe to. The unfortunate calling of my station."

She sighed and leaned her head against his shoulder. They stepped off the landing and paused.

"And I still have someone I am to meet, so shan't be leaving quite yet. Do try to keep yourself out of trouble."

"I would say as much of you, but you handle yourself well enough I doubt it will find you."

Elsabeth chuckled ruefully, clasping his hands between hers.

"One thing you will learn about me, love, is that I am always in trouble. But at least it keeps my sword and wits sharp."

Heinrich edged closer to her.

"Then we say farewell. For now, at least. Should you ever find yourself in Goslar you must be sure to find me, if I am at home."

"Tch, so you can make a bigger fool of yourself?"

He quirked a grin that set her heart to fluttering in spite of herself. "At the very least it gives me something to apologize for."

"Mmm, I could certainly do with another round of your apologies. But your friends, I am sure, are eager to be off, and to hear all manner of sordid tales of what we were up to last night."

"That I think is a memory, on my honor, that shall remain between us," he said, pressing his hand over his heart.

She flashed him a mischievous smile. "Very good; you are learning."

Heinrich took her hand between his and kissed it lightly on the fingertips. Her face heated, and she glanced past his shoulder at his comrades watching from their table. Without a word of warning, she took his face in her hands, and kissed him deeply on the mouth. He kissed her back fiercely, and her legs threatened to buckle beneath her. Dead silence fell across the inn at the shamelessness of their display, and when they finally parted again her breast heaved in a desperate bid for breath.

He backed away from her with a particularly satisfied, crooked smile. However, any attempt at poise or dignity was quickly cheated when he caught his heel on one of the tables and nearly tumbled over backwards. Elsabeth buried her face in her hands in a valiant effort not to laugh, which failed at his sheepish grin.

"Go on! Shoo!" she said, waving him away with an exaggerated turning of her head to hide her laughter.

Heinrich rejoined his friends, and the party walked him out the door with hearty slaps on his back. They passed out the door and into the yard, and their voices soon faded away.

Elsabeth found herself left virtually alone in the common room. The innkeeper gathered up the leavings of Heinrich's companions' breakfast, and retreated from the room with stacks of platters and bowls balanced in either hand. Two of the locals talked quietly over tankards of small beer, and the wandering of their eyes in her direction suggested their topic of conversation.

The only other person in the room that morning sat at one of the back tables with his back to the wall stuffing his face with a breakfast of buttered bread and sausages. He was a slovenly, short, and portly fellow dressed in the travel-stained black mantle and white gown of an Olivian friar. The braided cord round his waist strained to contain his ample belly. Wild white hair framed a round and heavy face with a bulbous nose, and black streaks shot through his unkempt beard. The only decoration of note upon his person was a pendant of the Wheel, suspended by a chain round his neck. His staff of office, engraved with more symbols of the Wheel along with other religious imagery in haphazard fashion, leaned against the table. An arming sword and an old battered steel buckler lay atop the table beside him.

Elsabeth heaved a sigh and turned in that direction. She made her way across the common room and dropped into a seat across from him upon reaching the table. She shifted uncomfortably in her seat, deeply conscious of her exposed back, but she had no mind to sit beside him.

"How lovely for you to join me, Hieronymus," she groused.

Hieronymus grunted dismissively, and jabbed a half-eaten sausage at her in annoyance. "I could say the same of you, Tetty."

"Oh please. Just where have you been, anyway? I was expecting you all last night, and instead you left me alone to be pawed at by every man here."

"Hah! And I am sure you did a considerable amount of pawing of your own, or was I mistaken about the nature of your dealings with that wet-nosed princeling of yours."

She rolled her eyes and grabbed a piece of bread and a slab of bacon off Hieronymus' plate. The bread was sweet, soft, and warm, and paired well with crispness of the bacon.

"Oh don't give me that," she said between mouthfuls. "He was a decent enough fellow, if a bit unrefined in his treatment of a real woman. If I am any judge, he has overly relied on his breeding and station to work his way into their beds. I merely took it upon myself to teach him some manners."

"I am sure you did, and most of those manners were of a most vulgar and unsavory sort."

"You are one to talk, love. Need I remind you of the lesson on etiquette you gave to that girl in Jena? You know, the one whose mother hired you to teach the vespers to prepare her for the convent?"

An indignant scowl crossed his heavy features.

"I'll have you know that girl was quite godly when she knelt before me," he said, spraying breadcrumbs across the table. Elsabeth brushed one off her arm in disgust.

"Oh, no doubt. And yet her father nearly ran you through over your ministrations."

"Hmph. 'Twas such a waste to lock a girl that lovely away behind cold stone walls."

"At any rate, you still have not answered my question: Just where have you been?"

"If you must know—"

"I must, which is why I have bloody asked twice now!"

"—I was looking into a lead for a bit of work," he continued, ignoring her interruption. "In fact, I have found us something quite reputable for a change."

The innkeeper finally arrived with a tankard of beer and set it on the table, along with a platter of breakfast for Elsabeth so she need not poach from Hieronymus' plate. Elsabeth swallowed the last pilfered bite and washed it down with a swig of beer.

"Well, that is certainly a change of pace. Have you run out of folk to swindle in this part of Boehm?"

Hieronymus twisted his lip.

"I don't swindle, Tetty."

"Oh, perish the thought."

"And this one will do you some good," he said. "Lord of All knows you could use something to wipe away your many sins."

Hieronymus promptly made the sign of the Wheel, and Elsabeth rolled her eyes.

"If we want to keep score, love, you have quite the head start on me. Care to get on with it?"

He leaned in and lowered his voice conspiratorially.

"I hear there was some trouble in Friuli up the road. Seems some enterprising sorts broke into the Abbey and stole a reliquary from the church. Can you imagine that, Tetty? Stealing from the church!"

"Beat you to it, did they?"

"Blasphemous harpy! I'll have you know that nothing is more sacred to me than my vows to the Lord!"

"At least so long as you can screw them to your advantage," she muttered, earning another dirty look from her companion.

"The Abbot — a Father Garnerius, as I recall — has offered quite the generous reward for its safe return."

She quirked an eyebrow.

"Would you not be obligated to see it safely restored to its rightful place?"

"Bah! My dear girl, you have much to learn about the workings of the world. Why I have seen monks and priests come to blows within the halls of the church itself over who is the rightful owner of such relics! 'Tis quite the unseemly goings on. And such a reward could do a fair bit of good for the poor souls I minister in my travels."

Elsabeth grunted and took a bite from her own plate.

"And you could certainly use some hush money for the next family whose daughter you scandalize."

He threw up his hands in exasperation. "I don't know why I ever agreed to this partnership! Here I am, using my none-too-inconsiderable respectability to find us work along the road, and all I get from you for my trouble is such vile slander!"

"First, because I saved your life. Second, because your tongue may be quick, but the rest of you is not, and you need me to do all the hard work. And third, you'll not shut up about the charms the Lord of All graced me with." She stabbed a sausage at him. "Even though I have more than made it plain you'll not have so much as a peak at them!"

"Give it time, my dear Tetty. I shall wear you down one of these days."

"Let us just focus on the task at hand, shall we?"

"Oh fine!"

"Do we even know anything about these thieves?"

He shrugged. "Very little, I am afraid, though a suspicious lot was last seen heading on the south road out of Friuli."

"When was the theft?"

"Three days ago."

Elsabeth considered. "We are about a day's ride south of Friuli, as I recall."

He nodded. "Indeed. The first stop along the road, I believe."

"Well, I have not seen any suspicious characters round here since I arrived last night."

"Assuming you were not overly distracted by your lordling."

"Oh hush. Are they afoot, or did they have horses?"

"On horse, I believe."

Elsabeth considered for a moment. "That complicates things a bit. There are two other roads out of this place: one to the west, and the other to the south. However, we are not so far behind that we would not be able to catch them."

"If we should pick the right road. The question, then, is which way?"

"A reliquary is no small thing to be moving," she said. "I don't rightly know the market for relics, but I imagine 'tis worth a few coin. The reliquary alone is liable to sell for a considerable sum, if made of gold."

Hieronymus nodded, and stroked his beard. "True enough, and the relic within is priceless. They won't be able to sell it just anywhere; they need a buyer with considerable coin to spare, and 'twill likely be done with discretion."

The friar eyed the innkeeper making his rounds of the common room. This early in the day he was alone to tend the establishment; the serving girls were either at home in their own beds, or earning an extra bit of coin in the rooms upstairs. Elsabeth watched Hieronymus for a moment, and followed his gaze.

"What are you thinking?"

"Well," he said. "If I were to want to unload something of such value—"

"Which I am certain you never have in your sordid past."

"—I certainly would not wish to do so directly. I would do it through a third party. If they already have a buyer, that is who would make the arrangements. If not, they would sell it to him instead."

"The innkeeper?"

Hieronymus chuckled, and took a long drink from his beer. "My dear Tetty, after the years you claim to have spent on the road, I would think you would know the sort of business an innkeeper does behind closed doors by now."

She scowled at him indignantly. "I am not a common thief, love. Yet another thing that separates me from those doing the Lord's work."

"As I see it, all things in this world belong to the Lord in the end, so what matter is it how He claims what is His?"

When the innkeeper's rounds brought him past their table Hieronymus waved him over. He casually flipped a cloth over his shoulder and approached.

"Good morning, Brother. Gnädige Frau," he said pleasantly, with a nod to them both. "Is everything to your liking?"

"Quite, my son, quite!" Hieronymus said. "I particularly compliment you on the quality of your drink. 'Tis not, of course, to the standards of the craft of my Order, but marvelously quenches the thirst nonetheless."

"I'll certainly accept the praise of an Olivian in such a matter."

Elsabeth chuckled, and took a pull from her tankard.

"Brother Hieronymus has certainly been at the bottom of enough barrels to have become a keen judge of the brewer's art," she said.

Hieronymus spit her with a glare.

"Perhaps in lieu of coin I could persuade you to take this irreverent and troublesome harpy off my hands! She certainly has her value."

The innkeeper's cheeks colored. "With respects, Brother, after seeing what she did to Herr Heinrich when he approached her unbidden last night, I'll not take my chances. Your coin will be fine."

"A wise choice, love," she said.

"Hmph. A pity, that, as most men I think would consider her worth the trouble. But! I do have some other business for you." The last he said with lowered voice, and he leaned conspiratorially towards the innkeeper. The innkeeper humored him, and bent closer so they might converse in hushed tones.

"It seems there was some trouble up in Friuli, and I wonder if anything might have crossed your keen ears of some folks seeking to rid themselves of an ill-gotten trinket of quite some value?"

The innkeeper heaved a sigh, and settled onto the bench next to Elsabeth. She watched his brow furrow in annoyance, and he pinched his nose between meaty fingers.

"Forgive me, Brother," he said, "but I am just a humble innkeeper and don't trade in such commodities. Here I sell only drink and food, and a few supplies to see travelers through to their destination. And there is gossip enough in this place among the travelers that I shan't indulge in it myself. Tales have a tendency to grow wildly out of control, and I am sure your companion's antics of last night will soon be the talk of every inn from here to Bremen by nightfall."

"Yes, she does indeed have a knack for setting tongues to wagging wherever she goes," he said, and Elsabeth impaled him with a dirty look. "And I assure you, sir, that I don't mean to imply that you indulge in such disreputable business. But 'tis said that there is no better place for news than from the mouth of an innkeeper, who might overhear any number of secrets when the drink is flowing and tongues begin to wag."

Hieronymus' hand slipped into a pouch at his belt, and he withdrew a few silver *pfennig* from within. He left the coins on the table between him and the innkeeper.

"I do pray that you are not an exception to your worthy trade," he continued.

The innkeeper furtively glanced at the small group of locals, then swept the coin into his hand and pocketed it.

"As I said before, I myself don't abide such business within my walls; 'tis an honest establishment that more than pays for itself in the quality of my beds and table. But," he said, before the protest forming on Hieronymus' mouth could spill past his lips, "you might try south along the road. Some disreputable-looking fellows departed here yesterday morning before your lovely companion arrived and set out in that direction, or so I hear from one of the locals. About a day's ride in that direction you will find a place less discriminating of their business. Perhaps you will have some luck there."

Hieronymus smiled, and made an exaggerated sign of the Wheel. "Thank you, my son, and may the Lord's blessings be upon you!" He smirked in her direction, and Elsabeth rolled her eyes. "As you see, my dear Tetty, 'tis all a matter of knowing the right man to ask, and the right incentive to offer."

She drained her tankard with one long draught, and thumped it down on the table top. "Every day I think the Lord of All looks down upon you and wonders disbelieving what manner of monster he wrought and set loose upon the world."

3

LSABETH GREETED HER HORSE, AN OLD Lizarran jennet, and giggled softly when she nuzzled her hands and jacket in search of a treat. Her brown-and-white pinto coat was graying in places, and she was no longer up to the rigors of the hard riding of battle. But she was still spirited and sure-footed, and stamped eagerly at the prospect of the day's journey.

"Good morning to you, too, Felis," Elsabeth said, and pulled an apple from her pouch. "I trust you passed a quieter night than I did."

Felis nickered softly and took the apple from her hands. Elsabeth gave her a loving pat on the side of her neck before hanging her bags and sword from the saddle.

The morning was a pleasant one; the sun still climbed into the eastern sky, but it was already quite warm. The midsummer breeze carried the rich and fragrant smell of turf through the widely-spaced trees of the surrounding beech woods. A low wood-rail fence encircled the small village. Columns of golden light pierced the ceiling of greenery overhead and dappled the road running through the center. Here and there she caught the silver glint of sunlight on the strands of spider webs, and the air was alive with the singing of birds.

Elsabeth adjusted the angle of her hat to shade her face from the morning sun, and lead Felis by the bridle from the stable and out into the yard. Hieronymus waited for her there with his bay Hackney, Josephus. She arrived just in time to watch him leverage his ample bulk onto the poor horse's back, but true to his even temperament, Josephus bore him without complaint.

"You do know where we are headed, don't you?" Elsabeth said. She stepped up into the stirrup, and easily swung herself into the saddle.

"Of course!" Hieronymus said, allowing his indignation to color his voice. "I have been wandering the roads and trails of Boehm since you were still toddling along behind your mother's skirts, girl."

"I just don't want this to end up like that little adventure in Damme, when we wandered in circles for three whole days."

Hieronymus urged Josephus forward, and the horse set off in a brisk and distinctive high-step trot. Elsabeth gently dug her heels into Felis' flank, and followed after him in a smooth and rolling amble.

"Well, we were being followed," he said. "I thought it best we lose our pursuers."

"We nearly lost ourselves in the process."

"'Tis just a straight day's travel down the road, my dear. You have nothing at all to worry about!"

Elsabeth rolled her eyes, but said nothing more as they ventured out onto the road. The track ran north and south through the heart of the woodland that dominated the Grünwald Uplands region of west-central Boehm. The ground rose and fell gently beneath them, and the road meandered keeping to the easiest ground in the troughs between the occasional forest-clad hill rising above them on either side. After a few miles, the woods to their east gave way to rolling farmland stretching away to the north and south. The road itself was empty, but laborers worked in the fields, and thin columns of smoke curled into the clear blue sky from the farmhouses dotting the landscape.

Felis' gentle amble barely even jostled her in the saddle as she followed along behind Hieronymus and Josephus. The old Hackney kicked up a sizable cloud of dust from the road, and in the rain she suspected it would quickly become a quagmire of sucking mud. The path was well-worn and rutted from the trundling of wagons and carts and narrow enough that riding two abreast would require a remarkable feat of horsemanship. The woods on her right grew up to the edge of the road, though as they gave way to the farmland on the left it opened up some room for passing.

A few small footpaths, most of them leading eastwards into the farmland, split off from the main road, and Elsabeth also spied signs of game trails leading into the woods. The beech woods climbing away on their right were open and spacious, offering few places where outlaws might set an ambush for unwary travelers, but she kept a hand near the hilt of her sword nonetheless.

The ride south was uneventful, however. Their destination loomed up ahead of them just as the sun began to slip westward behind the trees, and the heat of the afternoon faded into evening. To call it a village would be generous. The small hamlet (if it had a name, it was so insignificant that it bore no repeating) consisted of a few rustic huts and a stable clustered around a tavern. There was not so much as a fence to offer even the most rudimentary of protection from wild animals or outlaws.

Elsabeth spurred Felis up to crowd next to Hieronymus on the narrow path and surveyed the scene with a frown.

"This is it?" she asked.

Hieronymus grunted the affirmative.

"Quite the lovely little place, is it not?"

She shrugged. "'Tis not the most backward of places, though I expected something more if 'tis the hub of illicit dealings the innkeeper back there made it out to be."

"My dear Tetty, did you truly expect such a place to hang out its shingle?" The friar offered a chuckle at her expense, and Elsabeth's face heated indignantly. "'Tis a perfectly innocuous place that, I imagine, the local sheriff largely leaves to its own devices. If I were seeking to offload any ill-gotten goods, 'tis exactly the sort of place I would look for."

"Something I am sure you have more than your fair share of experience with."

"Hmph! I am merely worldly and well-traveled. When you get to be my age, you will learn a thing or two yourself."

Elsabeth scrutinized the lay of the place closely as they drew nearer. The tavern — and to her dismay there was not a proper inn to be seen — was the largest building. A communal stable stood at the southern edge of the village. A few workshops occupied the outskirts, and the ringing of a smith's hammer cut through the stillness of the approaching evening. A few folk returning from the fields on the east side of the road trudged through the village, children chased each other through the common, and women started the cooking fires or hung their laundry from lines beside their plain houses.

The village seemed to house no more than a few dozen residents, and their arrival immediately drew considerable interest. Men returning from the fields stopped and stared, and Elsabeth shifted under the eyes settling on her — and particularly on her sword — in amazement. Hieronymus received a few respectful nods and the occasional "Good afternoon, Brother," from those they passed, but otherwise garnered little attention himself.

"Well, the good news is that if there are any other travelers about 'twill not be hard to find them," she said. "I would guess strangers don't go unnoticed in a place this small."

"Quite true." Hieronymus curled his lip in dissatisfaction. "Tch! They don't even have a proper church. I can't imagine they even have a priest in residence."

She shrugged. "Too little money for them to bother, I warrant."

"Blasphemous harpy! My heart aches for their poor souls."

"Well, just remember that we are not here for their souls. We have a job to do."

Hieronymus skewered her with a glare. "My dear Tetty, you well know that ministering to such unfortunates is my foremost vocation."

She sighed and rolled her eyes. "First things first, love. Then you can proselytize to your heart's content, unless we overstay our welcome. Do mind yourself with the local wives."

"And I could say much the same of you. 'Twas not I who was left to flee stark naked from that mob of angry wives in Bielefeld."

Elsabeth's face heated.

"Oh don't you even start with that. 'Twas not a mob, and I was not naked! That fellow had not even gotten my shirt and hose off."

"Nonetheless, the whole town got quite the eyeful as you were run out of town over that business with the blacksmith. So do try not to scandalize yourself until our work here is done."

They pulled up their horses outside the tavern and dismounted. Elsabeth retrieved her sword from her saddle, hung it from her belt beneath her jacket, and gave Felis a gentle pat on the neck. Felis nickered softly in return. Hieronymus slid awkwardly out of his saddle, and grumbled irritably under his breath about the soreness in his backside.

Elsabeth then took a firm hold of Felis by the bridle, and turned to consider the tavern. It was a long, two-floored building of half-timbered construction, with white plaster walls and a steeply-peaked roof of red tile. A simple sign of an ale keg hung over the door. Smoke curled from the red brick chimney, and light within glowed through the shuttered windows and spilled invitingly out of the open doorway. The aroma of baked bread filled the air, and Elsabeth's mouth watered at the prospect of a meal after the day on the road. Iron hitching rings were driven into the timber frames along the front of the tavern for riders to secure their horses.

"Since you have this all thought out, what is the plan?" she asked.

"I should think first we ought to check out this fine establishment and determine whether the thieves have indeed come this way. And if they have, if they are still here," he said while scratching himself in a most unholy manner with the end of his staff.

Elsabeth led Felis to one of the hitching rings and secured her fast. Hieronymus did the same with Josephus.

"And if they are?"

"And if they are, my dear Tetty, between the charms the Lord of All saw fit to grace you with, and my own none-too-inconsiderable wit, we shall determine whether they are still in possession of our quarry, and if they are, relieve them of it!"

She clicked her tongue and rolled her eyes.

"You make it sound so easy."

"Have I ever steered your wrong?"

"Frequently, in fact. But 'tis your venture, so lead on. Just don't climb too deeply into the kegs before recalling why we are here!"

Hieronymus harrumphed as he pushed past her and waddled into the tavern. Elsabeth followed after him.

The interior of the tavern was the typical sort; rush matting lined the floor, and heavy timber columns and beams supported the ceiling. Much of the lower level was dominated by the common room, with tables spaced evenly across the floor. Bare plaster walls glowed under the light of lamps affixed to wooden columns or set out upon the tables. A fire blazed in the hearth along the wall opposite the door, and the fragrance of burning wood helped mask the sour odor of sweat and beer. Elsabeth's nose wrinkled at the realization the floor rushes were well overdue to be changed out, and she was glad for the pattens lifting her feet off the floor. Doorways to their right led to the kitchen.

Locals finished with their labor gathered round the tables with tankards of ale to share the news of the day. They all dressed in simple homespun, and their hands and faces were rough from a life of toil in their workshops and fields. Elsabeth was the only woman in the establishment, and she quickly garnered the attention of every man in the room upon entry, with Hieronymus drawing only a cursory look. One particularly rowdy table in the back corner was occupied by three rough-looking individuals clearly not from the local population.

The tavern keeper, a tall, curly-haired fellow with a stained apron straining to contain his thick middle, pulled himself away from a table of locals chattering amicably over a game of nine men's morris. He threaded between tables and chairs with practiced grace and approached them nearly as soon as their feet touched his floor.

"Have a seat wherever you like," he said, "and my Nes will be along shortly with supper. 'Tis two *pfennig* for the meal and ale."

"Thank you, my good man!" Hieronymus said pleasantly. "Might we have a word in private, first?"

The tavern keeper glanced over his shoulder, then leaned in closely. Hieronymus lowered his voice conspiratorially.

"My companion and I were due to meet with some fellows here. They may have arrived within the past day, and I was wondering if they might be here?"

Hieronymus slipped a coin into the tavern keeper's palm, and the man jerked his head surreptitiously towards the group in the corner. Elsabeth gave them a cursory looking-over; all were armed, and while their eyes at times strayed in her direction, their attention was mainly focused on their plates and tankards.

"Those are the only travelers who have been through the past week. I beg you finish your business so they are on their way, and soon. The big one has tried to put his hands on my Nes more than once, but I daren't say anything."

"Thank you, my son, we shall see to it. Oh! And if I might inquire where we might find lodgings and a place to put up our horses for the night?"

He grunted. "There is not a proper inn here; the village is too small for it. But the locals are good folk, and willing to put up travelers for the night for a bit of coin. There is a communal stable at the far end of town, as well. Your friends have set up there, but there ought to be room to spare if you are not troubled by the stink of horse flesh."

"Blessings of the Lord be upon you, my son!" Hieronymus said, and made the sign of the Wheel. Elsabeth merely sighed and folded her arms across her breast in exasperation at his performance. "My dear, a word with you?"

The tavern keeper inclined his head at the unspoken dismissal and returned to his business. Hieronymus took her by the arm and led her away towards the door, where they could speak without being overheard or observed.

"Well, he was quite helpful," she said.

"Indeed," he said with a nod of agreement. "And I am professionally quite disappointed; I needed no more than a *pfennig* for him to open up."

Elsabeth considered the men. They laughed uproariously over their drinks, and occasionally cast some dice onto the table. "Even that can go quite a ways in a small village like this. But that must be them, if no one else has been through."

"Doubtlessly. So, at least we can assume they have yet to unload their treasure."

She nodded stiffly. "How do you want to play this?"

Hieronymus bunched his brows. "Do you see any sign of baggage on them?"

"No," she said. "They are armed, but none of them have a bag that I can see. Certainly nothing large enough to carry the reliquary. Could they have it stashed inside their coats?"

His jowls wobbled as he shook his head. "I doubt it. 'Twas not a small thing, and even from here we ought to see a sign of it. So if you were thinking of convincing them to remove their doublets to have a look 'tis likely you will come away empty-handed. They must have it stashed somewhere."

Elsabeth chewed her lip thoughtfully.

"What about the stables? The tavern keeper said they had set up there, rather than finding lodgings with one of the locals."

Hieronymus nodded and rubbed his chin, the wheels of his mind spinning.

"'Twould be easier to keep a watch on it, without risk of one of the locals discovering it by accident." He paused, and a smile crossed the friar's features that started an icy tingle racing down Elsabeth's spine. "Keep them busy here, I think I shall have a look."

She scowled down at him. The tingle set all her finer hairs on end, and she spoke the question to which she already guessed his answer: "What do you mean, 'Keep them busy?'"

"I should think that my meaning is quite plain, Tetty. Give them a little something to keep their attention here in the tavern."

Her face heated, and she planted her hands on her hips.

"So once again you chastise me for what I do for my own entertainment, and yet you are perfectly content to ask me to do the same for one of your schemes?"

"Tch. Come now, Tetty. I have had my eye on that fellow since we walked in, and though he has tried to hide it, his have not left what the Lord of All saw fit to grace your best side with."

She clenched her fists and teeth and silently fumed, but the determined set of his jaw made it clear there would be no disputing his plot.

"And what will you be doing while I am letting those ruffians paw at me?"

A mischievous grin crossed his features. "Me? Why, I shall take our horses to the stable, and perhaps see if there are any poor souls about in need of a priest."

4

LSABETH GLARED AT HIERONYMUS' BACK as he waddled out the front door supported by his staff. He turned a corner and disappeared, leaving her alone in the tavern.

Raucous laughter reminded her that she was not, in fact, alone, and Elsabeth heaved a sigh. She adjusted the hang of her sword at her hip, turned on her heel, and sauntered back into the common room with an exaggerated swaying of her hips. Every eye in the establishment fell on her at once, and the tavern keeper pulled himself away from the locals again.

"My companion is seeing to our horses," she said. "And I shall be having a chat with our friends in the meantime."

"Very good, Gnädige Frau."

She fished into her purse for a *pfennig*.

"A tankard of your house's finest." He pocketed the coin and started away, but Elsabeth brought him up short with a hand on his arm. "And keep them coming until I have had my *pfennig's* worth."

I'll bloody have need of it.

He offered her a curt nod, then stepped away to see to her request. Elsabeth sighed again, tugged her doublet straight, then continued her stroll across the common room. The locals' conversation died down when she passed them, and their eyes lingered on her. They watched her with curiosity, and though they were not open with their thoughts, she had little doubt just what was on the lips of the youngest whenever they leaned into their companions with a muttered remark.

The three strangers in the corner, however, were a different sort. They made no effort to disguise their leers, and openly looked her over from head to toe. Even with her long coat swirling around her legs and obscuring the shape of her figure, Elsabeth felt naked under their searching eyes, and a great swell of pity for the tavern keeper's Nes filled her heart.

I have had many a ruffian lay a hand to me uninvited, but this lot may be the worst I have ever seen.

All three men were rough-featured and unkempt, with shaggy hair and poorly-groomed beards and mustaches. Their garb was of finer quality than the plain homespun of the locals, but nonetheless rumpled and stained from the wild. Their hair was bleached by the sun, and their eyes ogled her from weathered faces. The largest of the group was of marginally better grooming, though his doublet was cut a hair too small, and his hose clung more tightly to the shape of his lower extremity than she found pleasant. He nursed a tankard of ale from the bench with his booted feet kicked up on the table, and kept his back to the corner so he could watch the door. An old kriegsmesser in a battered leather scabbard leaned against the table beside him, while the others stood their weapons — an old wood axe and a tall ashen spear — against the wall. A pile of empty tankards was stacked upon the table, and she was astonished to find them sitting upright after the quantity they had already imbibed.

The big fellow's lips spread into a toothy grin, and Elsabeth fought to keep a sneer of disgust from displacing her forced smile. He might have cleaned up better than his companions, but the bar they set was quite a low one; his teeth were yellowed from lack of care, and heavily stained from drink.

"Well, what have we here?" he said, with a humorless laugh. "Too prettied up to be one of the local whores, eh, Duchess? Maybe they brought you in special so we leave the rest of this hovel's quims alone."

Elsabeth clenched her jaw to swallow the more cutting remark forming on her lips and forced herself to smile.

"Merely a fellow traveler on the road, love. Do you mind if I join you?"

He stood away from the table, and sketched a mocking bow. Elsabeth's face heated at his exaggerated display over her reasonable effort at basic hygiene, but said nothing.

"Your table is ours, Duchess," he drawled.

Elsabeth unhooked her sword from its belt, and leaned it against the table. The lamplight flickered along its steel fittings, and the eyes of the brigands seated around the table fixed warily upon it. She allowed a satisfied smirk to tug at the corners of her lips at having so put them off their guard. Elsabeth then lowered herself onto the bench next to the leader of the band with exaggerated fluidity, draped her arms along the back, and made a show of crossing her long legs in front of her. Her companions of the moment fell into stunned silence at the display, and her smirk broadened to her most smoldering smile.

The two men opposite were considerably younger than their leader, and their features behind their rough growths of beard heated in a manner that left her with no doubts she had them wholly within her thrall.

'Tis almost unsporting. I could have them polishing my boots with a simple word.

The third, however, was not so easily enchanted. He dropped heavily onto the bench beside her, and sidled up much closer than her nose liked. She forced the disgust from her features despite the pervasive stink of horse, drink, sweat, and other unpleasant odors clinging heavily to him like a cloud. Fortunately, the tavern keeper arrived promptly with her ale, and Elsabeth took a drink to distract herself. It was not the best — harsh and bitter, and overly strong — but she tilted her head back and downed a considerable portion in one long swallow.

If that impressed him, it did not tell on his features. Instead he reached across her to tap the pommel of her sword, and Elsabeth was not sure whether she was more alarmed at the way his arm now blocked her onto the bench, or incensed he would lay his hand on her weapon. However she kept her expression pleasant as she watched him over the rim of her tankard.

"'Tis quite a long knife for a lady," he said, and this close to him the ale on his breath was nearly as potent as what was in her tankard. "What do you be needing with that? You'll only cut yourself."

Elsabeth offered him a demure smile. "One can never be too careful on the road. And I assure you, your concerns are unwarranted. I am more than capable of wielding it at need."

He chuckled, sat back on the bench, and picked up his tankard for a drink. "I am sure you are, Duchess. I do hope the fact you travel with a priest is not indicative of anything. 'Twould be quite the waste."

"'Tis merely a penitence for some past indiscretions. For the good of my soul, you see."

She injected just enough playfulness into her voice to elicit a toothy smile from the brigands, and all three leaned in closer.

'Tis certainly an ordeal Hieronymus is putting me through. I do hope the Lord of All is paying close attention to this.

"And what does he do about the good of the rest of you, I wonder?"

Elsabeth, in the midst of another drink, nearly choked. She forcibly banished the horror of the unwelcome image projected into her mind.

"Nothing at all."

"'Tis quite the tragedy then, that you go on your knees before him with nothing but the Lord's judgment to show for it."

Elsabeth drained her tankard with one last gulp, and thumped it on the table.

"I don't think I have had quite enough to drink yet to endure that sort of talk, love."

"Well, we shall have to do something about that," he said with a grin, and whistled loudly. "Hoy! Another drink for the Duchess, here, and keep them coming, you slug!"

The tavern keeper looked away from his conversation with the locals, who eyed the table in the corner with expressions ranging from annoyance, to curiosity, to disdain, and no small measure of pity on her account. Their host heaved a sigh and pulled himself away once more to fetch her a fresh tankard.

"So what brings such an upstanding woman as yourself to such a piss-hole hovel as this?" he asked.

Elsabeth fluttered her lashes at him. "I could ask the same thing of a gentleman such as yourself."

He leaned closer to her, and lowered his voice. "I daren't say around this lot, Duchess, but I can promise you once my business is done, I'll have more than ample coin to make the night worth your while."

"Tch. Save your *pfennigs*, love, I am not for sale for any price. At least not for coin."

He chuckled coarsely. "You hear that, lads? Apparently, my coin is not good enough?"

"Your coin is not," she said. "But I did not say nothing else was. What trade brings you to so out of the way a place?"

He took a drink from his tankard, and lowered his voice. "That is between me and my companions, and I mayn't speak openly of it. Suffice to say, I am an acquirer of things for folk of means."

Well, at least that confirms that this is not a colossal waste of time and my patience. Hieronymus better bloody well make this quick.

She smiled and leaned as close as she dared. "You must have some interesting tales to tell, then."

"And always looking for more, Duchess. I am sure we could make quite the tale together."

The tavern keeper arrived at the table and set a tankard down for her. He glanced askance at her — the brigand looming over her did not take notice — but she sent him away with a slight shake of her head.

"Oh, I have my share of tales, 'tis for certain. But I am not here to make more quite yet."

"You may have your share, but I'll warrant none the likes of me," he said, and laid a hand on her thigh.

Elsabeth tensed at his touch, and tightened her hands around her drink. If he noticed her response he said nothing.

"Love, your hand seems to have fallen onto my thigh."

He flashed her a greasy smile.

"Clumsy me."

"Yes, clumsy you. What, pray, is it doing there?"

"One must take the measure of an unfamiliar mare before a ride, eh, Duchess?"

She gave him a wicked little smile of warning. "Careful, love, this one bites, especially when an unfamiliar rider rushes to mount up."

"Promises, Duchess." The others at the table laughed, and their leader's hand strayed higher up her thigh. "Never seen a woman what wears hose so well, you know. I almost don't need to imagine the rest."

She took a steadying drink from her tankard, and thumped it hard down on the table. "I would suggest, love, that you keep it within your imagination."

"Come on now, Duchess, can't we be friends?"

"My friends are generally a bit more respectful of my personage."

"I respect your personage quite a bit. In fact, I would rather like a closer look at it." His hand ventured closer to the space between her legs, and he gently squeezed her thigh. Elsabeth's stomach churned at the uninvited contact so near her intimate places. She gritted her teeth and spit him with a warning look, but he gave no indication he noticed it. His companions howled gleefully, and pounded their fists on the table.

"Love, I think you—" she picked up her tankard once again, but rather than take a pull, she upended it and dumped its contents over his head "—need to cool off!"

Ale splashed everywhere; down his face, soaking his doublet, and a few stray drops splattered in her lap.

The tavern fell silent. The soft drone of conversation among the locals ended abruptly, and the tavern keeper stared aghast at her table. The leader of the ruffians sat rigid with ale dripping from his hair and beard, his features frozen in astonishment. His companions blinked in shock at what she had done, before they exploded into laughter and hammered the table with their fists. Their chief's face turned a brilliant shade of crimson, and a strangled growl clawed its way from the back of his throat.

He rounded on her with surprising agility given his inebriated state and the close confines of the bench, and her only warning of his hand flying was the sharp slap and the sudden sting of pain as the back of it struck her cheek. Elsabeth's head snapped around.

"Cunt!" he snarled.

Elsabeth's face heated from the blow and the insult, and she returned his strike in full measure and then some. The brigand flailed for the handle of his kriegsmesser and scrambled to his feet. Elsabeth vaulted from the bench, and snatched up her sword on her way over the table. His companions were in motion now as well, and scattered empty and half-drained tankards everywhere in their haste to seize their own weapons.

"In God's name, no blades! No blades!" the tavern keeper squealed. He dove for cover behind a table. The rest of the locals fled the establishment and threw chairs aside in their mad stampede for the door.

She now found herself staring back at the messer, axe, and spear of the outlaws with no room to maneuver. The younger two watched her uncertainly, but the leader's eyes blazed with wrath.

"'Tis three of us against one of you, Duchess," he snarled. "What are you going to do?"

Elsabeth swept her eyes across the three of them and tightened her hand on her scabbard, but did not draw.

Bugger this all went crooked. I knew this was a bad idea. I won't get round the table to deal with the other two before that spear skewers me good.

Before her opponents could make a move, she seized one of the discarded chairs in her free hand, swung it with all her strength, and let it fly. The outlaws stumbled over one another in a mad scramble to dodge the incoming furniture. They went down in a heap, while their leader hurled curses at her back.

Elsabeth, however, did not wait for them to regain their footing. She turned and ran, and vaulted over scattered and upended chairs on her way to the door. Ragged footfalls from behind alerted her as the outlaws regained their feet, and she put her head down and charged through the open doorway.

And as she burst from the tavern, she ran headlong into a body coming from the opposite direction and went down hard in a tangle of limbs.

5

IERONYMUS STEPPED FROM THE TAVERN and leaned heavily on his staff. He looked both ways up and down the road running through the heart of the hamlet. Laborers returning from the fields made their way to the collection of simple huts lining both sides of the path. Most had already vanished inside and left the common area largely deserted. Several of the local folk loitered around outside, but aside for a few curious glances paid him little heed. Birds sang in the dying light of the day, and the wind carried the indistinct murmur of many voices lost in their private discourse. Dogs barked in some nearby corner, punctuated by the clatter of a cowbell in one of the fallow fields given over to pasture.

He adjusted the hang of his sword and buckler at his side, then turned south along the road. He passed a carpenter's workshop and the smithy tucked out of the way on his right, where any accident with the forge could be contained without burning the whole place to the ground. Not one of the ramshackle collection of buildings was a church, nor did he spy any sign that a priest dwelled in the hamlet. He harrumphed indignantly at such a lapse in faith among the residents, and determined that once his and Elsabeth's business here was concluded he would hold a proper service for the locals.

Perhaps the tavern would suffice for a hall of worship. He furrowed his brow in sudden irritation. Perhaps he ought to have sent his companion out to investigate the stables, while he relaxed with a good, cool tankard of ale in his hand.

Hieronymus banished the thought from his mind and continued down the road. Workers making their way from the fields to their homes nodded in passing or offered him the occasional "Good day, Brother." At times he paused to offer a meager blessing.

The communal stable was not a difficult building to find. It stood on the east side of the road at the southern end of the little hamlet as part of a small complex of structures including a storehouse and cattle shed. It and the tavern were the only buildings of appreciable size in the town. Cats relaxing from their long night of hunting mice lazed in the sun in the open doorways of the three buildings. The stink of horse and manure hung thickly in the air, and Hieronymus wrinkled his nose and tread carefully upon his approach.

The door at the gable end of the stable stood open. Hieronymus looked about but found no one around outside, so he hitched up his staff and quietly slipped inside.

Three aisles ran the length of the structure. The six bays in each lower aisle were enclosed into a stall that opened out into the stable aisle by means of a gate. Troughs for feed and water hung on the interior walls of each stall next to the gate. A bed of straw covered the hard-packed earthen floor, and rush mats ran the length of the stable aisle. Open windows provided ventilation and allowed a cool breeze to circulate through the structure and flush out the worst of the stink. Hieronymus wrinkled his nose at the odor nonetheless.

Most of the stalls were occupied by *affrus* and cart-horses. Their harnesses, collars, and other gear hung from the heavy timbers supporting the ceiling. Buckets, brushes, pitch forks, brooms, and other equipment were stacked neatly in one corner nearest the gable door through which he had entered. At the far end, however, Hieronymus spied a number of palfreys of finer breeding than the working animals of the town. A man of average height and dressed in a travel-worn doublet tended them in their stalls. Saddles, bags, and packs were piled in a corner nearby.

Hieronymus took hold of his staff and started down the stable aisle towards him. *One guard ought to be simple enough to deal with. So long as Tetty does not run into trouble, this ought to be easy.*

He did not make it far down the stable aisle before his quarry noticed his approach. The man stepped out of the stall and closed the gate behind him. Hieronymus took the opportunity to give him a quick looking-over; he wore a knife at his belt, but the only other weapon he carried was a simple truncheon hanging from a thong of leather at his hip. His shoulders sagged from boredom, and though he noted Hieronymus' sword and buckler, he stood relaxed and at ease, and gave no indication Hieronymus' sudden arrival put him off his guard. Nonetheless, the fellow spit him with a stern glower and moved to bar the path with his hands planted on his hips.

"The stable is full, Brother," he said in a rough voice once Hieronymus drew within reach of his staff. "Best you be moving along."

"Good evening, my son!" Hieronymus said. "I beg your indulgence, but surely there is space enough for an old man seeking shelter for the night?"

"Are you deaf? I said this place is full!"

Hieronymus harrumphed, thumping his staff against the packed earth of the stable aisle.

"I assure you, lad, my ears are working quite well. But I ask you, what sort of man would turn away a humble servant of the Wheel with night falling and all manner of brigands about?"

"One who has a lot of work to do before he can relax with a good bit of drink and no time to spare for this debate. Now move along!"

Hieronymus clicked his tongue and shook his head. "My, what a state this world is in! Why, there was a time when folk would fairly trip over one another to offer a place beneath their roof in exchange for a word on behalf of their souls with the Lord of All!"

"Perhaps you ought to trouble one of the hovels yonder," the fellow said, and waved vaguely back the way Hieronymus came. "Farmers have more need of prayers than I."

Hieronymus eyed him closely. "Surely that is a lie, my son. You carry the burden of sin upon your shoulders, as plain as the nose upon my face! Perhaps some dalliance with a local maid weighs upon your heart? Or mayhaps an ill thought towards your fellow man? My ear is open, my son, should you wish to avail yourself of it."

The other folded his arms across his chest and levelled a stare at him. His change in posture took his hands away from easy reach of his weapons.

"There is no resident priest in this community. Nor even a proper church."

Hieronymus swept his arms wide. "My son, all the earth beneath the sky is the house of the Lord! I, by your good fortune, am of the noble Order of St. Olivus, tasked with wandering beneath His glorious hall to minister to souls in need."

"What I need, Brother, is some peace and quiet and a good stout drink."

"Tch! What can drink provide that the Lord's blessing cannot?" Hieronymus thumped the end of his staff again, as much to distract the fellow from his own disbelief that he might utter such an absurd thing as to emphasize his point.

"A cure from this headache, for one. Now go! I have work enough to do."

Hieronymus stumped forward a little closer, and shook his staff. "Now listen here, you impious villain! Here I am, offering you my services from the goodness of my heart only to be rudely cast aside!"

"And I'll do more than that if you don't get lost. I would rather not strike a priest, so good day to you!"

And with that, the fellow turned his back to retreat to the stall. That was the opportunity Hieronymus was waiting for, and with speed belying his bulk he rushed forward and struck a solid blow with his staff across the back of the ruffian's knees. He yelped and went down in a heap when his legs collapsed under him. Hieronymus delivered another solid stroke to the back of his head before he could scramble back to his feet or reach for the truncheon hanging at his side.

The brigand collapsed face-down in the dirt, and moaned pitiably as he clutched the back of his head. To Hieronymus' consternation, the blow did not quite knock him senseless, but for the moment he was unable to move.

"Hmph! Irreverent bastard," he said, and brushed past him into the stall. "Perhaps next time you'll show a bit more courtesy to a man of my station!"

The horses snorted and danced in agitation over the confrontation, but Hieronymus ignored them and waddled past to the saddle bags piled in the rear corner among the five bedrolls. He frowned — five bedrolls, but only four of the ruffians were accounted for.

"Damn," he murmured under his breath, and quickened his pace. He hastily rummaged through the bags, casting aside changes of clothing and other odds and ends until he found a small bundle wrapped in cloth about the length of his forearm. Hieronymus glanced over his shoulder at the fellow writhing in the stable aisle outside the gate, then carefully undid the wrappings. As he laid it open, the dying sunlight beaming through the windows glinted upon a delicately-engraved golden tube. A smile tugged at his lips.

"Ah! Here you are! The Abbot will be glad to see you again," he said, and quickly made the sign of the Wheel over the reliquary. He wrapped it back up again, then snatched a bag from among the thieves' baggage and stuffed it inside.

Hieronymus levered himself back to his feet again with his staff, and quickly retreated from the stall. He scowled down at the fellow lying at his feet and gave him a quick jab in the ribs with the end of his staff.

"The Lord of All has a special punishment waiting for such blasphemers. Consider it a blessing I don't send you to meet Him right here and now!"

And with that, he turned up the stable aisle and hurried for the door through which he entered.

He did not, however, make if far before a cry of alarm went up behind him. Hieronymus spun around to see another figure silhouetted against the light streaming through the gable door at the opposite end of the stable. Though he could not make out the man's features, the truncheon gripped firmly in his hand as he stooped over his falling comrade left him with no doubts that this was the owner of the fifth bedroll.

"You there!" the man shouted, his voice echoing among the rafters. "Stop! Stop!"

Hieronymus uttered a most unholy oath under his breath, then turned and bolted from the stable.

He rushed back up the road towards the tavern, and dared not look back to check the progress of his pursuer lest he slow and give him a chance to catch up. Farmers returning from their fields stopped and stared in bewilderment as he huffed and puffed along the road, with his staff in one hand and fumbling for his sword with the other, while the bag with the reliquary bouncing against his hip. Angry shouts and cries echoed through the air behind him, not quite lost in the rushing of the wind past his ears at the speed of his flight.

His breath came in labored gasps, and his legs and lungs burned in agony even before he reached the tavern looming steadily larger ahead of him.

Lord grant me endurance, and my eye shall never stray to a woman's shapely rear ever again!

The shouts at his back grew louder, and he wheezed and gasped from the redoubled effort of moving his bulk along the road. He managed to get his sword free of his scabbard just as he neared the tavern. Their horses were still tied up alongside, and locals scattered at the sight of him barreling towards them.

As he reached the tavern a tall figure exploded out the door at a dead run and slammed directly into him.

Hieronymus cursed as they both went down in one tangled ball of limbs. Somehow he managed to keep hold of his sword and staff, but all the air was driven out of his lungs in a sickening grunt from the weight settling hard on his stomach.

"Bugger!" Elsabeth snarled, and when Hieronymus' vision cleared he found her lithe figure sprawling across him, with her backside almost in his face.

Hieronymus glowered up at the sky wheeling overhead while his head spun from the blow. "How is a man expected to keep to his vows when you place such a temptation in front of him?" he grumbled.

However before he could act upon their current orientation, Elsabeth scrabbled off him on her hands and knees, and rolled with her peculiar grace back to her feet. She spun round to face the tavern door in time to draw her sword and challenge the three figures emerging from within. Hieronymus scrambled madly away from them and took cover behind her.

"There you are, Tetty! Marvelous timing as ever!" he wheezed.

"Oh, shut up! What are you doing back here already?"

"I ran into a small complication."

Hieronymus pushed himself back to his feet, and leaned heavily on his staff gasping for breath. His heart hammered against his breastbone, and sweat plastered his hair to his face. The three ruffians from the tavern stood before them with weapons drawn.

"I see you had one as well," he said.

"You could say that."

The two men pursuing him closed in behind them, cutting off any hope of escape that way.

They were trapped.

"IF WE SURVIVE THIS," SHE MUTTERED, "remind me to kill you."

Elsabeth discarded her scabbard to take her sword in both hands, stepped out of her pattens, and peered at the three men pursuing her from the tavern from beneath the brim of her hat. From the corner of her eye she spied two more closing on them from behind, each carrying a truncheon in his hand. The locals scattered in terror at the brewing confrontation. Some fled back into the tavern, and others flew for their homes or whatever other cover was to be had.

"You worry too much, Tetty," Hieronymus said from her back. His voice wavered as he labored to regain his breath after his sprint from the stables. "The Lord of All will see us through. Have faith, my child."

The leader of the band glared, and his knuckles turned white around the grip of his kriegsmesser "You are about to chat with him face-to-face!"

"We caught the fat one in the baggage," one of the men behind them said. "Check his bag!"

His face heated. "If you have our property, Brother, I want it returned, now!"

"Bah! The cheap horse piss you lads have been drinking has dulled your wits, my son. I am but a humble man of the Wheel come to minister to your souls in these troubled times."

"Right, I am sure that has them convinced, very well done," Elsabeth said.

He turned his glare on her. "Be silent, child, I'll not take such insolence from you."

She rolled her eyes and shook her head. "No, but you are only too happy to drag me along on your little schemes. Why do I even listen to you?"

"Well, I did not see you trying to talk me out of it," he huffed.

Elsabeth turned on him and glared. "I spent all day on the road while you dragged me out here trying to talk you out of it!"

"But you did not, because it was a good job."

"I did not because you are too stubborn to let anyone else put a thought in once you have it in your mind to do something foolish. I only agreed to this to keep you out of trouble."

"How dare you! I am too old to need a nursemaid, girl. I had everything well in hand had you just played your part." Hieronymus waved vaguely at the men standing on the road in front of them. "All you needed to do was keep their attention on your abundant charms!"

The leader of the group tightened his hands on the grip of his kriegsmesser and glared. "Quiet! B—"

"Half a moment!" Elsabeth cut him off before he could continue, turned, and stretched to her full height to tower over the friar. The leader of the thieves blinked at her in disbelief. "If he would have kept his hands to himself then I would not have needed to empty my ale tankard over his head!"

"You spoiled everything!"

"Me? What about you? You could not even take care of those two?" she motioned vaguely at the two men who had pursued him from the stables. They looked between each other with bemusement over the argument shaping up in front of them. The two youths standing with the leader were turning red from their efforts to contain their laughter; one bit at the head of his axe, and the other buried his face in one hand. "Instead you came running back here huffing and puffing, and in need of me to save your prodigious backside yet again!"

Hieronymus glared back and shook his staff at her. "I'll have you know I can more than handle myself!"

"Still your tongues, both of you!" the ringleader cried. "You argue like a bunch of women!"

"You keep out of this," Hieronymus snapped. "This is a matter between me and the girl, my son. Once I have finished with her, I will see to you."

"I have heard enough! I want my property returned now. Hand it over and I'll let you keep your fat head." He turned his eyes on Elsabeth and leered as they wandered the length of her body. "You I may keep a while longer as compensation."

Elsabeth rolled her eyes and glanced at her companion. "We can discuss this later, but we really ought to deal with them first."

Hieronymus nodded in agreement. "Very well, I will have words with you later. Which ones do you want?"

"I'll take the loud one and the other two ahead of us, can you manage the others without tripping over yourself?"

"Don't insult me, girl! I am more than capable of handling these ruffians without your help at all."

"Well, you have had quite a run is all, and I would hate to see you collapse in exhaustion now. If I must contend with them all, I would greatly prefer knowing in advance."

"And I don't wish to be troubled by the weakness of your sex. Don't let me turn around and see you on your back with that lice-infested whoreson between your legs!"

"My sex? What do you know of anyone's sex, eunuch? You have not been a man since before you took your vows."

"Blasphemous harpy! I'll bless these men myself for taking you off my hands if you do not still your tongue!"

"And I would leave you to them if I could even fathom what use they could have for a fat friar who cannot even get himself up from the ground after his own prayers."

"Enough!" The ringleader's voice cut across the hamlet like a thunderclap, and he buried his face in his hands. The men on either side could no longer contain their amusement and burst into laughter. "I have heard more than my ears can bear. Just kill them both and be done with it! Now!"

Elsabeth was on the move before there was even a flicker of motion from their opponents. She lunged to her right and whipped her sword around in a falling cut at the nearest outlaw, while Hieronymus moved to contend with the men behind them. The harsh ring of steel broke the peace of the village as her blade struck the shaft of her opponent's axe, and the shock of the impact shook her sword in her hands. The ruffian hastily hooked her sword blade down, but Elsabeth sprung back to her left, and raked her sword along the top of his thigh. The blow sheared through muscle and tendon, and she took advantage of his collapsed leg to wheel her sword around in a high traversing cut that sheared off the top of his head. She stepped past his falling corpse, darted to the right once more, and twitched her sword into a hanging guard to cover herself from the leader's kriegsmesser whistling toward her left shoulder. Steel rang against steel as they exchanged a flurry of blows. Every step Elsabeth took was a little bit further to the right to keep her third opponent from bringing his spear to bear against her.

Her opponent proved quite skilled, but much like Heinrich the night before, he preferred the flourishes of a tournament fighter. Elsabeth bore into him; every movement short, precise, and simple. The speed of her attacks and counters wore him down, and the showmanship that impressed the crowds on the tournament field soon worked against him.

He wheeled his messer around in a blow to her left shoulder. She met his attack with an overhand cut of her own, and as their blades met, she flipped her sword into a short rising cut that sliced the undersides of his wrists. He cried out and lost his hold on his weapon. Elsabeth reversed her strike, and cut back down into his right shoulder.

She quickly surveyed the scene around her. The first of Hieronymus's opponents lay still in a spreading pool of blood. Her companion turned his attention to finishing the other, his staff abandoned in favor of the buckler. Her remaining opponent took note of his leader dying at Elsabeth's feet, then dropped his spear and took off in a dead run for the outskirts. The thud of steel tearing through flesh echoed across the space in front of the tavern, and Elsabeth turned to find Hieronymus withdrawing his sword from the chest of the last of the ruffians.

For a moment the din of the fight echoed across the hamlet, then died away. Elsabeth's arms burned with the exertion of the fight, and her stomach churned from the rush of battle. She mopped the sweat beading on her brow with the back of her hand, and wiped the blood from her sword on the garments of one of their fallen adversaries. Then she looked to Hieronymus.

"Weakness of my sex?" She stooped to retrieve her scabbard from the ground and slammed her sword back home in irritation.

"What have you to complain about? It worked, did it not?" he said dismissively. "The churl was so irritated that by the time he finally got around to ordering his lackeys to kill us, we caught them unprepared."

Elsabeth rolled her eyes, and nudged one of the fallen men with her boot.

"Just remember that I still owe you a thrashing for getting me into this in the first place."

Hieronymus chuckled. He hung his buckler from his belt once more, sheathed his sword, and reclaimed his staff from where he had discarded it. He reverently wiped away the soil and detritus of the town square. "Would a drink suffice to placate your wrath, my child?"

She twitched one corner of her mouth into a smirk. "Well, that would be a start at least. This trip would be worth it just to see you pay for once."

And with that, they turned together for the tavern and left the corpses for the townsfolk to deal with.

LSABETH CLUTCHED HER HAT IN FRONT OF her, and waited impatiently while the Abbot carefully scrutinized the reliquary clasped in his meaty fists.

Father Garnerius was a rather stocky fellow. Graying hair framed heavy, clean-shaven jowls twisted into a superior scowl. He narrowed his blue eyes as he turned his prize this way and that, and made no effort to disguise what he was doing when he gingerly opened one end and peered inside, with only a casual signing of the Wheel to sanctify his action. Hieronymus, leaning on his staff beside her, tensed in indignation at both the Abbot's lack of trust and the breach of sanctity in so opening the reliquary in front of them.

They gathered in the Abbot's private study, a small chamber outside his solar in the east range chapter house of Friuli Abbey. It was lavishly appointed, with a finely-carved oak desk dominating the center of the room, and a plush carpet spread out upon the hardwood floors. Garnerius sat in a high-backed wooden chair behind it, and his stout figure nearly vanished behind the stacks of books, parchment, and other paraphernalia piled atop it. Bookshelves lined the entirety of the wall on Elsabeth's right, laden with a diverse variety of manuscripts on as many subjects — both secular and ecclesiastical — in as many languages. On her left stood a row of shelves and display cases. Most contained accoutrements of the Abbot's office: a gold and gem-encrusted crucifix and a richly-decorated communion set of gold and crystal most prominently among them.

Fading sunlight streamed through open windows allowing a cross-breeze to cool the chamber. The town of Friuli sprawled at the foot of the hill from which the Abbey looked down upon the laity, and a distant echo of activity from below managed to reach them through its thick walls. The bell in the nearby church pealed out the hour, but the rest of the claustral complex was filled with reflective silence.

Finally satisfied that the reliquary he held in his hands was the genuine article, Garnerius sealed it once more and reverently returned it to one of the wood and glass display cases on his desk.

"Well, then," he said, "you have my thanks for your good service, Brother."

Hieronymus inclined his head graciously.

"'Twas merely my duty as a servant of the Lord, Father," he said, and Elsabeth nearly scoffed at his affectation of humility. Hieronymus spit her a glare from the corner of his eye as if he sensed her brewing impropriety, and she stilled her tongue with effort.

Garnerius then shifted his eyes to her, and Elsabeth quirked her lips into an amused smirk. Her appearance in the Abbey had caused no small commotion among the sequestered brothers, so she had put a little extra sway into her hips when she strolled through the grounds on her way to this meeting. Even the Abbot's eyes wandered, and she peered down her nose at him when his eye strayed down the length of her figure. His face colored when he caught his glance lingering too long on her legs, and he folded his hands tightly together on the desk and leaned forward.

"But I must protest your companion. 'Tis an impropriety that she even enter within these walls to tempt my cloister, particularly in this violation of sumptuary law. I cannot abide that you permit her to traipse about with her hair so uncovered — and of length beyond her station! — and in such fashion as this."

Elsabeth grunted. "I beg your pardon, Father, but Brother Hieronymus has no say over either my dress, or my comings and goings. I am an equal partner in this enterprise, and 'tis as much because of my sword-arm you have your relic safely back in your possession."

Garnerius heated. "I did not bid you speak, *woman*!"

Hieronymus heaved an exaggerated sigh.

"My apologies, Father, but my companion is overly free with her tongue."

"Tch, if you only knew, love," she said, with a lascivious and playful lifting of her brows. "And as for my dress ..."

Elsabeth reached inside her doublet, and removed a folded sheet of aging parchment safely tucked away inside a pocket within. She stepped forward and offered it to the Abbot. Garnerius eyed her doubtfully for a moment, then accepted and unfolded it. She waited patiently, a triumphant smirk still tugging at her lips, while he read it. When he finished, he glanced up at her in irritation, then turned the paper over a couple of times.

"Signed by his Grace himself, I see," he said, and chagrin over his defeat colored his voice. He casually tossed her letter of dispensation on his desk, and Elsabeth retrieved it, neatly folded it, and made a show of tucking it safe and secure back inside her doublet.

"His Grace saw fit to recognize that I must be able to protect my virtue as I travel—" Hieronymus barked a sardonic laugh, and she delivered a sharp kick to his shin. "—and 'tis ever so much easier to do if an assailant must fight past men's fashion than merely lift a skirt."

"As if any man would need to fight to get at what lies 'twixt your thighs, Tetty," Hieronymus groused as he rubbed his shin. "In any event, Father, I can vouch for the veracity of that letter."

"I don't agree with such business in the least," the Abbot said, but conceded with a sigh. "However, that is a matter to address with his Grace. You again have my thanks for your service."

Elsabeth leaned one hand on her hip.

"As I recall, Father, there was a bit more of an earthly reward promised for that bauble's safe recovery," she said.

Garnerius' features colored again, and even Hieronymus blushed.

"Tetty! We agreed that I would handle the matter!" Hieronymus said, aghast.

"No, you merely said you would handle the matter, I can't recall having agreed to it. You may be content to feign you did this entirely out of the goodness of your heart, but 'twas my neck on the line as well."

The Abbott curled his lips into a sneer. "Your companion is quite the impious mercenary, Brother,"

Hieronymus leaned on his staff and shook his head. "That she is, Father. Alas, my counsel often falls on deaf ears! But nonetheless, she is quite the skilled sword-arm, and worth every *pfennig*. And surely you would not offer restitution for such a dangerous venture and renege once the job was completed?"

Garnerius turned his glower on Hieronymus, who received it with a gracious bow of his head, and Elsabeth rolled her eyes at the display. Recognizing he would not win any further argument, the Abbot pushed away from the desk with a creaking of his chair. He tucked the reliquary's case beneath his arm, and padded across his office to the locked cabinets along the left wall. His robes of office trailed to the floor, and even beneath their voluminous drape it was evident the Abbott rivaled even Hieronymus in girth.

"I trust the thieves were dealt with appropriately?" he inquired. Garnerius fished a key from beneath his robe and unlocked one of the cabinets. He safely placed the reliquary inside, and withdrew a small chest. "The Lord of All shall see to the punishment of their souls, but I expect that they receive just retribution in this life, as well."

"One had the good sense to flee when it was clear he was thoroughly outmanned," Elsabeth said, and casually studied her nails. "The other four were being buried by the locals when we departed the village where they were holed up."

Garnerius frowned at her over his shoulder.

"One escaped, you say?"

"I wager he shan't make it far without his horse and only the clothes on his back, as I suspect he'll not reclaim it from the townsfolk. He certainly shan't come back *here* any time soon, either."

The Abbott grunted and returned to the table. He set the chest on his desk and spit them both with a warning glare when he opened it. Elsabeth craned her neck a little and was rewarded with the glimmer of lamplight on the coin within. The clinking of coin tinkled musically in her ears as Garnerius filled a small leather pouch. He then cinched the purse closed and tossed it towards her. Elsabeth reached out to catch it, but Hieronymus's hand unexpectedly snatched it out of the air just as it was about to reach her palm. He tested its weight, then secured if fast to his belt.

"The reward as promised, and a little extra for dispatching the culprits."

"God's blessing be upon you, Father!" he said cheerfully, and ignored Elsabeth's eyes boring through the back of his skull.

Garnerius grunted and waved his hand. Booted feet scraped along the floor behind them, and Elsabeth turned to regard the guard approaching from the door. He casually leaned a halberd against his shoulder.

"You are dismissed," he said, then turned to the guard. "Please escort them out of the chapter house."

The guard bowed his head stiffly and waited for them in silence. Hieronymus genuflected to the Abbott upon their dismissal and turned for the door. Elsabeth offered him a sweeping bow in turn, then strutted after him with just enough waggle of her hips that Garnerius' eye followed in spite of himself.

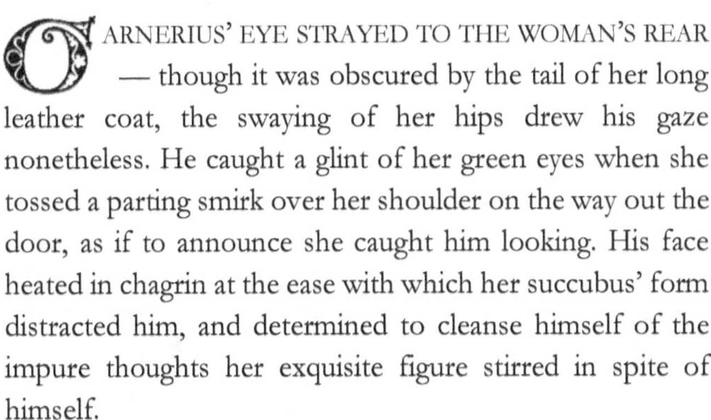

ARNERIUS' EYE STRAYED TO THE WOMAN'S REAR — though it was obscured by the tail of her long leather coat, the swaying of her hips drew his gaze nonetheless. He caught a glint of her green eyes when she tossed a parting smirk over her shoulder on the way out the door, as if to announce she caught him looking. His face heated in chagrin at the ease with which her succubus' form distracted him, and determined to cleanse himself of the impure thoughts her exquisite figure stirred in spite of himself.

The Olivian and his unconventional companion departed, and the prior — a slight, mousy-looking little man — entered and closed the door behind him. He scurried across the floor and stuffed his hands into opposite sleeves of his voluminous robes, then bowed deeply upon reaching the desk.

"You asked to see me once our guests departed, Father?"

Garnerius nodded. "I did. Tell me, what do you think of our esteemed Brother?"

"Honestly, Father?"

A tight smile tugged at the corner of his lips at the thinly-veiled disdain in the prior's voice.

"By all means."

"Well, Father, a most uncouth fellow. I can hardly imagine that even the Olivians would accept such an individual among their number."

Garnerius grunted. "You don't know many Olivians, do you? And what of his companion?"

The prior blushed fiercely. "Ah ..."

"Quite the fetching creature, you agree?"

"I would not know, Father," he said, but stumbled over his words in such a manner as to reveal his true thoughts about her.

"Oh, there is no need to mince your words; her effect on you is as plain as the rosary round your neck. And I imagine 'tis much the same among the rest of the cloister. 'Twould not have been my choice to admit her had I known the particulars of Brother Hieronymus' companion. To think that his Grace has given her dispensation to roam around in such unseemly attire! 'Tis a sordid business altogether."

"Yes, Father."

He stabbed one meaty finger at the prior. "Put her from your thoughts. In fact, I suspect everyone who has seen her has need of mortification. Remember: She is no woman, but surely a demon put on this earth in fair guise to tempt us!"

"Yes, Father. If I may ask, the reliquary was returned intact?"

Garnerius sat back in his chair and folded his arms over his belly. He offered the other a stiff nod. "It has, and what it houses is still safe within. Mercenaries they might be, but at least they were honest ones. Nor did the thieves have an opportunity to cause any damage."

"God be praised! Should I return it to the altar?"

"No, not yet. I'll keep it here in my office for now. See to it that the door is guarded around the clock until we can address the security of the altar and assure such a desecration cannot happen again."

The prior bowed. "Yes, Father. Is there anything else?"

Garnerius leaned his elbows on his desk, and thoughtfully tapped one finger against his lip. He considered the chest of coin, and fumed silently over the woman's insolent insistence on claiming the proffered reward. By all rights, she *ought* to have declined, and accepted a blessing for her deeds. Lord knows such a creature had a multitude of sins to wash away.

"Yes," he said. He rummaged through the papers on his desk for blank pieces of parchment and took up his quill.

The prior watched without speaking while he scratched out a note. "Have these delivered to Dietrich and Michel."

The prior's face paled. "Dietrich and Michel, Father?"

He nodded. "Yes. I have work for them tonight."

Let those two fools waste their precious coin. I'll take no chances with them.

8

RAVELERS MAKING THEIR WAY ALONG the road between Leyen and Ortenau filled the common room of the inn of Friuli to nearly overflowing that night. Elsabeth and Hieronymus, their purses heavy with the Abbot's coin, joined with the men of the town in drinking and gambling the night away.

This was no rustic village inn, but a true and proper establishment at the heart of a sizable town. The roar of the revelers boomed among the wooden beams and plastered walls, and shook the whole of the inn while musicians played a jaunty dance tune in one corner. Oil lanterns hanging from the great oak columns filled the room with golden light, and windows along the outside walls let in silver moonlight from the courtyard. Women and girls in common dress threaded their way through the patrons to deliver platters of food and tankards of ale, and slipped just beyond the reach of men seeking to pull them into a dance or kiss. The rich fragrance of herbs and cooking food lent the common room an earthy air. Merriment was the rule of the evening, and Elsabeth and Hieronymus dove into the frivolity with zeal.

The friar sat at a table in the corner with a tankard of ale in one hand, and the other around the waist of a local woman. His voice carried above the din of the other patrons as he regaled any who would listen with the details of their fight with the outlaws (with his own part greatly embellished). His antics ensured him an eager audience while he alternately took great pulls from his ale and molested the woman at his side to the roar of approval from the men around him.

Elsabeth plunged into the merrymaking with zeal. Her hair rippled freely behind her like a copper banner as she passed from one waiting lap to another, and drank her fill from both her own tankard and those of the men gathered in the common room. She danced with them and added her share of Hieronymus's haul at the gambling tables. She then approached the musicians to share a deep kiss with one, before turning her affections to another, and soon drew the attention of those gathered away from the serving girls. The inn vanished into a dizzying haze of light, color, and sound as she reached and exceeded her capacity for drink.

The revelry continued late into the night. Time passed, and the common room slowly emptied. The townsfolk returned to their homes and the travelers staggered up to their rooms. Elsabeth was left alone with one of the musicians after the others packed up and headed for their beds. She sat in his lap, plucking awkwardly at a lute under his direction, and giggled from time to time when his hands wandered from guiding hers along the strings of the instrument to rest on the inside of her thigh or on her bosom. She soon tired of plucking only the lute, and took his hand and started for the stairs leading to the private rooms above. Hieronymus remained at the table draining the last of the ale from his tankard, and then thumped it down to join the mountain of empty ones stacked at his side. Elsabeth paused.

"You were right," she said. "The pay was quite worth the hassle." Elsabeth swayed unsteadily on her feet from the quantity of drink she had imbibed over the evening. Her new friend caught her before she could fall and pulled her against him.

The friar gave her a self-satisfied smirk. "As I told you, Tetty, nothing to fear at all. Now, if you will pardon me, the lovely lass here has requested that I bring the bishop round for an audience at her nunnery."

Elsabeth chuckled. Her companion nuzzled the back of her neck impatiently, and she squealed when one of his hands slipped to the inside of her thigh. She jabbed her elbow into him playfully in response. "Go on, wait for me upstairs!" she said, and then turned her attention back to Hieronymus once the lutenist departed after a quick kiss of her hand. "Can you make it on your own, or should I summon a litter for you?"

Hieronymus grunted indignantly and levered himself to his feet with effort. "You need not worry about me, my love. It shan't be me upon my knees for these ministrations."

"Your devotion to your faith is an inspiration to us all, Brother." She sketched a mocking bow.

The friar barked a short laugh before bowing to her awkwardly. The woman in his company seized his soiled robes to ensure he did not collapse on the floor. "Good night, my child, and may the Lord bless and watch over you."

Hieronymus made the sign of the Wheel to her and shuffled out of the inn with the woman supporting him. Elsabeth waited for him to go before turning toward the stairs leading up to the private rooms. She swayed on her feet as she crossed the floor, and nearly ran straight into a cloaked and hooded figure who suddenly appeared in her path. A gloved hand shot out to catch her wrist when she began to fall and steadied her on her feet again. Elsabeth struggled for a moment against his iron grip.

"Hey! Take your hands off me!" she snapped, and aimed an unsteady blow at him. In her inebriated state she swung wide and nearly fell again.

The hooded man easily ducked back from her strike, and his hand on her wrist kept her on her feet. His features were lost in the shadow of his deep woolen cowl. "Easy, girl," he said in a low, gravelly voice. "I am not seeking you for my amusement."

Elsabeth threw his hand off once she steadied herself. "What? Why not... I mean, good! Touch me like that again, and the only satisfaction you will know is my sword. If I could remember where I put it last..."

He ignored her threat. "I come with a message: You and the friar turned over something to Father Garnerius of the Abbey this afternoon."

She scowled at him. "Our business arrangement with the Abbot is none of your concern."

"On the contrary, 'twould be most wise if it did not remain in his possession."

"Then you are welcome to address your concerns with him directly. We were hired to recover it and we did. The job is done, as am I with you. I have no desire to stand here and conspire with mysterious cloaked figures in the middle of a tavern at night, as that is far too much like some awful minstrel's fancy for my taste. Now if you will excuse me, I have had a long day and am rather in need of a release with the charming gentleman awaiting me in my room."

He sketched a mocking bow. "Then I shall keep you no longer. I warned you fairly, and whatever danger befalls you now is on your own head."

With that, he turned and strode from the inn with a swirl of his cloak. Elsabeth watched him go, then made for the stairs and followed after the lutenist.

THE CREAK OF THE FLOORBOARDS WAS HER ONLY warning. Elsabeth dozed naked in her bedmate's arms beneath her blankets. The moon was just beginning to slip beneath the horizon in the west, and only a faint shaft of weakening silver light spearing through the window illuminated her room. Her head was still heavy with drink, and she nearly missed the sound. Only the shifting of her companion in bed roused her enough to be aware of it.

She remained still. Elsabeth peered into the darkness, and in the faint light she just made out a hunched figure drawing nearer to the bed. A gleam of white briefly flared in his hand when the moonlight caught the blade of the knife he held in a fighting grip.

With no weapon near at hand, Elsabeth tensed and seized the covers. The assassin drew within a springing step of her, and she vaulted from bed and threw the blanket over his head. Elsabeth took advantage of the distraction while he struggled to free himself. She slammed into him low around his middle, driving him to the floor. After a moment's struggle to throw her off with his strength, he stabbed at her blindly through the blanket. His stroke missed, so he tried to cut his way out instead. She seized the knife as it slashed through the blanket. With a quick twist of her wrist, she wrenched it from his hand and plunged it down into the struggling intruder. He grunted as the blade pierced his belly. She withdrew her arm and pulled the covers off him, then finished him with a slash across the throat. He vainly tried to staunch the flow of blood oozing between his fingers, and he gasped and gurgled desperately for a breath that would not come.

She collapsed backward on her rear for a moment to regain her breath and watch her assailant's writhing still. By now, her bedmate was fully awake from the disturbance, but she ignored his cry of alarm at the man dying on the floor and the blood splattered across her naked body. Elsabeth quickly searched the assassin and found a folded slip of parchment tucked away in the pouch at his belt along with a leather drawstring purse containing a few silver *pfennig*. She ignored the inquiries of her companion, and instead hastily dressed and retrieved her belongings and sword from a wardrobe in one corner of the room. Her doublet rattled slightly as the small metal scales concealed between its linen lining and velvet outer shell moved against each other. Elsabeth tied her assailant's purse to her belt and stuffed the note into a pouch, then hurriedly gathered up her belongings and crammed them into her pack.

The musician seized her by the shoulders when she brushed past in her haste to depart. "Elsie, love, will you stop and tell me what is going on?"

Elsabeth leaned in and kissed him fully on the mouth before pulling away and continuing her preparations. "I am rather sorry to be running out so suddenly, but when someone comes for me in the dark of night with a weapon, I prefer not to wait for his friends. You may wish to leave yourself. I think 'twill be unwise for you to linger here."

"Where do we meet again?"

"We don't, I am afraid. Take care of those hands of yours," she said. Then she threaded her arms through her jacket, slipped her pack over her shoulder, grabbed her sword and hat, and was out the door before he could respond.

VERY SHADOW STRETCHING OUT INTO THE darkened streets of Friuli held unseen enemies. Half-timbered buildings frowned on her with their windows gazing down like empty black eyes. Their fronts crowded the dirt streets, while shadowed alleys stretched back in between them. A few lamps sputtered along the walls of the town, but she had only her own night vision to guide her through the winding maze between the inn at the main gate and the brothels in the rundown southern quarter of Friuli. The rush of her fight quickly snapped her drink-addled mind back to clarity, and she cursed at herself for ignoring the warnings of the hooded man. The message she found on the body of her assailant was short and concise:

> *Brother Hieronymus has served his purpose. He travels now with a woman of immoral character. I know not how much they truly know of this business, but consider this purse of twenty pfennig an advance on having them removed as a liability. I will double it upon proof your task is completed.*

There was no signature, but the letter was marked with the sign of the Wheel crowned with a tasseled galero. As the words blazed in her mind, she prayed she was not too late for Hieronymus.

The south quarter of Friuli was little more than a collection of hastily constructed, simple wooden shacks crowding around each other within the town's outer brick wall. Narrow and ill-lit streets wound between blocks of buildings thrown up with no regard for planning, and made for a confusing maze of alleys and dead-end streets cluttered with refuse and hovels. During daylight hours a few stalls offered goods more affordable to the destitute residents of the quarter than those of the market near the main gates, but after sunset the chief commodity was sin.

Finding which establishment Hieronymus chose to patronize took little time; the drunken friar stood out from the normal clientele. The two-story building was one of the south quarter's more ostentatious, with brightly painted wooden framing, timber-clad walls, and glazed windows lit from within by the golden glow of lanterns. Two rough-looking men guarding the entrance leered as she approached and looked disdainfully at the sword hung at her hip, but let her pass without hassle. The interior was no less gaudy than the exterior, with painted walls and furnishings, and the overwhelming scent of perfume hanging thickly in the air. An open common room greeted her upon entry, and the establishment did its best to take on the appearance of any other inn.

Stairs on her right led up to the lodgings on the second floor, and a door opposite the main entrance disappeared into the darkened kitchens. The trestle tables lining the wall were empty at this hour, as all the patrons were now continuing their business in the private rooms upstairs. Almost as she entered, a woman screamed on the floor above, and Elsabeth sprung into motion.

Her sword cleared its scabbard with the whisper of steel on wood and leather, and she charged up the stairs and turned a corner when they reversed back on themselves. A cloaked figure stood on a landing on the second floor, and spun around to meet her. He held a knife in his hand and rushed into her to close the distance before she could bring her sword to bear against him. He struck at her with a level thrust. Elsabeth stepped to her left and pressed her back against the wall. She slapped his wrist away with the flat of her sword to pass his knife harmlessly past her, then seized him roughly by the shirt and threw him over an outstretched leg. The assassin cried out and tumbled down to the floor below in a tangled ball of limbs. He struck the landing below with a sickening crunch, and lay there unmoving.

Elsabeth spared him only a long enough look to assure herself he would not be getting up again, then turned and sprung the rest of the way up, taking the stairs several at a time on her long legs. The commotion drew the attention of the women working the house and their clients, and people in various states of undress emerged from the rooms. The sight of her naked sword gleaming coldly under the light of the lamps sent most of them fleeing back into their chambers, while others rushed down the stairs to see to the fallen man. Elsabeth pushed past them, and spotted the woman Hieronymus left with earlier peering out from one door at the end of the hall. The woman panicked when Elsabeth started for her and tried to close the door, but she struck it hard with her shoulder and forced her way into the room only to find the friar lying naked and still on the floor, with his robes and other belongings discarded around him.

"God!" she said. Elsabeth dropped her sword with a sharp metallic clatter and knelt beside him.

"Hieronymus?" Elsabeth shook him by the shoulder, and her heart leapt into her throat when he did not respond. A bit of drool frothed around his mouth, and he continued to lay with his eyes slightly closed. "Hieronymus!"

The friar snorted and began to snore, and Elsabeth let out a relieved sigh.

She looked up at the woman, who had shrunk back against a corner opposite the door after Elsabeth broke into the room. "What happened?" she demanded.

The woman shook at the sharpness in her voice. "Nothing, I swear! He came up here, undressed, and fell asleep right where he was standing!"

Elsabeth sighed and rolled her eyes. "Well, good to know he is still himself. Go on, out!" She waved towards the door, and the woman scurried out in a fright, and with no further need of encouragement.

Elsabeth picked up her sword and returned it to its scabbard, then crossed the room to a dresser where a bouquet of flowers in a vase was set out. She discarded the flowers and dumped the water over the dozing friar's head. He snarled a stream of curses in protest at the shock of cold and wet rousing him from sleep.

"Lord damn you to torment, when I get my hands on whoever you are!" he snapped, and tried to shield his face. Hieronymus panted heavily as he forced himself upright. "What in the name of the Dark One am I doing down here on the floor?"

"You fell asleep, you drunken lech," Elsabeth said. "Get up, we have trouble."

"Elsabeth? What are you doing here? Finally came to your senses about me, eh?"

"Only in your prayers, love. I have seen rather more of your orb and scepter just now than I would ever like to again in my life."

Hieronymus tried to stand, but sunk back to the floor with a groan when his drink and sleep-addled limbs refused to cooperate. "Help an old man to his feet, will you, love?"

Elsabeth rolled her eyes again and took hold of his hand. With an effort, and Elsabeth straining on his arm, the friar managed to regain his feet. He clasped his hands on his prodigious belly. "You should show some respect. The Lord of All has made this body a temple. 'Tis a thing of beauty."

She chuckled and went about retrieving his garments. "In that case he may wish to execute his architect. Get dressed, and quickly, we need to get out of here."

He groaned. "What? Why? I have not done a thing."

Elsabeth handed him his clothing, and he took his time getting dressed.

"I'll explain later, but your night is not the only one to be spoiled. You are just lucky I got here when I did, or else you would never have woken again."

"All right, all right," he said. "And where are we going, then?"

"Like I said, I'll explain shortly. I would rather not say it here," she said.

"Fine, fine, Tetty. You certainly know how to ruin an old man's night."

ELSABETH AND HIERONYMUS MADE THEIR way along the darkened streets of Friuli. The friar huffed at her pace, and she wove through several alleyways and cross-streets to lose anyone who might try to follow them from the brothel. She only stopped when they finally emerged from the southern quarter and stood at the base of Abbey Hill, which occupied the entirety of the northern quarter and straddled the main line of the wall encircling the town. The base of the hill itself was beyond another wall of equal height, which intersected the main fortifications and created a bulge on the northern end of Friuli. A turret guarded each juncture between the hill and main walls. The Abbey itself looked down from its complex behind a second wall of brick at the summit.

The two pulled up just short of the wall and took shelter in an alley across from the gate. Hieronymus leaned on his staff and glared up at her.

"Well girl, would you mind explaining what all of this is about, and why we are sneaking around like a couple of common thieves?"

Elsabeth reached into her belt pouch, pulled out the note she recovered from her would-be assassin, and handed it to him.

"I was attacked as well. And right before I went up to bed, some strange fellow in a hood and cloak stopped me and warned me that we should not let the Abbot have that reliquary."

Hieronymus puzzled over the parchment and frowned. "You think the Abbot sent those men to kill us?"

Elsabeth shrugged. "Either that, or someone sent them in his name. Regardless, I am starting to think there is more to this than just recovering stolen church property."

The friar grunted and handed her back the message. "And here I thought it would be an easy bit of coin."

She quirked a grin. "Easy is not quite as fun. What do you think? Would he have returned it to the high altar by now, or will it still be in his office?"

"I don't know for sure. But I would be surprised if the guard has not been increased since the theft."

Elsabeth nodded her agreement. "And if the Abbot is at home, we can't just walk in ourselves. We need another way in."

"Well," the friar said, "I can think of one way, though 'twill likely not be a pleasant one."

ELSABETH WRINKLED HER NOSE AGAINST THE stench of excrement as she climbed the brick shaft leading up into the Abbey from the sewer tunnels running beneath the hill. She wedged her body into its narrow confines — the shaft was just a little over half again the breadth of her shoulders wide — with her back against one wall, and her feet jammed into the one across from her. She slowly shimmied upwards in this manner, while Hieronymus waited below.

She could just make out the distant circle that was her only light overhead, and any view of the torch held by her companion below was blocked by her own body. Elsabeth steadily climbed higher. Her legs ached from the effort of driving herself upwards, her shoulders burned from the strain of supporting her weight, and every breath filled her nostrils with the stink of human waste. She might have mused on the irony of a house of God being built atop such a cesspit, but all her effort now was focused on the climb and getting out of that malodorous passage.

Fresh air. Just think of the lovely fresh air when you get the bloody hell out of this hole.

Long minutes of climbing passed before she finally reached the end of the shaft. The opening at the top was a small round hole, just large enough for her hips to pass through the cut in the wooden planks with some squeezing. *Bless the Lord of All for not gifting me with an overabundance of padding round my backside.*

She tensed and strained her ears, listening for any sound of someone in the chamber beyond, but heard nothing aside from the gurgle of water in the drainage tunnels far below. With great care, Elsabeth reached through the hole with first one arm, then the other, and levered herself up. Her head surfaced, and she gasped at the draught of fresher air from the Abbot's garderobe. While not the most wholesome of chambers, it nonetheless smelled sweet as summer rain after her long climb up the privy shaft.

Elsabeth strained and pulled herself out of the shaft, wriggling a bit to clear her hips and backside, and for a moment sat on the lip of the bench to catch her breath. Then she slowly crept to the door and listened. Silence greeted her once again, so Elsabeth carefully took hold of the handle, pulled it open a crack, and peered through into the darkness beyond.

At first she could see little of the Abbot's chamber. Not even the fading light of the moon found its way in to illuminate it. Elsabeth waited until her eyes adjusted as best she could hope for, and slowly the indistinct shadow resolved itself into a four-post bed in the middle of the room, and other furnishings along the walls. An extensive wardrobe occupied much of the northern wall of the chamber, with a large desk and ornate chair opposite it. A round table and four chairs stood in another corner, where the Abbot could take his meals in private, and a large trunk sat pushed up against the foot of the bed. The floors were bare wood, but a plush rug covered much of the space. Of the Abbot himself, she could see no sign.

Elsabeth slunk round the door of the garderobe and slipped the rest of the way into the chamber. She crept across it — her soft-soled leather boots hardly a whisper on the wooden floor — until she reached the door leading out into the Abbot's private office. Again she stopped and put her ear to the door, but only empty silence greeted her.

She tested the handle of the door and found it unlocked. She opened it a crack, satisfying herself that the well-oiled hinges would not squeak and give her away to anyone in the hallway outside. Inky blackness spilled around the door; not so much as a single lamp or candle shone in the Abbot's office, leaving her to work with no light whatsoever.

Elsabeth slunk through the office, finding her way by memory to the glass case now on her right. She could just make out the shape of the cabinet, and found the place where the Abbot had left the reliquary during their earlier visit. She squinted and peered inside. What little moonlight found its way into the darkened office glinted off her golden quarry, and it almost seemed to glow in the gloom.

A quiet sigh of relief escaped her lips; fortune was with her finding the reliquary still where the Abbot left it. Had he returned it to the altar she might never have been able to get to it.

She reached into the pouch at her belt and withdrew a folded leather toolkit containing a small hook-shaped pick and a torsion wrench. Elsabeth started work on the lock, and it took her little time before the case was open. She reached within, removed the reliquary, and tucked it safely under her arm. Elsabeth closed the case and locked it again. Stuffing the reliquary into her belt as best she could, she hastily and silently retreated back across the office. Upon returning to the garderobe, Elsabeth worked herself back through the hole, into the shaft once more, and awkwardly made her way down again.

This quickly proved more difficult than her ascent, and several times she nearly lost her grip and fell. Her progress slowed significantly, and the stench of sewage and waste quickly became unbearable. Her lungs burned for want of clean air, and her shoulders and legs were afire from the effort of descending the length of the shaft. She was perhaps a good story from reaching the bottom when her hold on the sides of the shaft finally slipped, and she slid the rest of the way down with a yelp.

Elsabeth struck the floor of the sewage tunnel hard on her side, and landed with a splash in a slow river churning with foul water and human waste. She strangled a cry of disgust as she regained her feet and checked herself for any sign of injury. Hieronymus was nowhere in sight with their torch, so she carefully felt her way along the darkened tunnels back toward the dim light of predawn at the tunnel entrance. She emerged from the drainage gate and limped off to a dark corner nearby, where she found the friar dozing propped against the wall. She prodded him roughly with her toe and he awoke with a start.

"God damn you, Tetty!" he snapped. "I would have thought you of all people would have learned by now how to properly wake a man."

Elsabeth scowled down at him. She stepped into her pattens, and retrieved her sword and hung it from her belt once more. "Even if I had the desire to, we would not have time, love. I have it. We should probably make ourselves hard to find."

Hieronymus pushed himself back to his feet with the support of his staff and wrinkled his nose in disgust. "God in heaven, what is that smell? You should consider a bath."

"I have been knee deep in the blessed shit of the Abbot, which I hope is good enough to wash away at least a few of my sins. And next time, you can climb the privy shaft if you would not plug it first."

"I am a Brother of the Wheel, child, I do not wallow in excrement."

They hurried away from the wall encircling Abbey Hill, but did not get far before the shadowed figure of a man appeared in front of them. Elsabeth's hand went to her sword hilt, but three other figures closed in suddenly around them and she spied the faint glint of metal in their hands as blades were drawn. A familiar voice broke the silence of Friuli's darkened streets.

"Well," the hooded man said, "I see you finally decided to heed my warning."

Elsabeth released her sword and scowled. "You would be amazed how convincing someone trying to stab you in your sleep can be."

The man chuckled, a low, throaty sound.

"Indeed. I am pleased to see you had not abandoned all of your wits over drink and a little romp with wandering minstrels. Just the one, or did you have your way with them all?"

She scowled. "My sleeping habits are none of your concern. What do you want?"

"The reliquary. I assume that you decided to retrieve it?"

Hieronymus glared. "Listen here, my son, I don't know what this matter is about, but if you intend to make accusations against a fellow man of the Wheel, I think I am entitled to hear it."

"In time, Brother," the hooded man said. "And then you can go back to your wenching and drinking, which I am sure his Grace the Prince-Bishop finds quite becoming of one of his friars. Now. The reliquary."

He extended his hand, and the armed men around them closed in. They were too close for her to draw her sword, and they left her with no room to maneuver if it came to blows. Elsabeth sighed and retrieved the reliquary from her belt. She and Hieronymus gasped at the sight of it: It was now twisted and flattened from her fall, and a veneer of gold plating flaked away in places to expose the thin lead making up the bulk of the tube.

"A fake!" Elsabeth said in surprise.

The hooded man nodded and snatched it out of her hand. "Had it not been for you two fools killing the men I sent to retrieve it in the first place, this would be well on its way to the Bishop by now. I did not count on Father Garnerius noticing it missing so quickly. That was my mistake." He easily tore the soft lead sheet of the reliquary apart, and removed several pieces of rolled parchment concealed within.

"What is that?" she asked.

"Deeds and titles, pretty. Father Garnerius has been buying — or extorting — property from some of the lesser landholders around Friuli for some purpose. The Bishop has heard rumors of this, and would like to know why." He held one of the pieces of parchment close to his face to better study it in the dim light. "Interesting... Freiherr von Leyen."

Elsabeth frowned. "Von Leyen?"

"Baron Cuncz von Leyen, pretty. It seems that most of this land was acquired by the Abbot on the Baron's behalf." He quickly folded up the papers and stuffed them into his pouch. "The Bishop will be most pleased, but I believe in being thorough." The darkness of predawn and the shadow of his hood masked the man's features, but Elsabeth felt him regarding her and Hieronymus carefully. "You two seem to have no trouble taking coin for a good deed, perhaps you can be convinced to take his Grace's as well?"

Elsabeth folded her arms across her breast. "What do you have in mind?"

"If Father Garnerius is acquiring this land on Freiherr von Leyen's behalf, quite likely the Baron himself may have certain incriminating information in his possession the Bishop may greatly desire to see. I would like you to retrieve it for me. And I can promise that you will be much better rewarded than with a knife in the dark."

10

HE CITY OF LEYEN STOOD ON THE SOUTH bank of the Nebel River, situated in the point bar of a bend in the watercourse as it meandered westerly across the plain. The land on both sides, owned by Cuncz, was rich and fertile, and cultivated farmland stretched for miles in all directions before giving way to forest-clad hills rolling away into the distance of the Grünwald Uplands. The city, which occupied a low rise behind a wall of red brick, was a maze of cobbled streets threading between clustered blocks of homes, markets, and workshops. Inns crowded near each of the town's gates, and a cathedral with vaulted arches and expansive windows of colored glass dominated the town square.

Cuncz's castle and residence, a fortified manor on a lawn of green grass, stood beyond a series of walls on the north end of Leyen. Its encircling wall intersected the town's main fortifications in a manner much akin to Friuli's, with turrets spaced at regular intervals around it. A channel cut from the river passed through the wall on either side of the castle by means of grated culverts below the surface to form a moat around the inner wall. It was spanned by a drawbridge which was accessed by a white cobbled path lined with trees leading up from the town. The pathway continued through the well-fortified gatehouse, and past the gardens and ornamental fish pools that filled the bailey within the manor walls.

Elsabeth and Hieronymus arrived after a two day ride from Friuli, in the waning hours of the afternoon. The city was still alive with the calls of merchants and beggars, and the steady drone of foot and cart traffic along the narrow winding streets. She sat astride Felis, dressed in a cotehardie of deep red wool, with her hair braided under an organza veil. Hieronymus rode beside her on Josephus, clad in a green brocade doublet and woolen hose. His garments strained to contain his bulk and fit him closely, displaying rather more of his shape than Elsabeth found pleasant. Her sword hung from his saddle, and he kept his own sword and buckler at his hip.

"Well," he said, as they followed the flow of traffic in from the gate, "here we are. 'Twas not so hard to get in as I feared."

"Only because the guard at the gate paid more mind to me than he did your story," she said. A smug grin crossed her features. "I could have had every man at that gate with just a batting of my eyes."

Hieronymus grunted. "When the Lord of All blessed you with your charms, Tetty, I don't think he expected you to waste them on every marginally handsome man you came across."

"Oh what are you complaining about? My charms have extracted your prodigious rear from plenty of trouble."

"Leave my rear out of this!"

"At any rate, I am merely relieved that the Schwertbrüder don't maintain a presence in Leyen. They would recognize me too easily, and then this whole venture would be for naught."

He heaved an exaggerated sigh. "One of these days your little feud with the Brotherhood is going to cause us all manner of trouble, Tetty. I would rather prefer you left me out of it."

Elsabeth glared across at him. "'Tis not my feud. At least not one of my making."

"Oh, I am sure they want to chop your lovely head off for no particular reason. Quite a tragedy that would be, too."

"I did not say there is no reason for it, but merely 'twas not a fight that I started. And don't you think we have more immediate concerns at the moment?"

Elsabeth put enough edge into her voice that Hieronymus said nothing more on the matter, and she fumed silently over bitter memories threatening to well up and drown her. She forcibly drove them back down where they could not trouble her further, but she felt them there nonetheless, gnawing at her belly.

"All right, all right! But one of these days you and I must sit in confession and talk about this." Hieronymus shifted in his saddle. "It strikes me we have a formidable task before us. Anything incriminating Cuncz has in his possession is likely to be kept in the castle, and I daresay even the ample charms the Lord blessed you with are unlikely to let us just walk in and search for them."

Elsabeth considered the towers of the manor looking down upon the town and frowned. It was indeed a formidable edifice of well-guarded brick. She reluctantly conceded his point with a nod.

"You and I have broken into many a place," she said, "but even at our best such a mark would be beyond us."

"I don't suppose we can just call the matter off," he said.

"Somehow I doubt that fellow who 'hired' us will let us off if we don't see this through."

Hieronymus harrumphed. "Then we best figure out something. I think we ought to first make for the nearest inn."

Elsabeth glared across at him. "Oh no. I just know the moment we set foot inside, you'll forget all about our purpose here and be up to your armpits in the innkeeper's kegs, and chasing serving girls round the tables. We have a job to do!"

Hieronymus returned her glare in full force, and even she was forced to flinch at the intensity in his gaze.

"And if there is even the hint of a singer of even modest skill in attendance, he will have your skirts up round your head before the sun sets. But unless you can think of a better place to hear the goings on in this city, 'tis our best option.

"At any rate, 'twill give us a quiet place to discuss matters without doing so right smack dab in the middle of the street where anyone can hear us."

Elsabeth sighed, and conceded his point with an aggravated nod.

"All right, all right. Just remember we are trying not to draw too much attention to ourselves. So no swindling the locals at the gambling tables!"

Hieronymus twisted his lip.

"My dear Tetty, you certainly know how to deprive a man of a good time."

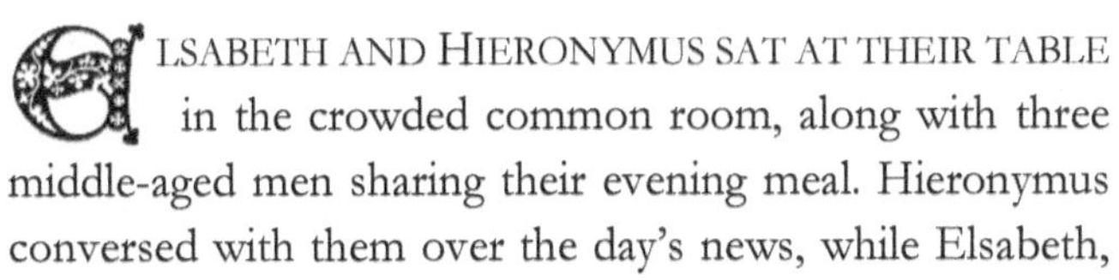

E LSABETH AND HIERONYMUS SAT AT THEIR TABLE in the crowded common room, along with three middle-aged men sharing their evening meal. Hieronymus conversed with them over the day's news, while Elsabeth, seated with her back to the wall, watched them closely and flashed demure smiles whenever it seemed Hieronymus was not paying attention to her.

They had set themselves up for the night in an inn a few blocks away from the west gate. Their chosen residence was more opulent than the inn at Friuli, but their arrival passed without fanfare and only a cursory interest as they settled in, for the place was crowded with merchants seeking a meal and shelter for the night, or drinking, gambling, and exchanging the news of the day. More than a few made eyes at her — her dress was chosen carefully to best draw their eye — even those traveling with their wives. So the men appraised her appreciatively, and she earned more than a few envious glares from the women in their company.

There was no music, much to her regret. But though she would not admit as much to Hieronymus, she acknowledged to herself it indeed was for the best.

I truly can't resist the strains of a well-sung tune. God, that will get me into trouble some day!

Evening soon passed into night, and the five of them now sat quietly together, with the four men nursing tankards of ale, while the patrons of the common room began to disperse to their own rooms or homes.

"Thank you again for sharing your table with my daughter and me this evening," Hieronymus said. "'Twas so crowded tonight, I feared we would be confined to our room!"

"You chose a rough time to visit Leyen, friend," said one of the men. He had a lean face, dark blue eyes, and a neat blonde beard, with hair to his shoulders. He called himself Jacobus. "Midsummer is the busiest time for trade in the town."

Hieronymus nodded and raised a finger pointedly. "Perhaps, but I imagine 'tis the most lucrative."

Another of their new companions, Clement, who was clean-shaven and green-eyed, with brown hair cropped short, chuckled into his tankard of ale. Elsabeth flashed him a coy smile and the traveler smiled back, leaning in slightly to ingratiate himself. "Indeed it is. Fortunately, there are a few good places left to put up a stall in the market. You will want to start your day rather early to make sure to claim one, however."

"Well, I am not precisely here to set up a stall like any common merchant," Hieronymus said, and injected just a touch of indignation into his voice. "I happen to be here to represent the League of Free Traders!"

Elsabeth glanced shyly at the third. His face was broad and plain, with a thick brown mustache and beard, shoulder-length brown hair, and piercing blue eyes. He introduced himself as Thadeus. He nodded eagerly, "Truly? We don't often see representatives of the League this far south."

Hieronymus made a show of eyeing his tankard. "'Tis a mission of rather some urgency, in fact. They are looking for a new supply of silver."

Thadeus leaned back and stroked his beard thoughtfully. "Well, in that case I might still be of aid to you. 'Twould be my pleasure to help a fellow traveler find his way about."

"Then I would be greatly indebted to you, my friend. Tell me, this is a safe city, yes? I would hate for my daughter to be set upon by some manner of ruffian when she takes her air while I am away."

Jacobus leaned back in his chair and swirled his tankard thoughtfully. Elsabeth watched him carefully from the corner of her eye for the slightest hint of deceit or hesitance in his response.

"The Baron certainly keeps the peace," he said. "I have heard scarce word of trouble with such lawless men within the walls of Leyen."

Hieronymus leaned in, took all three men in with a solemn glance, and continued with lowered voice.

"Tell me, what manner of man is he? 'Tis frightfully difficult upon the road. And sad to say that in these days there is often little means to tell the difference between the Barons and the local highwaymen. Road taxes, escort taxes, inspections. Many are the days I felt that there is less profit in trade than in taking up arms and joining the ruffians preying on the roads myself." He made a show of taking Elsabeth's hand and stroking it. She quickly and quietly kicked his shin under the table in response, but he ignored her. "If 'twere not for my dear child, of course. I could never subject her to such a life, or men of such distasteful disposition. Better to send her off to a convent than to think of her dallying with such rabble."

"I must confess we see little of the Baron," Thadeus said. "He spends much of his time in solitude within the castle, and I cannot recall having seen him set foot beyond its walls in any visit I have made here. Though I have heard he at times can be seen walking the outer walls during the morning hours, and takes the occasional ride just to remind the locals he is still here."

"No one to my knowledge has ever received an audience with him either," said Clement. "All matters between the town and castle are handled by the chamberlain or the Captain of the Guard."

"You must have wax in your ears." Jacobus scoffed. "I have overheard some of the gate guards say that at times during rides he spies a young lass that takes his fancy, and has her brought to the castle for the night. Then there are the stories of a sealed carriage arriving late at night that is taken all the way to the castle. No one seems to know who the passenger is, but it always leaves again before dawn."

Hieronymus chuckled and took a swig from his tankard. "Even I could venture a guess at that. 'Tis probably nothing more mysterious than some other mistress paying a visit. Perhaps the wife or daughter of the neighboring lord, and he wishes to keep tongues from wagging."

"I wonder who that might be, then, as Emrich von Ortenau, who is the nearest, has no official issue. Of course, there is Friuli as well, but the good Father has no... nieces of his own."

Clement chuckled into his ale. "Then I suspect Father Garnerius is the only resident of the Abbey with no such near kin. There seems to be a plague of men of the Wheel left to care for unfortunate nieces and nephews of mysterious pedigree. Still, I suspect our friend here is correct, that the Baron has found some lady he fancies. And good thing too, for Leyen still harbors uneasy memories of Rupertus von Leyen."

Elsabeth quirked an eyebrow. "Rupertus?" she asked. The three men looked her way at her unexpected intonation, for she had spoken little in her part in their masquerade, and all three showed great eagerness to respond to her.

Thadeus found his voice first and leaned in conspiratorially. "The Baron's father," he said in a hushed voice. "And yet not. His wife died in childbirth many years ago, and rumor has it the child she bore perished with her. He was devastated by this, and never took another bride, nor even showed interest in another woman for the rest of his life."

Clement broke in to take up the tale before the other could finish. "Some years later, however, he presented Cuncz von Leyen as his son, with the tale that the lad was sickly for much of his youth, so kept sequestered away. Thus he assumed the title of Baron when old Rupertus died."

"That sounds rather curious, does it not?" Hieronymus asked.

Jacobus shrugged. "'Tis certainly the subject of much speculation, as he merely appeared one day at Rupertus' side." He finished his tankard with one last draught. "There is sadly little else to say on the matter, as the Baron guards his privacy closely, and even his subjects scarcely know him. Now if you will excuse me, the hour grows late and I wish an early start setting out my wares on the morrow. Good evening to you all."

He pushed himself away from the table and bowed politely at the waist. His eyes lingered on Elsabeth's for a moment, and she coyly glanced away with a tight-lipped smile for his benefit. Then he turned and strode from the common room. Their remaining companions grudgingly acknowledged the deepening night and begged their leave as well. Elsabeth offered each a shy smile in the manner of the first, and they too departed to their private rooms, each certain that they alone shared an unspoken promise with the traveler's demure daughter.

Hieronymus levered himself to his feet and turned to her. "Well daughter, I think 'tis time to see to our own rest. If you would be so kind as to help an aging man to his room."

Elsabeth stood as well, and threaded her arm through his as they made their way toward their room. She leaned toward him and spoke with a low voice, "I think you are rather overplaying it."

"Nonsense, Tetty. And you are certainly one to talk. I have seen strumpets in a nunnery act with greater subtlety. No daughter of mine should be seen batting her eyes about an inn like a common bawd."

"Watch who you call common! Besides, it got us a meal without having to dip into our own purses, and kept them more focused on me than the questions you were asking. Better to send them off to their beds with lustful dreams, than for them to remember a pair of strangers prying about Cuncz."

Hieronymus grunted. "Well, then perhaps you should make your rounds to give them something to really remember. That should ensure all they have to recall are the charms the Lord of All has blessed you with. And when you are finished, your dear father could certainly do with some company for the rest of the night."

Elsabeth rolled her eyes. "When you say it in such a way, I can hardly imagine why I have refused your bed for so long. Regretfully, I must decline. After all, you have an early start tomorrow to see about that silver and whatever else you can dig up."

They reached their private room, and Elsabeth opened the door. She playfully shoved Hieronymus through before following after and closing it behind her. The friar stumbled forward and caught himself with a curse, which he followed with the sign of the Wheel. "And what do you intend to do all day while I am hard at work?"

Elsabeth smirked at him and crossed the room. In one corner stood a full-length mirror, and she made a show of admiring her figure in it. "I think I shall take in the sights of the town, and see what I can find out on my own."

HE INTERIOR OF FRIULI ABBEY'S GRAND church was of typical construction, if more opulent than common houses of worship. The nave consisted of a long central processional aisle running east and west along the axis. Imported stone made up the floor beneath the vaulted ceiling, supported by a frame of carved and painted timbers. An arcade separated the central aisle from a lower aisle on either side. At the far eastern end stood a large circular chamber, with doors in the middle of the northern and southern walls leading to the grounds and east range, respectively. The western half of the chamber was ringed with pews around an open space containing the pulpit. A rood screen behind the pulpit separated the nave and chancel. Even further beyond this lay the sanctuary where the altar and Tabernacle were kept.

Carved timber columns supported the arcade separating the aisles of the nave, and a carpet ran the length of the floor before disappearing beneath the rood. Marble statuary of the Saints decorated with gilded ornamentation occupied niches in the walls. Sunlight filtered in through a skylight in the dome over the pulpit, and through the large windows of stained glass where the walls of the main circular chamber came together at the apse.

The church was mostly empty that morning, with only a few novices at work polishing the stone floor, statues, and gilded fixtures. Garnerius stood before the altar and Tabernacle, with his arms stuffed through the opposite sleeves of his robes of office, and glowered at the craftsmen stomping about the sanctuary and putting the finishing touches upon the reinforced case of gilt wood and glass that would soon house the reliquary. A heavy gilt iron padlock, richly embellished so as not to detract from the grandeur of the case by its plainness, secured the doors. Gilt iron bars reinforced the glass set in the face of each door, so even if the panes were broken, one could not reach inside.

The wooden case was bound with an iron frame ingeniously disguised as decorative gold work. And yet, he was assured, the whole thing would be strong, secure, and impossible to break into by any means once it was firmly anchored to the altar upon which it rested.

He had no intention of allowing it to be put to the test, but the craftsman staked his life and soul upon his pronouncement, and that was sufficient for him. However, with the original thieves dealt with, and the friar and woman following them to the grave last night, Garnerius contented himself the secret of the reliquary was now safe.

Still, he had little liking for the laymen swarming around the altar in this sanctuary to the Lord of All. He gritted his teeth while he supervised their work, and doubted all the holy water in Friuli would be enough to cleanse them inside this most sacred of spaces.

Unfortunately, it was work that needed to be done, and all had the good sense to decline pay in exchange for lending their time for the betterment of their souls.

Honest laborers are truly a gift from the Lord after the past days' outrages.

Garnerius heaved an impatient sigh, and shifted from one foot to another. The workmen barked orders at one another in voices better suited to back alleys and darkened taverns than such a holy place. More than once one forgot himself and uttered some crude vulgarity, followed by a panicked sign of the Wheel, and a look over a shoulder at the stern glower of the Abbot, or the visage of the Saints looming over them from their alcoves along the walls. Fortunately for them, there was no sign a bolt of divine retribution was imminent, and they quickly returned to their work with red faces and only slightly greater care as to their choice of vocabulary.

The soft squeak of light slippers on the floor behind him drew his attention away from the workmen. Garnerius glanced over his shoulder and spied the prior rushing down the aisle through the rood screen. His mousy face twisted in dismay, and judging from his hurried pace, Garnerius mused whatever matter brought him to the church that morning would not be put off by his need to supervise the work on the case. He heaved another sigh and squared his shoulders. As if he did not have enough concerns this morning.

He turned to address the prior the moment he threaded past the screen and bowed respectfully but stiffly.

"I beg your pardon, Father," he said, his tone quite aggravated, "but there is a message from the office of the Constable."

Garnerius frowned. The Constable of Friuli seldom needed to consult with him directly. Though Friuli had not been granted full town privileges, he nonetheless granted the Constable and town council considerable leeway in the running of their affairs.

"Speak up, then," he said, allowing a hint of impatience to leak into his voice. "What is it?"

The prior eyed the workmen nervously, and Garnerius glanced behind them. Some had paused in their work during the interruption and now tried to watch this new development without being too obvious about it.

"Forgive me, Father," the prior said, "but 'tis a matter best spoken of in private."

Garnerius' belly turned uneasily at the tightness in the prior's voice. He spit the nearest worker with his most commanding glare.

"Get back to work! I'll only be a moment."

"Yes, Father!" the workman sputtered, and scurried to resume his work.

Garnerius turned and strode past the rood screen with the prior falling into step beside him. They emerged into the nave, and he waved to one of the novices at work on the floor nearby.

"Go and watch over them," he said, pointing vaguely back towards the sanctuary. "See to it they remain focused on the task at hand and don't touch anything!"

"Yes, Father!" the boy said, and quickly vanished behind the rood screen to carry out his task.

Garnerius and the prior made their way up the aisle, and he was conscious of the novices following them out with their eyes. The prior's urgency upon his arrival had not gone unnoticed, nor did they miss his own trepidation over the yet to be revealed message. They passed out the grand processional doors and into the Abbey's grounds. These were mostly empty that morning; the caretakers had long ago finished trimming the grass, trees, and hedges within, and had gone on to other work. The distant rumble of activity in Friuli below Abbey Hill echoed beyond the walls, but did not disrupt the contemplative silence of the outer cloister.

Garnerius led the prior to a private space in one of the many gardens, away from prying eyes and bent ears.

"What is it, then?" he said, once he was certain they were alone. He nonetheless kept his voice low, lest it carry.

"There was an incident in the town last night, Father," the prior said, so quietly that Garnerius had to lean in to hear him clearly. "A fight of some sort at one of the inns left a man dead. And another body was found in the streets outside one of the nunneries in the southwest quarter."

Garnerius let out a relieved breath.

"Then 'tis nothing for us to worry about. Dietrich and Michel have done their work. Send a reply to the Constable's office that I entrust the investigation to his hands."

The prior's face paled in a manner that made his stomach stop turning and instead try its best to claw its way up his throat.

"But Father, the description given of the two men found dead matches Dietrich and Michel."

All the color drained from Garnerius' face at once.

"Are you certain?"

The prior nodded. "Yes, Father. Michel was found dead at the inn of a knife wound, and Dietrich was found hidden among the refuse outside the bawd house, his neck all twisted about in a most unnatural manner. No witness has come forward yet."

"Damn them. Damn!"

Garnerius did not even bother to make the sign of the Wheel. He immediately spun on his heel and raced back towards the Abbey, his robes flying madly around him.

"Father!" the prior huffed as he struggled to keep pace. "Father, what is it?"

"I want to see it!" he demanded, and his voice cracked with urgency.

After only a few paces his heart was hammering against his breastbone, and his breath came in heaving gasps from his sprint across the grounds. Those few abroad that morning stopped and watched his flight, with the prior nipping at his heels. Their habits flapped wildly around them, and in other circumstances he might have found the sight comical himself. But sudden panic washed over him, and now his only thought was to ensure the safety of his prize.

"I beg your pardon, Father," the prior said. He gasped for breath, and his voice was barely audible past the wind rushing through his ears. "But did you not see it this morning?"

"I did not think to look!" he wheezed. "I thought the matter addressed."

"But surely they would not have—"

"If you have anything more than wool between your ears, you shan't finish that thought!"

They reached the east range, and Garnerius threw open a side door and stumbled inside. He paused only long enough to catch his breath and to assume a more dignified pace lest he draw the attention of the whole cloister, and turned up the hall with the prior close behind him.

The sparsely-appointed living quarters passed him by in a blur on his way to the far end, then up the rickety old stairway to the floor above. They emerged just outside his private offices, and the guards in brigandine and kettle helms snapped to attention at his approach. He ignored their genuflection, threw open the door, and hurried inside. The prior caught it before it could slam against the wall, and gently closed it behind him.

Garnerius hurried to the display case, and his blood turned to ice when he reached it. He fumbled in his robes for the key, and his hands shook so badly he missed the lock several times before it slipped into the keyhole. The case swung open, and only confirmed what he saw through the glass: Where the reliquary ought to be was only an empty space.

His face heated, and he seized the edge of the door and slammed it closed so hard the glass fit into the frame shattered on impact. The guards outside responded immediately, and burst in with their halberds leveled. But finding no one within but the prior and Garnerius, they froze in confusion.

He balled his fists and gritted his teeth, but could not restrain the most unholy of curses. prior and guard alike looked upon him with astonishment — the former shrinking into his habit and trembling, the latter uncertain how to respond at all. Garnerius stormed around the room and tore at his hair, uttering a string of curses and oaths wholly unfit to spill from the mouth of any servant of the Lord of All. Finally he wheeled on the guards and stared them down.

"Are you blind? Deaf? You were here for a reason! You had one job, and one job only to do, and that was to safeguard this room! Yet you let intruders walk in here on a whim! What have you to say?"

Both men paled and hung their heads. Their bodies tensed, and they clutched their hands tight around the shafts of their halberds. Neither gave any indication they intended to answer.

"Well?" he demanded, his voice breaking when they did not respond.

"Begging the Father's pardon," one said in a small, quivering voice, "but other than yourself, no one has entered or left this room."

"Aye, not a soul," said the other, taking courage from his comrade breaking his silence first. "Not even the cleaning staff. Not since we relieved the night watch."

"And they reported all was quiet. Save for yourself when you came to bed, they said no one passed the doors since they were posted."

The prior edged towards the broken cabinet and peered inside, his features twisted with disbelief, and his face drained of all color.

"How then was this even possible? The windows are too narrow for even the slightest body, and there is no other way in or out."

"It does not matter!" Garnerius roared, and all three men flinched. "Send a message to the Constable: I want the Olivian and that...that woman found and brought to me at once, do you hear?"

The prior swallowed. "Do you truly think—"

"Who else would have even known, if no one else has been here since? I don't know how they managed it, nor do I care. But I want them brought to me at once, even if 'tis just their heads in a sack. And I want the reliquary returned!"

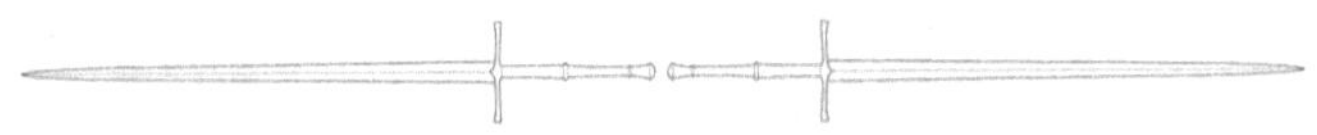

THE DAY PASSED SLOWLY, AND GARNERIUS SPENT much of it pacing his office, fuming in silence. Doubt and fear gnawed at his belly. He dared not reveal the truth to the prior or guards. If any of them were to learn what the reliquary truly contained, he doubted even the prior could be convinced to keep his silence, and with Michel and Dietrich gone there was no one left he could trust to carry out the grisly task required to keep his secrets safe.

If those two mercenaries were to read those documents, 'twould surely be my head on the block.

Garnerius paused and turned to the narrow slit window looking out onto the cloister. A warm breeze spilled through, stirring his finer hairs, but offering him no refuge from the thoughts racing through his mind. A new one clawed its way to the surface, and his lips twisted into a scowl. Mercenaries.

Like as not they will look for some way to turn this to their advantage. Yes, almost certainly they intend to leverage those documents against me for petty vengeance, in the hopes of draining my coffers dry.

He gritted his teeth and balled his hands into fists. God damn Michel and Dietrich for their incompetence! He heaved a breath. Or perhaps this was his own foolish mistake; perhaps he had underestimated the pair from the start.

Garnerius returned to his desk and dropped heavily into his chair. It creaked and groaned under his weight, and for a long moment he sat with his hands folded over his belly. He propped his head up on one arm, and gazed down at the light lunch set out upon his desk. There was wine in a plain pewter goblet, (with the bottle alongside it) a loaf of bread on a wooden board, and a clay bowl of broth for dipping. His belly rumbled, and yet he could not work up the desire to eat. Instead he reached for the wine, lifted it with a shaking hand, and brought it to his lips for a drink. It was a potent Navarrese vintage, and as fine an example of the vintner's craft as could be had. Yet Garnerius took no pleasure in it.

More time passed, and he busied himself with the paperwork of his office — an inventory of the Abbey's supplies, preparing sermons, reviewing the work of the scriveners charged with copying the manuscripts in the library — minutiae that could not distract him from the agonizing wait for news from the town. His bread and broth went untouched, but he drained first one goblet, and then another, until the bottle was empty. His head swam, and he buried his face in his hands. The heat of his office grew stifling, so he slammed his quill back into the ink bottle, pushed away from his desk, and unsteadily crossed the room back to the window.

The sun westered as afternoon slowly faded to evening. Bright golden light spilled down on Friuli and the Abbey, and though the breeze coming in through the window was warm, it still provided some relief from the close confines of his office.

His patience rapidly wore thin, and he was about to summon a messenger to inquire into the search when someone knocked heavily on his office door.

"Enter," he said, and made no effort to disguise the frustration in his voice.

The door creaked on its hinges, and the soft whisper of woolen robes announced the arrival of one of his brothers. Garnerius did not turn to welcome the intruder.

He sipped his wine and gazed out the window onto the Abbey grounds, and let them wait. They shifted their weight anxiously, the creak of the floorboards underfoot the only sound to break the tense silence. Once Garnerius satisfied himself the calculated time had passed, he slowly turned to address them.

The prior stood with his hands stuffed in opposite sleeves, not quite able to mask the impatience on his features.

"What is it," Garnerius said.

"Father, I have news from the Constable." His voice wavered and nearly broke. Garnerius frowned; the anxiety in his tone and features could only mean one thing.

"Go on."

"The town has been swept quite thoroughly. Every inn and tavern, every stable, every brothel, and the locals were questioned thoroughly."

Garnerius took a sip of his wine. "And?"

The prior swallowed. "I am afraid, Father, there is no sign of either the friar or his companion anywhere in Friuli."

Hearing the words did little to ease the blow of what he already suspected. Garnerius snarled, and hurled his goblet against the wall. Wine splattered across wall and floor, and the goblet clattered loudly. The prior squeaked in fright and ducked his head at the sudden outburst.

"Everywhere? They searched everywhere?"

"Everywhere, Father. The woman was last seen at the inn where Michel was found, and one of the whores in the

South Quarter confirms that Brother Hieronymus was there. But no one knows where they might have gone. And the stable master at the South Gate reports their horses are gone."

Garnerius narrowed his eyes.

"Are you sure of this?"

The prior nodded eagerly, perhaps hoping that any possible lead would spare him his wrath.

"Yes, Father! Brother Hieronymus rode in on a common Hackney, but there was no mistaking his companion's jennet."

He gritted his teeth, and pinned the man to the wall with his glare.

"And just where was the night guard at the gate?"

"I beg the Father's pardon, but I know only what the Constable saw fit to tell me. I don't know whether he questioned the night watch or not, or if they even saw them depart. But I venture 'tis safe to say they are no longer in Friuli."

"Of course they are no longer in Friuli!" Garnerius roared. His voice shook the office, and the prior's face drained of color. In truth he yelled as much at himself; how foolish of him to think they might still be found within the bounds of the town! "They would not break in here and steal from me and remain behind to be discovered!"

"Begging your pardon, Father," the prior stuttered, "but why then search the town?"

"Because I believe in being thorough, or had hoped that someone on the watch with more sense might have seen which way they were headed!"

"The Constable has already dispatched men to search the surrounding countryside, but they have nearly a full day's head start. I still don't understand why they would return the reliquary, only to make off with it again themselves."

Garnerius mopped his brow. "Perhaps they saw an opportunity; be paid once for returning it, then seeing its value, steal it again to sell elsewhere. Or perhaps ..."

He fell silent as his thoughts returned to the documents within, and he once more wondered whether the pair discovered its contents, and even now sped to Bremen to turn them over to his Grace. Garnerius' mouth went dry, and he balled his hands into fists. For a long moment he said nothing, and the prior watched him anxiously.

"Father?" he finally said. "Is there anything more that we should do?"

Garnerius turned back to the window, and leaned against the wall. He gazed outside without favoring the prior with a response, and his thoughts drifted to the leagues separating Friuli from the seat of the Prince-Bishop's power. He could imagine the ignominy of the trial, and wondered what punishment his Grace might hand down. Would he be neatly beheaded in deference to his station? Or would he be drawn and quartered first?

"Father?" the prior said again, interrupting the vivid imagery of watching himself being disemboweled and castrated before a madly cheering crowd.

"Ready my horse," he said, and turned from the window.

"Your horse, Father?" The prior blinked in confusion. "Surely you don't think to catch them yourself?"

Garnerius rounded on him. "Of course I don't, you daft twit! Just see to it, and have an escort prepared. I leave immediately!"

"Yes, Father!" the prior said. He bowed stiffly at the waist and scurried from the office lest Garnerius do something more rash.

He watched him go, and when the door slammed behind him, he turned and hurried to his desk. Whatever plans the two had for the reliquary it was for the moment out of his hands, and all he could do was pray the Constable might by some miracle have better luck with them than he had with the thieves he had hired them to find in the first place.

For now, he had only one course of action. He only hoped it was not too late.

THE NEXT MORNING DAWNED BRIGHT AND clear and, before the sun rose above the eastern span of the walls of Leyen, the denizens began their morning routines. Cooking fires in the hearths of homes and the kitchens of the inns filled the gloom of pre-dawn with pleasant aromas, and merchants prepared their stalls in the many market squares. Tents and pavilions of brightly painted canvas sprung up around the green gardens, like a field of garish flowers in the heart of the main square. Overlooked by the towering edifice of the Cathedral of Leyen, it was the most prestigious of all the local markets. A rosy blush bloomed on the horizon to the east as the sun appeared, and with it more of the townsfolk awakened and took to the paved streets to see to their morning business.

Elsabeth awoke early and dressed, while Hieronymus snored from the couch that sat along one wall of their room. She slipped into a simple gown of green wool fitted snugly down to her hips to best flaunt the curve of her figure, and covered her hair with a plain cap and veil. Once satisfied with her appearance, she quietly slipped from the room and across the inn. She stepped alone onto the streets of Leyen just as the sun crested the battlements of the wall to the east.

By now there was considerable activity around the town. A distant buzz of voices filled the air as merchants directed their servants in erecting pavilions and stalls, and laid out their wares for the pedestrians who would soon be crowding the streets. A few carts laden with goods trundled through gates, now opened to the world beyond the town walls. Small numbers of travelers dressed in fashion both fine and common mingled on the roads in a display of organized chaos. Exquisitely dressed riders on well-groomed horses made their way along elevated curbs, along with a few people of station who chose to walk. The rest of the foot traffic proceeded on the edge of the street with only their pattens to keep them out of the refuse strewn across the stones.

Elsabeth stepped out into the traffic and kept to the edges of the road nearest to the raised curbs. She cut a meandering path through the town, and stopped at times at the few stands where merchants were already hawking their goods. Anyone who might follow saw only a young woman taking the morning air and browsing the market.

It took her little time to reach the moat that encircled the inner wall around the central keep. The wall itself rose like a sheer cliff of carefully placed bricks from the edge of the water on the far side. She judged the moat to be some thirty feet across, with a green lawn stretching from the near bank to a tall hedge hiding it from view from the street. Decorative arches allowed access within the hedge, and created a secluded park on either side of the bridge leading into the bailey.

Elsabeth passed through one of the arches. A small number of women gathered within to make use of the moat to do their washing, or to fetch water for the morning cooking. A few trees provided shade, and Elsabeth found a place beneath a willow that was growing on the bank. She slipped her shoes and pattens from her feet, drew her skirts up around her knees, and seated herself in the embrace of the gnarled roots stretching down into the water. She let her feet dangle down into the moat, and reclined against the willow's trunk. The morning was warm, the water was cool against the bare skin of her feet and calves, and she took some time to relax and listen to the growing din as Leyen awoke beyond the hedge.

After some time Elsabeth yawned and stretched, and picked up her shoes and pattens before rising to her feet. With her footwear in one hand and the other holding up her skirts, Elsabeth walked the edge of the moat, and carefully scrutinized the defenses.

The castle was as formidable up close as it appeared from a distance, and she puzzled over how she and Hieronymus would gain access. She did not relish another climb up the privy shaft after the misadventure in Friuli. Anyway, from a quick survey it seemed such a point of entry would not be possible. Nor could they simply walk in the front gate uninvited, if the rumors from the table the night before were true.

She found a place where the grass grew all the way down to the water's edge and lowered herself with practiced grace. She folded her long legs beneath her. A gentle breeze stirred her finer hairs poking out from beneath her cap and veil, which flashed like streams of molten copper in the morning sun. Elsabeth gazed into the water and hooked her hair behind her ear. She remained there for a time and despaired as she considered her dwindling options. She slid her shoes back on her feet, rose and stepped back into her pattens, and retraced her steps through the garden and back to the streets.

The harsh cry of a horn rang out from the wall overlooking the moat as she stepped beyond the hedge once more. Elsabeth froze and instinctively reached across her hip for her sword but came up empty. Her heart hammered against her breastbone, and she whipped her head about for any sign of guards closing in around her. Had she aroused suspicion on her walk through the outer bailey? Or had Father Garnerius learned of their escape and sent warning to Leyen?

Elsabeth scrutinized every face in the crowd, but there was no sign of anyone watching her. Nor did any of the guard rush from the direction of the keep in pursuit. In fact, aside from a few other curious folks craning their necks in the direction of the horn call, hardly anything changed on the streets at all. She took a steadying breath to will her heart back out of her throat and into her chest where it belonged. Another horn sounded in response to the first, this time from the direction of the main gate. A small crowd, buzzing with excitement, began to form along both sides of the street. Elsabeth had just slipped in among the pedestrians jostling for a place nearest the street, when guards in coat-of-plate over mail and bearing large halberds emerged from the hedge and methodically pushed them back to clear the path.

"What is this about?" she asked a matronly woman balancing a basket of soiled linens at her hip. The woman, dressed in rough homespun quite at odds with the finer cloth most prominent so near the castle, had been approaching the garden when the guard emerged. Elsabeth ventured a guess she was on her way to do her laundry in the moat.

"Are you new to Leyen, Gnädige Frau?" the woman asked.

Elsabeth struck a suitably meek posture, with her hands clasped in front of her.

"I am afraid so. My father told me to stay close to the inn, but I wanted to see something of the town!"

"'Tis not my place to pry, but a lady of your standing ought to listen to what her father tells her." The woman gave her a respectful looking-over from head to toe, and carefully averted her gaze from Elsabeth's eye. "But you are in for a rare treat this morning."

Elsabeth regarded her quizzically.

"How so?"

The woman smiled. "Just wait and see, Gnädige Frau."

Another horn cry near at hand smote the city streets, and Elsabeth all but felt it in her belly. This was followed shortly after by the pounding clatter of hooves on cobblestones. Sure enough, a column of horse emerged from the bailey, thundered across the drawbridge, and stepped out onto the street. They were all fine coursers and among the finest animals Elsabeth had ever seen, all decked out in caparisons emblazoned with the arms of Leyen — *Argent, a dragon segreant Sable.*

Eight knights in gleaming plate armor led the column, carrying upright lances fixed with pennons bearing another blazon with which she was unfamiliar — *Sable, on a fess Or between three boar's heads erased Or two griffins statant Gules.*

"'Tis the arms of the Baron himself!" her new companion breathed, and a measure of awe played across her lined features. "Must be some official business. He don't ride out often, and keeps mostly to the castle. God is smiling on you this morning that you were walking here."

Elsabeth's heart fluttered with excitement in spite of herself. By chance or fortune she found herself at the front of the crowd, and the weight of bodies behind her pressed her forward into the waiting halberd shafts of the guards keeping the streets clear.

"Go on, back!" the guard barked, and shoved back against the surging mob straining for a better view of the procession emerging from the castle grounds. "Here now, you rabble! Back!"

"Easy now!" the woman beside her snapped when Elsabeth stumbled back from his halberd. A small tremor of panic surged through her over the thought of falling underfoot as the crowd strained against the guard, and she only suppressed the instinct to strike out in her defense by sheer force of will. "The poor girl is set to be trampled!"

"If this lot stays back, she won't be. Now back with you!"

But the mob crowding against the road would not be easily cowed, and they surged again. Elsabeth was thrust forward with them, and nearly fell atop the guard altogether. She blushed fiercely and choked back a curse undignified of her purported station after he availed himself of the opportunity for a quick grope when he shoved her back again.

A sudden cheer went up when another figure emerged from round the hedge mounted atop a black courser even finer than those of the guard. And when Elsabeth laid eyes upon him her breath caught, a flutter worked through her belly, and her heart climbed up into her throat.

Cuncz sat straight-backed in the saddle, clad in a knee-length coat of brocade velvet over a fine silk doublet and parti-colored hose. One hand held his reins and gently guided his horse along the street, the other was propped regally against his hip. A longsword with a functional hilt of polished gilt bronze and a waisted grip of tooled blue leather hung from his saddle. If she were of the sort for such idle chatter among other women, she might have described his face as painfully handsome, with a strong jaw and defined features. Brown hair flecked with gold and worn loosely to his shoulders framed his face, and he wore a short and neatly-trimmed mustache and a patch of beard on his chin.

But it was his eyes that drew her attention most. They were dark and dangerous, but playfully so rather than sinister. And they swept the crowd like a raptor seeking out its prey from above, missing no detail among the crowd as if his escort served no purpose but ceremony, and he would spy any threat amongst the sea of faces long before his retinue.

And for a moment it seemed that his dark eyes locked on hers as they passed across the crowd, and her heart seized up in her chest. It was just a fleeting moment until he released her gaze again, and yet it seemed as if he had looked clear through her. Elsabeth flushed as she stumbled against the crowd pressing forward, and a strange fear overtook her that in that brief meeting of their eyes Cuncz might have peered into her very thoughts and betrayed her purposes there. But he rode on, swaying in his saddle without a word. And yet, she caught a subtle movement of the hand resting on his hip, hardly even a twitching of his fingers, but enough that one of the courtiers trailing along in his wake astride a collection of fine palfreys broke away from the others, and for a brief moment rode at his side.

Elsabeth watched this with a frown, and bile worked its way into her throat when her fancy of impending doom returned. The courtier leaned in to Cuncz and exchanged quiet words with him. Then he turned his horse aside, and returned along the path whence he came while Cuncz and the rest of his retinue rode on. The courtier dismounted, and led his horse right to where Elsabeth braced herself against the bodies pressing her forward, lest she be pitched over the guard's halberd shaft and onto her face.

He stopped in front of her, and Elsabeth's blood froze. Then he bowed politely, reached into his doublet, and pulled a folded note from within. He extended it to her between his index and middle fingers.

"With Freiherr von Leyen's compliments," he said.

Breathless, Elsabeth accepted it from him with a polite incline of her head. Then he mounted again and swung his horse around with expert precision (much to the appreciation of a few other young women of the town who cared little that he was but a functionary). The courtier dug his heels into his horse's flanks, and hurried to catch up with the rest of his Lord's company.

"Well now, that was curious," the woman beside her said, with a playful lilt in her voice. "I can't say that I have ever seen that before!"

For a long moment Elsabeth stood dumbstruck and watched the last of the procession pass by. A rear guard of light horse in brigandine and carrying bows trailed behind the rest of the company, and soon the excited buzz of the crowd died away. The guards nonetheless kept a close watch so long as their Lord remained on the streets of Leyen, and though the crowd behind her dispersed, a sea of bodies filled every square along his route towards the main gate, and she suspected it might be some time before she would be free to make her way back to the inn.

"Well, are you not going to have a look?" her companion asked.

"Hm?" Elsabeth murmured absently, still too awestruck by what just happened to put her thoughts in order.

"That bit of paper in your hand, you silly girl! Tch! I know if I were handed something by Herr Baron's hand I would not be standing around in a daze!"

Elsabeth shook herself from her reverie with a blink and a shake of her head.

"Oh! Forgive me, I have never seen such a sight as this before," she said, allowing a carefully measured hint of breathy excitement into her voice. "'Tis all quite overwhelming."

Elsabeth made a show of fumbling with the note. And when she opened it two thoughts crossed her mind: The first, accompanied by a thoughtful smile, was the makings of a plan.

The second was how little Hieronymus was going to like it.

AVE YOU LOST ALL GRASP OF YOUR WITS, girl?" Hieronymus asked in disbelief.

Elsabeth rolled her eyes. She adjusted the fit of her blue velvet cotehardie, and carefully arranged the square neckline of the dress to bare a generous hint of her cleavage.

"Will you stop your complaining? I know what I am doing," she said.

"Oh, I bet you do. I bet you can scarcely contain your excitement at notching your bedpost with another nobleman."

She glared over her shoulder at him.

"'Tis not like you have room to talk, hypocrite. Or need I remind you about the daughter of the Graf of Ehrenfels?"

"That was not what it looked like! I'll have you know my only concern was for the soul of that poor girl."

He made the sign of the Wheel as if to lend divine support to his protest but, knowing better, Elsabeth could only bark out a sharp laugh.

"Yes, as I heard it, you started with her sole, then moved up her calves, and then her thighs, before settling betwixt them. You know that if there is anything incriminating against Cuncz he will likely have it in the castle. That means we need some way inside to look for it. I had a look about and saw no other obvious way in, and I am of no mind for a swim in the moat or another climb up a privy shaft. I am merely taking advantage of the opportunity that presented itself."

"And instead of climbing up one privy shaft, you decide to invite him up your own. Very clever, Tetty."

Elsabeth retrieved a small velvet bag from her pack, opened the drawstring, and emptied its contents into her palm. A gold pendant fashioned into the form of a six-spoke Wheel with the space in between each spoke filled with cloisonné work of red enamel fell out. She fastened it about her neck on a length of gold chain, and adjusted it so the wheel nestled itself in her cleavage.

"I would think you, of all people, would know when a man is at his most vulnerable," she said. "Remember that thief in Basel? She made off with half your collections after one night, as I recall. And this would hardly be the first time I have taken advantage of it myself." She thumbed the Wheel hung about her neck. "Besides, I do have this, so I am prepared."

"May the Lord of All have mercy on you for your impertinence, using the Wheel in such a manner!"

Elsabeth took a brush from her pack and began working on her hair. Hieronymus glowered at her back with his arms folded across his ample gut. He still wore his traveler's garb, topped now with a ridiculous floppy hat with a feather stuck into its band, from his day feigning work in the markets. She smirked at him in the mirror.

"This from the man whom I have seen use his staff of office to scratch an inconvenient itch in the most unholy of places?"

"My nethers are none of your concern—"

"Now that is a blessing from on high."

Hieronymus shot her a dirty look as he continued. "— and there are better ways than opening yours to a wet-nosed princeling. And I can tell you I have sown my oats in much fairer fields in the last month than he has in his lifetime. How do you even know this mad scheme of yours will work?"

She pulled her forelocks back from her face and secured them at the back of her head, leaving the rest of her hair to spill freely down her back like a banner of copper.

"'Tis no more mad than any of yours."

Elsabeth picked up the summons and deftly walked it through her fingers. She stopped, placed the note under her nose, and took in the rich fragrance of the perfume sprinkled upon it.

"Clearly I caught the Cuncz's fancy during his ride this morning, and so he summons me to the castle intending to use his charms on the simple merchant's daughter to entice her into his bed. It will work, of course — what choice have

I, truly? I am but a humble peasant girl and he a powerful lord — but what he does not know is that I am actually taking him in by letting him believe his attempts to woo me are working. I remain in full control of my faculties while I put him in my pocket. He has his bit of fun, and when he finishes and falls asleep, I am free to slip away."

Hieronymus threw up his hands in exasperation.

"The Lord of All needs no rival in the Underworld, for he has woman on earth to contend against him!" He sighed and let his hands fall to his sides in resignation. "Fine, do what you will, but I pray it does not end with me having to bury you after the hanging."

"Just gather up all our things and be ready for a swift exit from Leyen. Whether or not I find what we are looking for, I suspect we shall need to be away from here with haste. Meet me on the far side of the west bridge at dawn." She flashed him a mischievous smile that did little to assuage the friar's concerned expression. "And as I said: I know what I am doing. Trust me."

Elsabeth ignored Hieronymus's fretting and finished her preparations. The late afternoon waned into twilight, and a small thrill worked through her belly as the hour of her departure drew nearer. Soon the muffled tread of boots on the stairwell reached them from the hall outside, followed shortly after by a firm but polite rap at the door.

"Father, dear, I am nearly ready! Do see who is at the door," she said, just loud enough that their visitor would hear her voice. Elsabeth stood away from the mirror far enough to make a show of inspecting the fall of her dress, and how the lacing pulled it snug to follow the contours of her figure.

Hieronymus spit her with a glare at the playful smirk curling her lips, then without a word to her swiped the hat from his head, and waddled to the door uttering a few choice oaths beneath his breath. He swung it open so quickly that an official-looking little man dressed in a fine brocaded doublet nearly tumbled in after him. Elsabeth hid a roll of her eyes behind her hand while Hieronymus scrambled to catch the fellow before he could fall flat on his face. She craned her neck for a look out into the hall, and spied a pair of guards bearing halberds struggling to restrain a laugh at their companion's expense.

"Who is it, Father?" she asked, and stepped into full view of the guards beyond as a test of her appearance. Sure enough, both stiffened the moment their eyes fell upon her.

"Forgive me, my good man!" Hieronymus said as he scrambled to get back into character. "Allow me, sir, allow me! I did not think anyone would be leaning on the door after knocking."

He helped their visitor upright, whose face twisted with annoyance at Hieronymus' fat hands brushing down his doublet and only mussing it further. The fellow, who was perhaps half a head shorter than her, shook him off with forced politeness and straightened his clothing and hair himself. He glared back at Hieronymus, then turned to Elsabeth and greeted her with a graceful bow.

"Good evening. I am Conrat, chamberlain to the Freiherr von Leyen. I have been commanded to see you safely to his residence," he said.

"Respectfully, sir," Hieronymus said, petulantly folding his arms across his chest, "I am unaccustomed to this notion that a man's pride and joy can be so plucked from his side without so much as a word of introduction. How am I to know she will be safe whilst in your custody?"

Conrat bristled a bit at the suspicion in Hieronymus' voice, but retained an affectation of stern patience.

"I assure you, sir, that Herr Baron has the finest and most disciplined guard in all of Boehm. She will be well cared-for while she remains his guest, and I shall personally vouch that no harm shall befall her."

Hieronymus let out a dubious grunt that won him no friendship with the chamberlain, and Elsabeth stepped in before the friar might say something to jeopardize her opportunity to gain access to the castle.

"I am certain I'll be in good hands," she said, and his features heated at her choice of words and the wry curl of her lips as she spoke them. "You fret for nothing, Father."

"If you are ready ..." Conrat said, and offered her his arm.

Elsabeth plucked a short cape carefully chosen to match her dress from a hook by the door, and threw it about her shoulders with an elegant flourish. It settled around her and broke the spell her dress cast upon the guards standing outside. Both drew in a steadying breath and averted their eyes anywhere but at her.

Oh, this will be too easy.

She leaned in and gave Hieronymus a peck on the cheek.

"I will see you soon," she said. "Do behave yourself while I am away; try not to drink the innkeeper out of house and home!"

With that Elsabeth accepted Conrat's arm and fell into step beside him as he led her from the room. She keenly felt Hieronymus' aggravated scowl boring a hole into her back on their way to the stairs leading down to the lower level, but it soon faded when she was led from the inn with the guards close around her, leaving no illusion that the invitation she received was merely a polite formality.

The streets of Leyen were still rather crowded, and only slowly did the throngs of pedestrians disperse to the inns or their own homes. A few looked her way, but otherwise showed little interest at the sight. Sweeps and street-cleaners appeared to scrub away the refuse of the day's activities, and lamp wrights made their rounds to light the town's many street lanterns.

They reached the bridge leading into the castle grounds just before full darkness settled over Leyen, and the pale disk of the full moon peeked above the battlements to the east. Conrat led her over the drawbridge, and they passed without challenge through the massive gatehouse guarding entry to the outer bailey. A few courtiers of Cuncz's household strolled through the gardens and watched her pass, and the still waters of the fish pools lining either side of the path reflected the stars just winking to life in the deepening sky overhead. Barracks, stables, and storerooms crowded against the inside of the outer defenses, while another wall encircling the manor itself loomed up ahead of them. Turrets rose at the northeast and southwest corners of this rampart, both as a last line of defense, and to provide an admirable view of the town and river beyond the outer walls.

Conrat led Elsabeth through a last fortified gate into the inner bailey, and they emerged once more in another quiet garden encircled by the inner wall and the buildings within the complex. The manor itself sat backed against the wall in the northwest corner, while guesthouses clustered opposite it to the southeast. All were of brick, with narrow windows on the lowest two floors and larger ones gazing out from the upper levels, and peaked tile roofs.

The manor itself consisted of a large central structure four stories tall, with two short wings of lesser height on either side that each ended in a square tower the height of the central wing. The front entrance featured a vaulted arched doorway set in the center of the main wing. Golden light shone from the windows and beckoned to those in the gardens as night descended. At the center of the bailey stood a fountain of white stone encircled by matching benches on a lawn of green grass, and the quiet trickle of water splashing into the basin filled the air. Guards patrolled the inner wall of the bailey and manned the turrets at either corner of the complex. Servants passed between the guest houses, manor, and store houses. Groundskeepers finished their daily maintenance and departed for their own quarters and evening meals.

Elsabeth followed Conrat to the main entrance of the manor. A guard stood at either side of the door and opened it upon their approach, allowing them into the antechamber and out of dusk's gathering gloom.

14

LSABETH FOUND HERSELF IN A SMALL, LOW-ceilinged entry chamber opening out onto a broader hall with wooden floors and plastered walls. Gilt lanterns illuminated the interior with rich golden light, making the floors and furnishings seem to glow.

Servants waiting in the foyer took her cloak and pattens. Conrat directed her forward past guardrooms on either side of the hall to another doorway, and ushered her into the great hall itself before he and her escort departed.

Upon entering, the low ceiling of the passage gave way to a lofty and expansive chamber some three stories high occupying almost the entirety of the central wing. Carved wooden columns supported the ceiling high overhead, along with a balcony ringing the second and third levels of the hall. Doors centered in the walls on her left and right led to the east and west wings through carved stone archways. The floor of polished marble tiles formed intricate geometric patterns in a variety of colors, and reflected the light of lanterns hung from the timbers supporting the ceiling.

Elsabeth swept her eyes across the hall, and scrutinized every detail. A large gilt crown-shaped chandelier, with many candles covered by prisms of glass, hung over the center of the floor and provided additional lighting and lent the hall a golden glow. Large folded trestle tables stood tucked away in both corners. Atop a dais at the far end of the hall mounted by a flight of five steps, was another long table against the wall. A high-backed chair of ornate gilt wood stood at the center of the dais. The chair was vacant and Elsabeth's heart fluttered in spite of herself as she laid her eyes once more on the Baron of Leyen, standing at the foot of the dais with his hands clasped behind his back.

Now that she saw him on his feet, she noted he stood perhaps half a head above even her tall frame. His keen and intelligent eyes were a piercing blue, and Elsabeth felt as if his gaze could peer clear through her. But though she found his eyes unsettling, his smile was exhilarating. One corner of his mouth pulled up rakishly as he laid eyes on her. It was confident, superior, and welcoming, but with a slightly predatory edge that lent him a hint of danger. For a moment her breath caught and she maintained her composure only with a great deal of effort, though his searching eyes did not miss the slight catch in her measured pace. Though finely groomed, he dressed relatively simply in a burgundy doublet and dark woolen hose that fit him so closely Elsabeth's eyes could not help but stray.

Elsabeth reached the foot of the dais and curtsied deeply in a manner that afforded him a nearly unimpeded view down her dress. Upon returning fully to her feet, Cuncz stepped forward and took her hand.

"Welcome to my home," he said in a smooth and cultured voice. "I pray the manner of my summons caused you no alarm, but after I spied you on my ride this morning, I could not chase the thoughts of you from my mind. Such beauty is a rare sight in Leyen, and I could not bear for it to pass and only see it from afar." Cuncz brought her hand to his lips and gently kissed the back of her fingertips.

Elsabeth blushed fiercely, and her heart skipped at the touch of his hand. *Get hold of yourself, girl. 'Twas not that good. You have heard better than this from stable boys drunk out of their wits.*

"Herr Baron flatters me greatly," she said, and shyly turned her head away with embarrassment that was only partially feigned. "Surely in a magnificent city such as this, there are many women of much greater beauty than I, and certainly those of higher standing."

Cuncz's lopsided smile broadened and he stepped closer to her.

"Higher standing, perhaps, but certainly not of greater beauty." He threaded his arm through hers and walked her up the dais. At some unspoken command, servants quickly entered from doors concealed at the rear of the hall. They bore a small round table and chairs and placed them atop the dais behind the high seat. "May I ask your name, my dear? I don't wish for us to remain strangers to one another."

"Gwenhevare, Herr Baron."

"Ah, quite lovely and quite fitting. I must commend you on the skill of your tongue as well, then, for you speak our language quite well. Unless I miss my guess, you are from Coventry?"

Elsabeth chided herself. *That choice of name led him too near the mark.*

"I am," she said. "But my father travels widely, and desired I be well-learned in many languages." She favored him with a coy smile and a slight lowering of her chin so she could look up at him through her lashes. "My tutors found my tongue to be quite able to the task."

Cuncz's face colored slightly at the innuendo, but he maintained his composure and helped her into her seat. From the corner of her eye she caught him stealing a look down the front of her dress, and his hand lingered on hers for just a moment longer than protocol would deem appropriate. Then he released her and rounded the table to his chair. Servants reappeared from the hidden doors bearing silver plates and two crystal goblets — even from this better vantage, Elsabeth still could see no sign of their hinges or latches. They quickly laid out the table. With the plates were a matched set of a knife, spoon and, much to her wonderment, a utensil with three tines like a small pitchfork. She picked it up and eyed it uncertainly. Cuncz noted her reaction and chuckled with amusement.

"'Tis a new fashion coming out of the Free City-States," he said. "They have been replacing their skewers with forks at the table. That is, of course, whence this set came, and they are the first in all of Boehm. Even the Emperor himself has not yet commissioned a set."

Elsabeth blushed in genuine embarrassment, and she suddenly felt very unenlightened and uncouth.

"I have never seen such a thing," she admitted.

Cuncz's lopsided smile broadened. "I insist on staying at the very forefront of fashion, and I suspect they will displace skewers at all the tables soon enough. But we are not here to discuss the finer points of cutlery, though I daresay your father might have an interest. He does deal in silver, does he not?"

The coloring of her cheeks this time was much more intended for Cuncz's benefit.

"Herr Baron is quite well-informed."

"In my position I find it useful to know what goes on within my walls. I knew of your arrival in Leyen the moment you set foot within the gate, though I nearly punished the guard over the tales he spun of your beauty. Until I saw you for myself I thought surely the man was telling mad lies."

Elsabeth smiled shyly and forced a little more color into her cheeks. Before either of them could speak again, the servants returned once more. One filled her goblet with a strong red wine from the City-States, while others carried in three silver platters and two matching silver bowls. One tray was piled high with baked morels wrapped in pastry, upon another, buns of fried cheese and white bread rolled into balls. A third was laden with beetroots marinated in wine, spiced with anise seeds, coriander, and caraway, and layered with horseradish. The servants placed bowls of watercress salad dressed with oil and vinegar for each of them, while the platters were set in the middle of the table where she and Cuncz could select from them as they desired. Once all were placed, they retreated back through the hidden doors, closing out the aroma of spices, herbs, and roasting meat wafting from the kitchens beyond.

Cuncz popped a baked morel into his mouth and watched her closely — his lips quirked into that lopsided smile — as if gauging her reaction to the meal's opening course. *Well, he certainly is doing his best to impress me.* She allowed an expression of awed delight — not entirely feigned — to light her features while she surveyed the variety of food presented to her.

"I do hope you are hungry," he said, his own expression one of satisfied amusement at her reaction. "I am afraid my cooks had little time to prepare, so the starters might be rather more lacking than I would like, but I pray you find my table to be adequate nonetheless."

Elsabeth reached for her wine and took a sip. As she suspected it was a potent one, with a hint of apple and oak. *Best be careful with that, or I might be dancing on the table well before dinner is over.* She took just enough wine to leave him the impression of being overwhelmed by the victuals laid out before them, and set the goblet aside.

"Herr Baron is modest; I have never seen such a table as this, even on high feast days," she said, then chewed her lip and appraised the marinated beets eagerly. She hesitated a moment with one hand poised to snatch one from the tray, and glanced at him as if she sought his permission to proceed. Cuncz chuckled in amusement and waved for her to continue. Elsabeth took one with feigned excitement and popped it in her mouth. It was strong and spicy, and she made a show of sucking the wine marinade from her fingers with a playful smile. His eyes widened slightly in response, and he took a hurried drink from his wine.

A course of goose stuffed with onions, quinces, pears, and bacon roasted on a spit, applesauce spiced with wine, sugar, cinnamon, saffron, and ginger, and white cabbage cooked with chicken in spiced beef broth followed the starter course.

After this came the main course: deer that was first boiled and then simmered in pepper sauce, carrots roasted with beef broth, and cubed parsnips roasted in a mixture of the same broth and butter.

Once they finished with the main course, the servants returned one last time with trays of fruit tartlets, almond and raisin pastries, and a variety of nuts coated with sugar and spiced with nutmeg, ginger, and cloves.

Elsabeth ate her fill and allowed herself to enjoy Cuncz's hospitality. She privately admitted he provided quite an impressive table even under such short notice, and she could not recall having sat at so fine a feast since days long gone in Soest. She took great care with the potent wine, drinking only enough that might be reasonable for a merchant's daughter overwhelmed by an evening of dining far above her station, while still leaving her in control of her faculties. Even with that effort, she nonetheless found her head swimming as the evening wore on, and she fell into occasional giggling fits at the Baron's flirtations.

Focus, girl! Hieronymus will never let you hear the end of it if you pass out before you can do what you came here to do.

Elsabeth helped herself to another tartlet to distract herself from the wine.

"You certainly seem to fancy those," Cuncz said over the lip of his goblet, with that same lopsided smile on his face. There was a slight slurring of his speech from the impressive quantity of wine he had imbibed over dinner, and his eyes were half-lidded.

Elsabeth blushed slightly in genuine embarrassment; she belatedly realized that aside from a handful of the sugared nuts, Cuncz had scarcely touched the dessert course and already half the tartlets were gone. Elsabeth flashed him a playful smile and dipped the tip of her little finger into the filling — this one made with cherries — and withdrew it again. She then gave her fingertip a slow lick.

"They are wonderful," she said truthfully. "Especially the cherry ones. You should have a taste."

Cuncz's smile curled into an amused smirk. "I would rather like to, but it seems that you have laid claim to the last of them."

Tartlet still in hand, Elsabeth rose smoothly from her seat and glided with an exaggerated swaying of her hips around the table. When she reached him, she leaned over with a toss of her head to move her hair away from her face, dipped her little finger into the filling, and held it out for him. Cuncz took her finger in his mouth and sucked the filling off, before trying to pull her down into his lap. She giggled playfully and stuffed the tart in his mouth, then retreated out of reach, just far enough to force him out of his chair. He followed after her while quickly finishing the tartlet, caught her by the wrist before she could reach her own chair, and pulled her close. He kissed her firmly, but gently, on the mouth.

Elsabeth allowed him a moment, as if the wine had slowed her recognition of his intentions, then pushed him away with a feigned gasp of shock. "Herr Baron!" she exclaimed, hoping her tone sounded sufficiently scandalized to the ears of anyone who might be able to overhear. "This would not be proper of me." She let her cheeks color fiercely and ducked her head away from him shyly.

Cuncz cupped her chin and gently turned her head back to face him. He flashed that lopsided smile again, and her heart fluttered in spite of herself.

"There is no need to worry, my dear. Not a soul here would breathe a whisper of what might happen tonight."

She made a show of trying to push away, and stumbled awkwardly when she freed herself from his grip. "I really must return to the inn; my father worries so," she said, her speech slurred for effect. She swayed unsteadily and collapsed toward him. Cuncz darted forward to catch her, and he pulled her close against his chest. "Oh my..."

He helped her regain her feet, but a hand against the small of her back kept her pressed against him.

"I think you may have partaken too liberally of the wine." There was a note of concern in his voice. "'Tis a touch stronger than I suspect you are accustomed to, I fear. You are in no condition to make it all the way to the inn, and I cannot rest easily with the thought of some misfortune befalling you. I insist you remain here with me tonight, and I'll see to it that your father has no need to worry for you." He brushed her hair back from her face and stroked her cheek. "I would very much like to share the full extent of my hospitality with you."

His lopsided smile broadened further to hint at the meaning behind his words. Elsabeth hesitated a moment, before allowing a smile of her own to cross her lips.

"'Twould not be proper of me to refuse such a gallant offer."

He leaned in and kissed her again, and this time Elsabeth kissed him back fully, and with a carefully gauged measure of eagerness he returned in kind. She smiled inwardly as his hands caressed her back, and one dipped toward her bottom.

Hieronymus worries too much, everything is going just as I planned.

15

IERONYMUS STUDIED THE CARDS IN HIS hand, from left to right: Ober of Acorns, Unter of Hearts, Ten of Leaves, Eight of Bells, and Two of Hearts.

The common room of the inn was full, though not crowded, and the walls trembled from the rumble of many voices all talking over one another. Travelers and locals alike gathered to share the news of the day, or drink away their cares. More business would be done in the quiet corners away from the prying eyes of Leyen's constabulary and tax collectors, as goods both exotic and mundane were bartered and sold. Most of the company that night were menfolk, though a few women slipped from table to table, plying their flesh and company for a bit of coin. His thoughts drifted to Elsabeth against his will, likely up to all manner of unseemly escapades in the castle, and he forcibly restrained himself from crushing his cards in his fists.

His opponent glowered at him from across the table, and anxiously shuffled his cards about in his hands. Hieronymus paid him no mind. He took his time to consider his move, and even paused for a long draught from his ale. A few other folk sat round the table watching the game unfold, placing wagers among themselves, laughing over their observations of each round, and drinking heartily (which was the order of the night with nothing else to occupy them).

"'Tis your move, friend," his adversary finally prompted. He was a man of roughly Elsabeth's age, tall but of willowy build, dressed in a fine tunic and, if Hieronymus was any judge, had not worked a hard day's labor in his life. Nor was he of an aristocratic sort, being rough in dialect and with no title by which to introduce himself. So perhaps he was a merchant — Hieronymus glanced at the fellow's hands, and noticed the tell-tale callouses on his fingertips formed by long labor over a lute or harp — or worse, a musician.

"I am quite aware of that, sir!" Hieronymus growled, letting a bit of his indignity into his voice. No doubt were Elsabeth here, rather than most certainly tumbling about in a most undignified manner with Cuncz by now, she would be draping herself in his opponent's lap. If for no better reason than to rankle him at her lasciviousness. "Don't rush me!"

"Oh, I have no intention of it," Willow said. "But I would like to finish this game while the night is young enough for me to enjoy it."

Hieronymus grunted. "I don't see what there is to enjoy; I don't think you have won a round yet!"

"And I shan't unless you lead the trick."

"What was the trump for this round again? 'Twas Hearts, was it not?"

His opponent rolled his eyes and heaved an exaggerated sigh. "Yes, 'twas Hearts."

Hieronymus harrumphed and played his Ober of Acorns.

"There now, I have opened the trick. What have you?"

The other twisted his lip at the card lying on the table before him.

"Bah," he growled, and threw down an Eight of Leaves.

Hieronymus uttered a self-satisfied chuckle, echoed by a few low cheers from his side of the table, and the clinking of coin changing hand.

"Are you sure that the Free Traders were your rightful calling?" he groused, "I imagine you might make a healthy fortune at cards."

"'Tis merely a diversion and a way to put a little extra coin in my purse, especially with a good-for-nothing daughter whom I believe was placed on this earth to eat me out of house and home!"

One of the men sharing their table — a rough-featured fellow with hair like straw seated at his left hand — chuckled softly into his tankard.

"She has a taste for things beyond your means, has she?" Straw Head asked. "I sympathize with you, my friend. My own has had her eye on a brooch from one of the local jewelers this past fortnight, and I dread the disappointment in her eyes if I should tell her I could never afford such a bauble."

"What we do for our daughters!" Hieronymus grumbled. "And in the end 'tis only to see them married off to another household, though there are times I confess 'twould seem that I would gain more out of such a deal. A son, perhaps, would at least be able to follow me into the trade."

Willow shuffled the cards in his hand, and drummed his fingers impatiently on the table while Hieronymus took an exaggerated pause to drink from his tankard.

A chuckle came from an old silver-haired grandfather seated to his right. The lamplight tinted his hair golden.

"'Tis the truth indeed, friend," Silver said. I am oft surprised the lengths to which folks will go to have a son. Noble folks not least of all."

"Most of all, I would say," said Straw Head with a laugh. "There is certainly no shortage of lords with mysterious nephews turning up out of the blue."

Hieronymus grunted, and thumped his tankard down.

"My friend, I think you listen to a few too many wild rumors," he said, and considered his cards. "And I have certainly heard a wild one in my day, I assure you."

He played the Ten of Leaves. His opponent laid down the Ober of Leaves with a smile, and took the trick.

"Oh, no doubt, no doubt," Willow said, as he exacted a measure of vengeance on Hieronymus by taking his time to consider his cards and nurse the tankard at his elbow. "A fellow as widely traveled as you I imagine must be full of tales.”

Hieronymus chuckled into his tankard, rather than rise to the bait of his adversary’s deliberations.

“Indeed I have. In fact, I imagine I have heard tales enough to entertain you all from now until sunrise, and still have enough for the next fortnight. But I am but a guest in this fine city, and certainly you have not come all this way to hear me talk.”

“Your humility is refreshing, sir,” said another of the gathering — a redheaded fellow sitting at ease at Willow’s right. “Seems all manner of folk come through filling the place with their hot wind. You would think that Leyen was not a vital part of the Empire by the way they yammer on about this port, or that castle.”

“’Tis a veritable jewel in his Crown, is it?”

“Indeed ’tis,” Willow said, and laid down the König of Bells. “’Twas the old Baron who made it so, and ’tis fortunate the young Baron was born, else he might have died without issue, and we would all have fallen under the sway of Ortenau.”

Hieronymus played his Two of Hearts and took the trick without so much as a smirk of satisfaction, though his opponent curled his lip. “You make it sound like it was a narrow thing.”

“’Twas indeed,” said Red. “By all accounts ’twas a difficult labor, and the Baroness, God bless her soul, perished by the end of it. He was truly a changed man after that; political marriage it might have been, but he loved her dearly all the same, 'tis said."

"All of Leyen was in mourning, and we saw neither hide nor hair of Herr Baron for some time after," chimed in another voice from the other side of the table, at Willow's left. He was a heavy-set figure of even more impressive girth than Hieronymus himself, with heavy jowls that wobbled whenever he spoke. Hieronymus considered his next move over a draught from his tankard, and he listened closely to the gossip spilling from tongues wagging under the influence of too much drink.

"I confess it came as quite a shock the day he stood atop the walls of the castle and presented the young Baron, alive and well," Jowls continued. "I was there that day, and I recall many astonished whispers amongst the cheers, for all I suppose assumed the babe died with his mother."

Hieronymus heaved a sympathetic sigh. "I suppose I can understand the old Baron's heart on the matter. My dear wife died bearing my daughter, in fact, and for a few years after I feared that she would follow, for her health was always poor from the day she was born."

He played his Eight of Bells, and his opponent quirked a smile when he laid down a Nine of Bells to claim the trick.

"And you have my sympathies, as well, friend. But I confess some satisfaction that this round you shan't win, for I have been waiting 'til just this moment to play this card!"

And with a flourish he played the Seven of Hearts. A low murmur went up among the crowd at the Devil lying face up upon the table, and Hieronymus allowed a smile to cross his features.

"'Twas a well-played hand indeed, my lad, and a valiant effort. But—" and with no less of a flourish, he tossed down his Unter of Hearts down upon the Devil card "—the round is mine, nonetheless."

Willow stared open-mouthed at the Karnöffel lying atop his Devil, and sank back into his chair in disbelief. Hieronymus chuckled in satisfaction, and swept up the cards to return them to the deck. He shuffled them thoroughly.

"As I hear it, there were doubts about the Baroness's survival from the start. The Abbot of Friuli spent much time by her side, or so my wife — God bless her soul — said," said Silver. "In those days she did some occasional washing for the old Baron for a bit of extra coin, and helped with the Baroness's bedding."

Hieronymus quirked one eyebrow. This was certainly becoming interesting.

"'Tis quite the ride for the good Father, is it not? Especially with Leyen's cathedral already so near." Hieronymus finished shuffling, and dealt one card face up to Willow — Five of Hearts — and one for himself — Two of Bells. "Bells are the trump, it should seem."

Willow leaned in and fixed him with a determined glower. "I raise you three points for this round."

Hieronymus nodded. "I see your raise, and propose a further three points for an even ten!"

Willow considered and nodded in turn. "Ten it is, then!"

Hieronymus then dealt a pair of cards face-down upon the table, one for each of them. He drew the Three of Acorns. Willow peeked at his card.

"A ride, for sure," said Red over his tankard, "but he was always close to the Baroness, and the old Baron consulted him often, as well."

"Did he indeed?"

Willow considered his card. "I raise the bet for this round another three."

"I see your three, and raise you again."

Willow nodded, and Hieronymus dealt another pair of cards — an Unter of Leaves for him.

"Aye, indeed," Red continued. "But 'twas the Baroness he counseled most. And he often came round when the old Baron was away on other business."

Willow checked his card, but passed on the betting. Hieronymus considered. "I raise you another three," he said.

Willow sighed and acquiesced with a nod. Hieronymus then dealt them each a fourth card, for him the Seven of Bells. This time Willow did not hesitate with raising him three points.

"Very well, but you should know that with that I would win the game," Hieronymus said.

"Then at least I shall be put from my misery," Willow said.

And with that, Hieronymus dealt them each their last card — for him the Seven of Hearts — and they each gathered up their hand.

"Don't start in with those rumors again, my friend," Straw Head said with strained patience. "'Tis unbecoming to speak so of a man of Father Garnerius' station, or to slander the Baroness in such a manner."

Hieronymus raised an eyebrow as he shuffled the cards through his meaty fingers, then paused for a draught from his tankard. "What manner of gossip is this?"

Straw Head sighed, and reached for his own drink. "Idle gossip and poppycock, sir, best befitting the clucking of hens whiling away the hours while they tend to the housework."

Silver spit him with a glower. "'Tis hardly idle, lad. My dear wife heard much the same talk among the staff. The Father visiting her late into the night, and departing again early the next day. Always when the Baron was absent."

Hieronymus opened the game with his Three of Acorns, and considered Silver with interest.

"That does sound quite the sordid rumor, if I understand your charge rightly."

"And I stand by it! 'Tis a queer thing that the Baroness would consult so closely with Father Garnerius, with Leyen's own church so near at hand."

Willow laid down the König of Acorns, and collected his trick with a smug grin. "I am sure the good Father counseled her quite intensely, too."

Red laughed into his tankard. "There seems to be no shortage of Men of the Wheel giving such counsel these days. My own sister told me just the other day her last visit to the church ended most abruptly when the priest laid his hands in a most intimate place during the blessing!"

Hieronymus bristled, as much at the self-satisfied smirk upon Willow's lips, as Red's slander of the clergy.

"'Tis nonetheless an unseemly sort of accusation to level against a man of Father Garnerius' status and reputation," Straw Head said. "'Twould certainly be best for you that he not get wind of such a charge."

Willow considered his cards carefully, and played a Five of Hearts. Hieronymus quickly countered with his Seven, and claimed the trick. "Bah! He is away in Friuli, and I warrant he little concerns himself with such idle gossip so long as 'tis not done within his earshot."

"But surely if what you suggest is true," Hieronymus said, "'twould mean that Freiherr von Leyen is not the legitimate heir of the old Baron that he is claimed to be."

"True enough, and yet who could prove it?" Red said. He leaned over the table and watched the final round with interest. "The old Baron presented him to us as his own, and no one I know could present any claim otherwise."

"Who indeed?" Silver said. "The household staff certainly won't speak of it beyond whispers, for fear of the consequences."

"I can hardly blame them," Hieronymus said. He laid his Two of Bells upon the table, and the play of the Kaiser earned him a small round of applause. "Such a charge without evidence would likely lead to the rolling of heads, particularly if it came from the wagging tongues of common folk."

"And 'tis why I consider the whole matter to be nothing but twaddle," Straw Head said. "There is nothing to it, at all!"

Willow shrugged, and Hieronymus gritted his teeth when his adversary played a Six of Bells; the Pope trumping his Kaiser, and winning his opponent the trick. "True enough. But one does wonder how 'twould shake up the world if 'twere to come to light. One can imagine the scandal should Garnerius be exposed for breaking his vows with the Baron's own wife!"

Silver nodded. "His Grace the Prince-Bishop would like as not have a word or two to say of it."

"The young Baron would certainly be embarrassed by the affair," Red said. "But what 'twould mean for Leyen, who could say? His Grace, perhaps, but no one among us."

Willow studied his last two remaining cards, and glanced up from them to peer at Hieronymus with a triumphant smirk.

"I think I have finally got you, friend!"

Hieronymus considered his last two remaining cards; the Unter of Leaves and Seven of Bells. He kept his expression even from long practice both at the table and in confession, but a small thrill gnawed at his belly at the prospect of actually losing the round if his opponent should play anything but a low Leaves card; he had not had the right opportunity to play his Devil card before.

The door to the common room opened while he awaited Willow's play, and for a moment everyone turned away from the table to look upon the newcomers. Hieronymus blanched, and the gnawing ate clear through his belly when he spied the livery of Friuli Abbey upon the armed men who stepped inside.

"Well, is that not the coincidence?" Straw Head murmured into his tankard, and suddenly everyone at the table shrunk into their collars and turned back to their drinks. "I wonder what Garnerius' men are doing here."

"Father Garnerius has come to see the Baron, I warrant," Silver said. "His visits have been no less frequent since he succeeded his father."

Willow played the Ten of Leaves, and Hieronymus released his breath. Nonetheless, the bile clawing at his throat refused to settle back into his gut.

Damn the luck! If Garnerius is here and intending to drop in with Cuncz, Tetty has had it!

He played his Unter of Leaves and claimed the trick.

"A common occurrence then?" he asked casually, and hoped that no one noted his sudden distress. No one said a word, and Willow merely grumbled at his sudden reversal of fortune.

"Aye, though not as frequent as it was in the days when the Baroness was still alive," Silver said.

"But I don't think for a moment 'tis part of any grand conspiracy," Straw Head said. "The Father and Baron do share a mutual dislike of Emrich von Ortenau."

Red shrugged. "There are not many in Friuli or Leyen that do have a liking for Emrich. Especially with his efforts to petition the Prince-Bishop to grant him control over Friuli."

Hieronymus watched the men from Friuli carefully. They all took seats at one of the tables, and though they soon busied themselves with food and drink, he was also quite aware that they made no effort to sit at ease or disarm themselves. Whatever business brought them to Leyen, they were wary and ready for a fight.

"I can't imagine that would go over well with his Grace," Hieronymus said, and played his Devil.

Willow slammed an Eight of Hearts down in frustration, and uttered a most obscene oath under his breath. The rest of the inn craned their necks in the direction of their table, and the men from Friuli turned to look as well. But fortunately their view was blocked by the sea of bodies between them.

"Friuli has been a question for some time," Red said. "It has long been under the control of the Abbey, and both Leyen and Ortenau have been seeking to make it a vassal for some time. 'Tis not quite large enough to maintain its free independence, though, and 'tis only a matter of time before one or the other is able to claim it. The only question is to whom his Grace most wants to grant secular control."

"Hm. Well, my friends, such matters are quite beyond me," Hieronymus said, and looked significantly at Willow. "And that is the game! And since you did not score a point, I do believe the payout is thrice the wager."

Willow curled his lip, but tossed a purse of coin down upon the table. Hieronymus gathered it up with a chuckle, and tested its weight in his hand.

"I call it all good fortune," Willow groused, "and I would challenge you again for an opportunity to win it back!"

"'Tis hardly fortune at all, lad, merely the Lord of All providing. But alas! The hour is growing late, and 'twas a long day. I thank you for the game and the company, but now I must bid you all good night."

Hieronymus grunted as he rose from the table with exaggerated slowness, and tied his newly-won purse to his belt. He inclined his head politely, and his companions lifted their tankards in farewell. Without another word he turned for the stairs leading up to the sleeping quarters, and ducked his head lest the men from Friuli spy him from across the common room. But he reached the stairs without incident and hurried up.

Damn the Dark One for this ill-turn of luck!

He hurried down the hall to his room, slipped through the door, and rushed to gather up all their belongings. If Garnerius was in Leyen, it was only a matter of time before he discovered they were here as well.

Tetty better have everything in hand. I knew this was foolish from the start, but if things don't come off as planned, we may be finding ourselves a head shorter come morning.

HINGS WERE NOT, IN FACT, GOING AS planned.

Elsabeth lay naked in bed with her eyes closed, both attempting to slow her breathing and relax her body to feign sleep, and trying very hard not to actually do so. Cuncz's lean body pressed up against her back. He loomed over her with one arm propping up his head, and the other round her waist hugging her close to him. At times the hand about her waist slipped away to gently stroke her shoulder, or glide up her ribcage to fondle her breasts, or slip down her belly and caress the space between her legs. Then he would lift the fall of her copper locks away from the back of her neck and deliver soft kisses to her neck and shoulder.

And she lay there through it all, trying her hardest to feign sleep and not respond to his touch, while her mind raced for a plan.

She had underestimated both his stamina and his appetite, and Elsabeth now feared Cuncz would be able to go well into the night, and far too late for her to have time for a proper search for whatever incriminating evidence he kept at hand. She had already attempted this ploy of pretending to be asleep several times while she tried to think of a way out, but he quickly learned just where to touch her to force her own body to betray her, which unfortunately made focusing on the task at hand something of a challenge.

Just my bloody luck to try this on someone who actually knows what he is doing in bed...

His hand slid up her belly to caress her breast once more, and she forced herself not to tense her body against the telltale stirring — impossible not to notice with the way his body pressed against the length of hers — announcing he was ready for her again. Elsabeth gritted her teeth, squeezed her eyes shut, and desperately forced herself to ignore the warmth flooding through her, but his hand once more found the spot he was seeking. She choked back the low moan building in her throat, but her efforts to feign sleep would soon once more prove futile.

Then abruptly his hand slipped back down to her belly. He gave the ball of her shoulder a quick, nibbling kiss, and the bed behind her shifted as he slowly and quietly left it with a concerted effort not to disturb her.

Elsabeth strained her ears, and could just make out the soft padding of his bare feet circling around the bed in front of her, then the soft creaking of the floorboards as he made his way across the chamber. She risked cracking one eye open, and gave the scene a quick and cautious survey.

Through the hazy slit of her vision, she spied Cuncz silhouetted against the silver light of the moon streaming through the window, and threading his arms through a robe.

He wrapped the gown around himself and cinched it about his waist, then slid his feet into a pair of slippers before quietly making his way to the far corner. If she rightly remembered what little of the layout of the room she saw in their mad scramble from the door to the bed (she blushed at the recollection that they had not quite made it, and their tryst had begun quite scandalously on the floor) it was the northwest corner. Rather than meeting square, as did the other corners of the chamber, the wall there cut across at an angle instead. A bookshelf stood against that angle in the wall, and he regarded it thoughtfully. It was the only other furniture of note, besides the large bed she now occupied, and a quiet conversation circle of chairs around a low table in the room's northeast corner.

He turned slightly to glance over his shoulder to where she lay, still unmoving with the blankets cast down around her waist, then turned his attention back to the bookshelf. He drew one of the volumes toward him, and to her surprise a soft click just audible over the whisper of her own breath broke the stillness of the room. The faint creak of well-oiled hinges sounded as the bookshelf pivoted into the room, and revealed a black hole in the shadow of the wall. Cuncz gave her one last look, then silently slipped inside and pulled it closed behind him.

She waited several tense moments, daring neither to move, nor even open her eyes fully, and strained her ears for any sign of activity in or near the solar. When no other sounds presented themselves, Elsabeth slipped from the bed and quietly padded toward the bookshelf. Even knowing they were there, she spied no trace of the well-concealed hinges along its edge. She stared in amazement at the number and varieties of texts lined up on the shelves. Most were written in some dialect of the Boehman tongue, but here and there she found one in Navarrese, Lizarran, or her own native Coventrish, and still others she could not begin to name much less decipher.

Elsabeth ran her index finger along them, and read the inscriptions on their spines. Her breath caught in her throat when she came across a large blue volume labeled, *Examinations Upon the Longsword And Arts Of Defense, By Paulus von Soest, Master of the Longsword.* At the top of the spine, painted in silver and gold and brilliant blues and reds that almost seemed to glow in the moonlight, was an escutcheon bearing the same coat of arms as the badge fixed to the scabbard of her sword. She momentarily reached out and touched the image with a trembling hand, but forced aside the bitter memories it stirred within her to focus on the task at hand.

She continued her examination, not quite able to shake off the ghosts haunting her. The leather covers and bindings were aged but well cared-for, except for one resting in the middle of the second shelf from the top, with a bright red leather spine, and gold letters in an unfamiliar script. Elsabeth reached out for it and stopped short. The bindings on this book certainly looked new, and stood out so well among the rest of the collection it easily drew the eye. In fact it did so too well. She took a cursory look at the other volumes, and smiled tightly when her eyes fell upon a tall manuscript to the left of the one she had first reached for. On both its front and back covers she could just make out an arcing streak in the thin layer of dust the cleaning staff could not quite remove.

Elsabeth took a firm grip and pulled the book toward her. It resisted a moment, then naturally pivoted on yet another masterfully disguised hinge at the front of the shelf before reaching a stop. She once again heard the same quiet click. The bookshelf slowly swung away from the wall, and a dark, tightly spiraling stone stairwell yawned open in front of her. She chuckled softly.

"They always put them behind the bookcase," she said.

A chill gust of wind spiraled up out of the darkness, and set her finer hairs on end and made her bare flesh pimple. Elsabeth quickly withdrew to find her discarded chemise and shoes. She slipped into both, returned to the tunnel, and cautiously stepped onto the landing of the staircase inside. A handle on the back of the bookcase allowed it to be closed behind her and opened again from this side. A dim glow somewhere below provided just enough illumination to make out the edge of the steps as they wound clockwise around a stone column supporting the ceiling of the passage. She tried the latch experimentally to be sure she could leave the passage that way again, then carefully started down into the darkness.

The staircase descended sharply, but though it wound in a tight spiral and the steps were narrow, they were even and well maintained, with no cracks or broken edges waiting to send her tumbling. However, it was still dark and steep, and Elsabeth needed one hand on the wall to keep her balance, while the other held up the skirt of her chemise to keep herself from tripping on it.

She descended past the level of the third floor of the central wing, then down through the second, and finally the first. There were no other exits she could readily see, and it appeared as if the passage connected the solar directly to whatever lay at its bottom. The staircase continued to spiral downward, and gradually the dim golden glow she first noted at the top of the passage resolved into the flicker of lamps.

Upon reaching the level of the cellars, the brickwork walls gave way to bedrock. The temperature dropped noticeably, and the roughly-hewn stone walls of the lower level became cool and moist to the touch. Finally, she reached the bottom, and the staircase ended abruptly in a short tunnel roughly carved out of the surrounding stone. A sealed timber door framed with iron blocked any further passage. Lamps hung from iron brackets on either side dimly illuminated this part of the tunnel.

Elsabeth crept to the door, placed her ear against it, and just made out two separate voices. One belonged to Cuncz, the other spoke gravely and with an air of authority. It seemed familiar but she could not quite place it, muffled as it was by the door.

"...do not see what was so important as to keep me waiting," the unidentified voice said. "I'll not risk being missed."

"Calm yourself, Father," Cuncz said. Elsabeth quirked an eyebrow. *Father?* "I was entertaining a guest and 'twould have been rather unseemly for me to have her thrown from my solar."

The other made a sound that might have been a disgusted grunt. "What is more unseemly is your obsession with whatever passing harlot happens to catch your fancy."

Elsabeth's face heated indignantly at those words, and Cuncz's voice turned angry. "Do mind your tongue, Father. I'll not have a guest in my home insulted. And I am sure you have not come from Friuli to comment upon my choice of company. What may I do for you?"

"There has been trouble at the Abbey," the other said, his voice quietly indignant over Cuncz's warning.

"I see. Are your brothers helping themselves to the sacramental wine, or perhaps taking a more hands-on approach to the confessions of the female laity of late?"

Now it was the other who made no attempt to disguise his indignation. "Nothing of the sort! Someone has broken into the Abbey twice and made off with the documents in my keeping. I recovered them once and the thieves were dealt with. But this second theft is of much greater concern."

Ah, Father Garnerius. I thought I recognized that self-righteous condescension. So Cuncz is indeed involved with whatever game the Abbot is playing.

"And you let them just walk right into the Abbey and take them again?" Cuncz was clearly concerned, but he kept the other's rising note of alarm out of his own speech.

"Of course not! I had it locked in the display case in my private study."

Cuncz made a sound much like a short laugh. "Oh, of course. That only means 'twas perhaps the least secure place you could have put it. And since you are here now, clearly your security is more lacking than you realized. Who was it?"

"I suspect the fools I hired to recover them originally. They were the only ones other than my own prior who knew what became of it. I sent men to have them dealt with, but both were found dead, and those two troublemakers have vanished from Friuli. We are still trying to determine how they even got into the Abbey in the first place; after the first theft I ordered the entire complex sealed."

"Well, sending men to kill them no doubt made them suspicious. Maybe you should have let them have their coin and been done with it."

"I thought it best that the fewer who knew about that reliquary the better."

"Instead they decided to pay you back for your double-cross. Who were they? Perhaps some agent of His Grace?"

"One is an Olivian friar; a rather slovenly one at that. The other a woman of ill character. She dresses in men's fashion and claims to have dispensation from his Grace."

"A woman?" Cuncz said, his voice colored by sudden interest.

"Yes, a woman, but I warn you I'll not tolerate any such thoughts as you are doubtlessly entertaining! I want them both found and dealt with. If they are indeed working for his Grace, I don't want word of those documents reaching him."

"And you wish to know if I have some agent of my own I could lend you to track them down?"

"Yes. And also to tell you that we will be delaying our plans until the documents are back in my possession."

"That is out of the question. You know the urgency," Cuncz said. Elsabeth quirked an eyebrow and pressed her ear closer to the door.

"I don't need you to lecture me on expediency, boy," the Abbot snapped. "I have been working toward this for longer than you know, and I'll not see it unravel over your impatience. Those two must be dealt with — and what they have stolen must be recovered — before word of it reaches his Grace. What have you done with the documents in your possession?"

Elsabeth's breath caught in her throat, and she listened intently.

"They are in the locked drawer of my desk in the study."

The Abbot grunted. "Ah yes, so much more secure than my methods."

"Quite a bit, in fact. Had the first attempt been mere thieves, anyone who would rob an abbey would have gone right to that false reliquary you had them stashed in, thinking 'twas pure gold. And a skilled thief would also know anything hidden away inside was something of value even without being able to read it themselves. But just another stack of papers in a desk drawer? A casual thief would pay it no mind. An agent of the Bishop would need to be able to read them to know 'twas what he wanted. You would be surprised what people miss when 'tis lying in plain sight."

"All the same, I am done with having everything scattered about. I want it all moved to where it can be kept together and watched closely. I will send a man to collect them when I return to the Abbey."

"If you insist, Father."

"I do indeed, my son. Now I must take my leave. I must be on the road soon if I expect to reach Friuli before I am missed. I'll let you return to your whore."

Elsabeth quickly scrambled away, and muttered quietly under her breath at the Abbot's insult. Now she knew where to look, and it was only a matter of arranging an opportunity to do so. She idly fingered the Wheel pendant around her neck as a plan took shape in her mind.

17

IERONYMUS POKED HIS HEAD OUT THE window and looked both ways up and down the street.

His room with Elsabeth was at the rear of the inn and overlooked a narrow alleyway separating the building from one of the market squares. His view of the market was blocked by the back of one of the shops encircling the square, but fortunately it also shielded their room from view. Night blanketed the city, and except for a few widely-spaced lamps, the streets were cloaked in shadow. Hieronymus surveyed the ground below, but saw no sign of anyone standing watch.

Well, that is the first miracle of the night; it seems the Abbott's men are here entirely by chance, or at least did not recognize me from across the room.

He turned away from the window. Still dressed in his merchant's garb, his sword and buckler hung from his hip once more, and rattled noisily as he bustled about and gathered the last of their belongings. Hieronymus threaded both arms through his pack and slung Elsabeth's longsword across his back by its belt. Her baggage was something of a problem; not so much heavy but an awkward burden to shoulder along with his own bag.

She makes it sound so easy, yet while she is off rolling on her back for a night with that bastard of a princeling, here I am left to do all the work!

Hieronymus heaved a sigh, grabbed hold of her pack, and dragged it over to the window. He hefted it up onto the sill and looked both ways up and down the street once more. Satisfied that no one was about, he leaned out and let the bag drop to the paving stones below. It struck the ground with a dull *whump*, and for a moment he tensed and strained his ears for any sign it had been noticed. Nothing but distant voices echoing in the far corners of the city and the rumble of the patrons in the common room below broke the silence outside.

He scooped up his staff of office leaning against the wall beside the window, slipped it down between his back and his pack, and leveraged his bulk up onto the window sill. With a grunt, a wheeze, and much cursing over the tight fit, he wedged himself into the open window frame. Hieronymus carefully turned around, and, conscious of the empty space over which he hung his backside, gingerly squeezed himself out and hung by his fingers from the lip of the sill. His feet found purchase on the exposed frame of the half-timbered exterior walls, and he painstakingly clambered down.

The Lord of All was with him, however, and he reached the street without mishap or misadventure. Hieronymus huffed from the effort of his climb, muttered a brief prayer of thanks, and made the sign of the Wheel as he pressed his back against the outside wall of the inn behind him. The street was deserted, and he could see nothing beyond the backs of the buildings in front of him.

He retrieved his staff and stooped to heave Elsabeth's pack up and sling it among the rest of the baggage. Then, leaning heavily on his staff for support, he scurried up the street and made his way to the stables at the west gate.

Although the night was not particularly old, the streets were nonetheless all but empty. Dark shadows stabbed across the cobbled paving stones, broken up by dim circles of golden lamplight. Dogs barked in distant corners of the city, and faint voices and laughter echoed across Leyen from the inns, taverns, and common houses near the Gate. A few guards walked abroad patrolling for vagabonds and troublemakers, but with a practiced eye, Hieronymus skirted the most likely patrol routes and picked a careful, meandering path that would allow him to approach the gate without being spotted. He saw no further sign of the Abbott's men in the streets.

I supposed 'tis just a coincidence, then, that Garnerius came here, and his men at the inn were not part of a concerted search. Mayhaps 'twas merely to warn Cuncz of the theft after all. Good, so long as Tetty can keep her head down and not draw too much attention to herself — trying as she may find it —this may work out after all. God be praised!

Hieronymus wove between a few markets, but angled unerringly towards the west gate stables. Reaching them was a relatively simple matter; getting their horses out the gate to make his rendezvous at this hour without drawing suspicion was another altogether. He considered for a moment stopping to change into the robes of his profession, but with Garnerius' men on the lookout he dared not betray his rightful identity. Nor would the guards dismiss his departure at so late an hour without scrutiny.

A few plans spun through his mind as he huffed under the burden of his baggage, and his sword and buckler rattled uncomfortably loud in his ears no matter how he tried to still them. But thus far the racket had not drawn attention to him on his winding path through the back streets and alleyways between their lodgings and the gate. Not one vagabond slept in the shadows between buildings, a testament to the routine patrols by the city watch on the lookout for ne'er-do-wells and ruffians preying on those who might wander into the wrong part of the town. Nor did he hear the call of the bawds he might expect from the streets of a city of this size; no doubt such working women kept their trade to the nunneries and inns. The streets of Leyen were his alone, with only the occasional stray dog or cat darting across his path or crying out in the night.

After a few minutes he reached an open square and stopped in the shadow cast by the corner of a tall shop on his right. He judged from the lingering fragrance of recently-baked bread that it was a baker's shop, and his stomach rumbled in spite of himself. Hieronymus froze, put his back against the wall, and leaned out slightly to peer around the corner into the light spilling across the square. The well-fortified gatehouse of the west gate loomed up ahead of him. They stood open to an inky black portal into the countryside outside of Leyen. The echo of voices filled the open space in between, and his whole body tensed.

A sizable knot of armored men and horses stood in the open square. Coats of plate rattled as the men moved about, and the horses stamped and snorted with impatience to be off. Man and beast alike were adorned with the arms of Friuli Abbey, and lamplight glinted on the points of their halberds and the tops of their helms. Bile churned in his belly at the realization he would not be going anywhere near the stables without being spotted on his approach.

Hieronymus glowered into the star-dusted sky above. *Well, Lord, you saw me through this far, only to snatch away my hope of escape from this city. I don't know what lesson there is in this, but I pray it be a good one!*

The stars winked down impassively, offering him no answer.

"...'tis their horses, I am sure of it," one of the men beyond said, his voice just reaching Hieronymus' ears from his vantage. "I was stationed at the gates of Friuli when they departed and saw them myself."

Oh, bugger.

Hieronymus flattened himself against the wall as best he could, and cursed the protrusion of his prodigious belly.

"Then they must be here," said another, a fellow whose voice carried the weight of some authority. "The Father is meeting with the Baron and may not be back for some time yet, but 'twill be our heads if we let them slip our grasp."

Hieronymus edged closer to the corner and peered around once more to watch the exchange. He could not make out clearly who spoke, and it was only the acoustical quirk of the square that allowed their voices to carry this far.

"Summon the gate guard," the second voice said. "And the watch captains!"

One of the Abbott's men sped off towards the gatehouse to do as commanded.

"The rest of you gather into groups of four," he continued. "I want a search of the city; every inn and tavern. The Abbot wants both of them alive. The woman may try to use her wiles against you, and I'll have the balls of any man who tries to lay hands on her in such a manner hung on a string round my neck, and his head on a pike if in doing so lets her get away!"

Despite the threat, the gathering laughed, and Hieronymus rolled his eyes.

Hmph. He knows Tetty so well already. Though not well enough; four men, armed as they are, would not be much trouble for the two of us were we together. I suspect they don't know about Tetty's rendezvous, then. That is something, at least.

The men organized into their parties, and soon the runner returned from the gatehouse, bringing four men with him. Only one, whom Hieronymus suspected was the watch for this time of night, was armored. The others were dressed in their plain coats and doublets.

"The watch captains," the runner said. One of the men, whom Hieronymus supposed was the captain of the Abbott's retinue, stepped forward to address them.

"Two wanted fugitives from Friuli may be in your city. Their horses have been found in your stables; a brown and white Lizarran jennet, and a mangy bay Hackney—"

Hieronymus curled his lip into an indignant scowl. *Mangy, my arse! Josephus is as well-cared for as any noble beast could hope!*

"—I want to know when they arrived in the city, and where their masters might have gone."

"I know the horses you speak of," one of the captains said. "They arrived late yesterday afternoon, and after putting up their horses made for an inn not far from here. 'Tis a straight shot up the road, and I can take you right there."

"Right, show us the way. Four men with me, and two of you remain here to keep watch on the stables. The rest of you search the city; I'll not chance that they might be holing up elsewhere. Check the inns and the nunneries in particular!"

Hieronymus frowned as the search parties scattered into the streets, while the leader of the escort turned up the road towards the inn in company with his guide. He pressed his back against the wall and shrunk as deeply into the shadows as he could until the Abbot's men had cleared the square. All but two, who flanked the entrance to the stable in company of the watch captains. No doubt they would soon rouse their own men to join in the search.

God damn the luck! He promptly made the sign of the Wheel to beg the Lord's forgiveness. *I suppose I should be thankful I was at least graced the foresight to vacate the inn when I had the chance. Pray that the locals have already forgotten me by the time they get there.*

He frowned, and leaned round the corner again. Open ground stretched out between him and the stables and gate, empty of cover and brightly-lit by the streetlamps. Nor was there any other means of approaching the stables without being spotted. And even if, by God's Grace, he could, there would be no leaving through the west gate now that the watch was alerted.

'Tis a pickle indeed, but this old fox has slipped many a snare tighter than this. 'Tis but a matter of finding the loose knot.

With that, he snatched up his staff, and retraced his steps back along the wall. He paused at the far end of the building, found that the search parties had already moved on, and slipped back into the deeper shadow of the alleyways.

I do hope Tetty is enjoying herself, while I am out here taking all the risk fumbling about in the dark!

UNCZ'S RETURN CAME FROM AN UNEXPECTED direction.

Elsabeth waited for him in a small private dining hall on the upper level of the manor. It was situated along the southern face of the central wing, with tall windows looking out onto the bailey. A door in the eastern corner of the north wall led back to Cuncz's private study, and from there to the solar on the left or the bower on the right. A heavy timber trestle table, surrounded by chairs with padded leather seats and backs, dominated the center of the hall. A silver tray bearing a bottle of more of the wine from dinner and two goblets awaited them there. There were cupboards and shelves along the north and west walls for storing dishes and cutlery, and a fireplace occupied the eastern wall. A door to the right of the fireplace led east to a landing allowing access to the lower levels, and Cuncz returned to find her sitting on a rug laid out in front of the fireplace, while a small blaze crackled in the hearth.

She turned at the sound of his entrance, put on a welcoming smile, and rose quickly to her feet.

The passage must have another exit somewhere within the castle. I wonder what other secrets this place holds.

She let her hair spill freely down her back in a disheveled cascade of copper, and adjusted the neckline of her chemise to tease him with a glimpse of her breasts. She had left her shoes behind in the solar, and the polished wooden floorboards were cold and smooth beneath her bare feet. Elsabeth padded over to him, threw herself into his arms, and kissed him deeply. If Cuncz's conversation with the Abbot left him distracted he did not show it, and he kissed her back fully and eagerly, his hands wandering down to her bottom and pulling her tightly against him. Elsabeth forced down the rising thrill of the kiss, and gently pushed herself away from him.

"And what are you doing out here, my dear?" Cuncz asked playfully.

Elsabeth ran a finger down his chest. "I awoke and you were gone. I came to find you and bring you back to bed, but a servant said you would return shortly." She flashed him a smoldering and inviting smile. "I hope you don't mind, but I asked him to fetch us a bottle of wine. Go and sit by the fire, Herr Baron, I'll bring it to you."

Cuncz smiled back at her and kissed the side of her neck. He took advantage of the moment of closeness for another grope of her backside, then made his way over to the fireplace. For a moment he left Elsabeth alone with the wine, and she needed little more time than that. She quickly filled both goblets, and then carefully turned the chain loop atop her Wheel pendant until she felt, more than heard, the soft metallic click of the hidden latch, and the face of the pendant popped open. She carefully measured a pinch of the fine white powder within and sprinkled it into one of the goblets, then closed the pendant again with another inaudible click. Elsabeth swirled the doctored wine until the powder vanished, then returned to the fireplace.

She handed Cuncz his drink and lowered herself to the rug. Elsabeth adjusted her skirts as she folded her legs beneath her, baring her lower legs for him. Cuncz took a swallow of his wine and shifted closer to her so he could run a hand along her calf.

"I do apologize for leaving you, my dear," he said, and took another long drink. His hand reached her knee, and slipped under her skirts to continue up her thigh. "A rather urgent matter required my attention."

Elsabeth drank from her goblet, and allowed a giggle over his hand wandering to her hip before inching over to the inside of her thigh.

"I hope 'twas nothing serious." She swatted his shoulder playfully when his searching fingers edged even closer to the space between her legs.

He chuckled and took another drink from his goblet. "Not at all. And I swear, you now have my undivided attention."

Elsabeth smiled at him over the rim of her goblet. "Wonderful, I would hate for us to be interrupted further."

"Will you and your father be remaining in my humble town for long?"

She sighed heavily. "I fear not. My father prefers not to remain in any one market for long. He says 'tis poor business to sit in one place. I suspect he is already seeking a man to make arrangements for the sale of his goods in Leyen.”

“Ah, then perhaps I should have invited him to dinner as well. I prefer to keep a close eye on such arrangements myself. I find that there is much less incentive for such local contacts to cheat on the tariffs when I take a personal hand in the matter.”

She pouted. “But then I fear you and I would not have had as much time alone.”

Cuncz reached out to stroke her leg again and took another drink. He was slow in taking the goblet from his lips, and hesitated before responding.

“Which I would have deeply regretted,” he said after a moment, and when he did his words were ever so slightly slurred. “But if you will remain my guests another few days, perhaps I shall have time to speak with him before you depart.”

“I believe we may still be here a few days more at least, perhaps a week.”

“Excellent! All the better, since we shall have more time together. You will remain my personal guest here, of course.”

Elsabeth giggled. “Of course.”

Cuncz swayed a little, and mopped his brow with the back of his hand. “Wonderful! I will very much...” He trailed off suddenly, and his last words were so slurred together she could not make them out.

She allowed a look of concern to appear on her face. “Herr Baron, are you all right?”

He slurred something more she could not understand, then slumped onto his elbow before collapsing onto his back. Cuncz's head lolled about, and his eyes glassed over as they gazed sightlessly at the ceiling. Elsabeth casually drained the last of her wine and gave him a quick looking over to satisfy herself that he was still breathing.

"I am sorry about that, love, but had you only been concerned about your own pleasure and gone right to sleep when you popped off like I had counted on, we might have avoided this entirely," she said into the stillness of the dining hall.

She left Cuncz to lie unconscious next to the fire and headed for the study.

It was a chamber of modest size and not particularly opulent in its furnishings. A single wooden desk dominated the center of the room. In one corner sat a couch and two chairs around a table. A map of Leyen's surroundings hung on a board on the southern wall to the left of the door, and shelves laden with books, scrolls, and other odds and ends occupied the wall immediately to her right. A row of curtained windows looked out to the north across the bailey, and she could see the fading light of the moon glistening on the waters of the river in the darkness outside. Paintings, whose details she could not make out in the faint moonlight, hung on the east and west walls.

Elsabeth hurried over to the desk and quickly checked the drawers until she found the locked one Cuncz had mentioned to the Abbot. She slipped a hand into a pocket hidden within her chemise, withdrew the leather pouch for her lock picks, and quickly went to work. It took only a few moments for the lock to click, and she pulled the drawer open and rifled through the stacks of papers within.

Most were innocuous documents of little interest: correspondence with merchants and other nobles, trade ledgers, inventories, records of wages for the manor staff, minutes from meetings of the town's council, and other miscellanea. Finally, buried at the very bottom of the drawer in a leather case, she found what she was looking for, a nondescript sheaf of papers bearing the seal of Father Garnerius. Elsabeth stuffed them down the front of her chemise, slipped a few loose papers into the case until it looked reasonably full, then returned it and the rest of the documents to the drawer where she had found them and slid it closed. The lock clicked on its own, and she gathered up her picks, retrieved her shoes from the solar and slipped them on, and hurried toward the door leading back into the private dining hall.

As she emerged from the study, she found the chamberlain leaning over the prostrate form of Cuncz with three guards behind him, all turning to look in her direction as she stepped into the room.

"Fuck," she said.

"Seize her!" Conrat shouted, and the three guards charged her, drawing swords as they came.

Elsabeth retreated quickly into the study, seized its heavy timber door in both hands, and swung it closed into the face of the first guard to reach her. It struck him hard and he stumbled backwards under the force of the blow, entangling himself with his comrades and sending the entire group crashing to the floor, snarling curses in her direction.

She wasted no time in taking advantage of the distraction. She coiled her legs beneath her, sprung back into the dining hall, and dove over the guards while they fought to free themselves from each other's limbs. She struck on her shoulder and rolled back to her feet in time to meet a panicked dagger-stroke from the astonished chamberlain. She lunged to her left and guided his attack past her right shoulder with her forearm, then used his own momentum coming forward to throw him over her leg and into the recovering guards.

Elsabeth turned and ran for the fireplace, sprung over the dozing Cuncz, and snatched a poker from a rack of tools next to it on her way past. She rushed for the east door and hurriedly pulled it shut behind her as she fled into the hall, slid the poker through the handle, and wedged both ends as best she could into the frame before hurrying on her way again.

She found herself in a short hall that ended in a dead end to the north. Across from her were narrow windows draped with velvet curtains, looking out eastward a good two stories above the east wing. A short distance away she could make out the shadow of the tower at that end of the manor, black against the indigo of the dying night sky. More windows looked out onto the bailey on her right, and in the southeastern corner was a flight of stairs leading down to the galleries overlooking the great hall.

The door behind her shook when someone yanked on its handle. The poker dug into the wooden frame with a piercing squeal as it began to give way under the effort of the guards trying to force it open. Each tug on the handle from inside opened the crack between the edge of the door and the jamb just a little wider. Elsabeth let out a decisive breath and hurried to the window closest to the middle of the roof below her. She flipped the latch and threw the window open. A warm breeze from the bailey greeted her when she peered out and looked down. The roof of the wing below was rather steeply peaked, ending in a quite abrupt drop to the bailey below. Elsabeth turned suddenly at another squeal behind her, and found the door had opened wide enough that one of the guards was able to slip his hand through to try removing the poker.

"Bugger."

The windows were narrow and it took a little wiggling to clear her hips, but she was soon crouched in the windowsill with the curtain in hand. She made the sign of the Wheel, held her breath and dropped off.

For a moment she fell freely, then she reached the end of her slack and kicked her legs to throw her weight forward, aiming to swing near enough to the peak of the roof so she could grab hold of the ridge and stop herself from sliding down into empty space. The curtain began to tear free under her weight, and Elsabeth's momentum carried her right into the wall of the central wing. She grunted from the impact, lost her hold of the curtain, and fell awkwardly the rest of the way to the roof below.

One foot touched down first and to her dismay she went down on her rear, the ridge just out of reach as she went skidding backwards and downwards. Elsabeth managed to roll herself onto her belly and grabbed at the shingles with one hand to swing around until she was sliding feet-first. She bit back tears of pain as she dug her fingertips into the roof in hopes of gaining purchase. Instead, she slid all the way off the end of the roof, and it was only when her hands caught the gutter that she managed to stop her slide.

Her fingers found a grip on the edge of the channel, but the sudden stop jolted her shoulders, and she cried out in pain. For a moment she hung there, before looking both ways along the roof. The eavesdrip was too far out from the wall and the windows too far down for her to safely climb inside from here, and the roof itself was too steep for her to climb back up again. She was too far from the east tower to make her way in that direction, particularly in the time she had before Conrat could rouse the guard, and there was nowhere toward the main wing where she could reach another window or find a handhold to climb down. Elsabeth looked down and noted the ground immediately beneath her, two stories below, was a lawn of grass.

"Bugger it," she said, and released her grip, throwing her weight around to face away from the wall.

The fall ended with alarming suddenness. The moment Elsabeth's feet struck the ground, she allowed her legs to collapse under her and threw herself forward into a roll. She tumbled across the ground, arms shielding her head and neck, and stopped herself with a break fall. She checked herself for injury, but a quick survey revealed nothing more serious than scraped and bloodied fingertips from trying to stop her slide down the roof and a few bruises from the fall. Elsabeth double-checked the documents hidden away in her chemise and looked about quickly for a means of escape before the alarm was raised.

Only one gate led out of the inner bailey, and this was under guard, to say nothing of the men patrolling beyond. Elsabeth kept to the wall of the manor and used its shadow to hide as best she could from the guards on the battlements in hopes they had not noticed her cries or the noise of her fall. She edged her way toward the east tower. She rounded it quickly to the back side of the building and spied a well in the narrow court between the back of the manor and the inner wall. No one stood watch at a back door that she guessed led to the kitchens, though a lantern on either side of the entrance lit the surrounding area. She hurried as fast as caution allowed across the court and gave the well a quick looking over.

It was a simple brick shaft with a winch used to raise the heavy wooden bucket, which rested on the rim of the well. She could not see how deeply it descended, but with the river near at hand, Elsabeth mused some branch cut away under the hill, though whether its entrance and exit lay above the surface of the water she would not be able to tell until she found it.

The distant echo of voices shouting orders reached her from the other side of the manor; one, at least, was Conrat, and with no other options, she let the barrel drop into the shaft. Elsabeth seated herself on the edge, grabbed hold of the rope, and swung herself into the hole. The drop of the bucket suddenly accelerated under her weight, and the dim circle of the sky above vanished as she plummeted into the darkness.

Elsabeth did not bother to keep the time of her fall, and only the splash of the bucket hitting the water told her when it reached the bottom. She descended a moment more herself, when suddenly the rope attached to the winch above played out and she snapped to an abrupt stop that tore her hands from the rope. She fell backwards into the water below with a cry. It was quite deep and icy cold. Elsabeth shot back to the surface with a desperate gasp for breath and grabbed hold of the rope.

She allowed herself a moment for her eyes to adjust to the dark and to get her bearings. The faint circle of moonlight shining into the well revealed she had descended into a cistern lined with brick, and the water flowed past her, fed by some channel dug off the river. She could just make out a raised walkway running the circumference of the cistern, but the rest was lost in total blackness. Elsabeth swam in that direction, and hauled herself out of the water. She shivered in the darkness, and turned first one way and then another, listening intently for any sign of pursuit.

Well, this whole adventure will have been pointless if those papers are ruined. No time or light to do anything about that now, though.

Elsabeth chose to follow the flow of water, and carefully felt her way along the wall. The walkway was dry and the brickwork masterfully done, so she suspected even during a flood the water would normally be below the level of the walkway. Her spirits lifted: Surely this channel and the cistern saw regular maintenance, and anyone who came down here would have another means of entering than the one she had chosen.

The passage ran straight and relatively level for some distance until it ended at a blank wall of bedrock where she suspected the canal exited to rejoin the river by means of a grated opening somewhere deep below the surface to prevent an intruder from using this as a means of accessing the castle.

I suppose 'twas hoping too much Cuncz's security would be as lax as Friuli Abbey.

She felt around the surrounding walls seeking an exit, and her searching hands found a heavy timber and iron-bound door near at hand. She cautiously tugged on the handle and found it locked, but she needed only a moment with her picks to have it open. Not a shred of light from beyond escaped the crack beneath the door or through its keyhole. Elsabeth fumbled in the dark for the door handle and pulled experimentally. It gave easily and noiselessly. She slipped into the darkened chamber beyond and shut the door behind her, where it clicked locked again.

A thin silver light shone in through a narrow window somewhere high overhead. It mingled with the golden light of lanterns casting flickering shadows on the walls, and she reasoned she must be at the bottom of one of the towers ringing the outer bailey. Stacked crates and boxes, barrels, tools, and other supplies, along with a dozen or so feet of rope coiled on a box, filled the space beneath the spiraling staircase leading up into the tower. Elsabeth hung the rope over her shoulder, and started as quickly and quietly as she could up the staircase.

After a few stories she cautiously approached a landing at ground level, where a heavy iron-bound door allowed access to the tower from the inner bailey. When she saw it was deserted, she hurried past and continued up. She passed several arrow loops with embrasures too narrow for her to slip through, until she finally reached a small open window about halfway up the tower. The only place she found to secure her rope was an iron bracket bearing one of the lanterns filling the tower with muted light. Elsabeth made her line fast about the bracket, then with a great deal of effort squeezed through the window. It was a very close fit, and she very nearly caught her hips in the window frame before she finally managed to wriggle through. She was soon rappelling down the tower and muttering to herself about making yet another long descent.

Fortunately this time her feet reached the ground before the end of her lifeline, and she took off from the cover of the wall, her ears alert for shouts of alarm and warning. The commotion raised by the search of the grounds grew louder as the guards shifted their attention to the outer bailey, but for the moment she found herself clear and beyond the walls of Leyen. The rise on which she now stood descended a steep bluff toward the river below, and Elsabeth quickly slipped out of sight of the walls and onto the slope.

She picked a careful path down to the edge of the water, and angled off to meet Hieronymus.

IERONYMUS THREW HIS WEIGHT BACKWARDS and gripped his staff with his elbows for leverage. The hapless guardsman thrashed and kicked. He grabbed at the graven wooden shaft pressed across his throat in a vain effort to free himself after the friar assailed him suddenly from behind and dragged him into the dark shadow of the alleyway. A weak, rasping gurgle that died the moment it left the fellow's lips was the only sound to break the stillness of the evening during the struggle.

"Lord of All, come to meet this soul and guide him safely to your side in Heaven," Hieronymus whispered into the guard's ear. "Give him eternal rest, and may your Light shine upon him forever more."

Panic awoke in the guardsman's eyes when he murmured the Last Rites, and he renewed his struggle with sudden vigor. But with Hieronymus' ample weight to anchor the staff in place and the leverage of his position, there was no escaping his fate.

"All-powerful God, I commend to you this man, your servant. Let him know your mercy and love, as you expunge the sins he committed in his weakness. He has died from this world. Let him dwell now with you forever."

The guardsman vainly reached out for his fellows disappearing into the blackness of one of the back alleys of Leyen, having never noticed he fell behind during their search. And then suddenly his struggling ceased and his body collapsed lifelessly into Hieronymus' arms. He held his staff firmly across the fellow's throat for a few moments more to be certain he was not merely play-acting in hopes he would relax his grip too soon, then with reverent tenderness gently lowered the body to the ground.

Hieronymus crouched over him for a moment, and checked the guard for any signs of life. His glazed eyes stared sightlessly up into the night sky, and his face was blue in the silver light of the stars and moon. An ugly purple bruise marked the spot where his staff crushed the fellow's throat.

He solemnly made the sign of the Wheel, and he wordlessly uttered a prayer for mercy for the soul of this man who had died in the Abbot's service.

For a moment he sat back on his heels and considered the body lying sprawled upon the ground before him. He had come upon this particular patrol suddenly as he was working his way past the west gate for a point further to the south, and only just managed to take cover again before they could spy him lurking in the shadows. The other three passed him by, but this fellow by some quirk of fate had seen or heard something, and he paused and turned, as if to retrace his steps and investigate. Fortunately, he did not sound an alarm, allowing Hieronymus to catch him round the neck with his staff before he could cry out for his companions. If the Lord of All was still on his side, it might be some time yet before the others realized he was missing and turned back for him.

There is nowhere convenient nearby to hide the body, though, so once they notice he is gone they will almost certainly find him. 'Tis best I be well away from here ere they do.

He regarded the man's garb thoughtfully for a moment. If Hieronymus were not many times more the man the fellow lying on the ground before him was, he might have appropriated his gear and tried slipping out the gate. However, one of his stature would not be easily mistaken for a member of their company, and even if it did fit, almost certainly they would recognize him as a stranger by his face the moment he drew near (to say nothing of any passwords they might have for just such a happenstance). No, he had to make do with the clothes already upon his back.

Hieronymus sighed and levered himself back to his feet with his staff. He strained his ears for any sign the struggle had been noticed — by the guard's companions, by the night watch of Leyen, or one of the locals — but no one uttered so much as a peep, much less a cry of alarm. So, satisfied that stealth was still an option, he started off again as quickly as he could without rattling the gear on his belt or the packs on his back.

And this is but the easy part. There is still the matter of how in God's name I shall get beyond the damned walls!

He continued through the streets, cutting a meandering path to throw off any potential pursuit. At every intersection he listened carefully for any indication he had been spotted, or of guardsmen close behind, but was answered only by the distant echo of a dog barking in some corner of the town, or the night breeze stirring wind chimes hanging from a nearby roof. He made his way steadily towards the south wall.

This part of Leyen was largely occupied by warehouses and workshops. A few guards patrolled the streets between the buildings, but they were few in number and widely spaced. Were he the owner of such a business, he was of the mind he ought to complain about the poor security — it would be an easy thing for a thief to break in with such poor coverage by the night watch — but tonight it served his purposes well.

Ere long the arc of the wall loomed up ahead of him. His path dodging between alleyways brought him to a point roughly halfway between the west and south gates. He hunkered into the shadow of a warehouse at the edge of a small, open square that stretched between him and the dark shadow of the wall ahead. It was enclosed on all four sides by workshops and warehouses, and accessed by three main roads and the narrower confines of the lesser passages between blocks. The shops at the far end butted nearly right up against the wall, spilling dark shadows in the nooks and crannies, where one might approach the wall itself unseen if one could cross the square.

Hieronymus swept his eyes across it; it was not appreciably large like the markets in the inhabited parts of Leyen, and if he were any judge of the layout, it was used for the loading and unloading of goods coming into and out of the storehouses closing around it. Lamps spilled flickering circles of light down upon the street, with considerable stretches of shadow where a light-footed man might dance between them unseen. Nor did he spy any sign of guardsmen patrolling this stretch of the city streets. He strained his ears, but not so much as the squeak of a mouse could be heard in the eerie silence hanging over him.

He turned his attention momentarily from the market to the wall ahead of him. It was of considerable height, though not wholly unscalable (little as he liked the thought). More importantly for his purposes, it was not particularly well-lit, and he saw no sign that the night watch maintained a post at this stretch.

Not so much as the glint of lamplight upon a helm. Well, Lord, I shall commend myself to your benevolent hands, and trust that fortune is with me!

Hieronymus heaved a breath, snapped up his staff, and broke from the cover of his hiding place. He dashed, quick, quiet, and low as he could under his burdens, and dodged for the seas of darkness surrounding the pale islands of light around the lamp posts.

Upon reaching his next hiding place he froze and crowded his bulk as deep into the shadow as he could manage. Hieronymus strained his ears for any sound out of place and scanned the square. But no one cried out, nor did he spy a light in a window, or any other sign his passage disturbed the stillness of the night. He nodded in satisfaction, and crept along the front of a warehouse that smelled strongly of ale (*Curse the Lord for laying this temptation at my feet! Oh! What a cruel test he presents to me!*) before disappearing into the dark corner between two workshops and a small segment of the wall rising up in front of him.

He considered the stonework thoughtfully. The red bricks of the walls were masterfully laid and neatly mortared, with not so much as a single block out of place that might be of use as a handhold.

Hieronymus then regarded the buildings on either side. They were of half-timbered construction with red brick on the lower level, and their steeply-pitched tile roofs reached to just below the catwalk atop the town walls. But though the overhang of the eavesdrip would make reaching the roof somewhat of a challenge, they were nonetheless much more scalable than the sheer face of the town wall itself. So he slipped his staff down amongst the packs on his back next to Elsabeth's sword, rubbed his hands together, and faced down the daunting task ahead of him.

Well, there is nothing for it but to ascend as did the Holy Son, though I warrant the road to Heaven was much less grueling!

He braced his legs beneath him, rubbed his hands together, and with a mighty heave belying his bulk, leapt upwards and caught hold of a wooden transverse a short distance above his head. Hieronymus ground his teeth together and strained upward. His feet found purchase against the brickwork on the lower level, and he slipped one hand up to the joint in the X-shaped cross-bracing. He jammed his fat fingers into the lip of the frame and, with much huffing and wheezing and aching in his shoulders, he pulled himself higher.

He continued in this fashion, clinging for dear life to the wall in front of him, his face mashed so near he could smell the plaster painted over the infill of the second story. He would almost certainly walk away from his ascent with flakes in his beard. His arms burned and sweat beaded on his brow.

Tetty had best be enjoying herself. Here I am in mortal peril of dashing my head upon the paving stones, while she spends the night in the most undignified of positions for the benefit of that blasted Cuncz, and being waited on hand and foot. Bah!

Nonetheless, the climb proved more grueling than hazardous, and he soon reached the first true obstacle. Hieronymus craned his neck; the eavesdrip hung over his head just within reach of his fingers, but extended out far enough from the wall he would not have the use of his feet in clambering up. Reaching it would also risk unbalancing himself from the weight of the two packs slung across his back. He considered his ascent carefully, and with his weight as forward as he could manage, reached up and seized the edge of the roof with one hand and wrapped his fingers around the edge.

Once confident of his grip, he released the wall. His bulk swung alarmingly into the empty air. Hieronymus grabbed hold of the roof with his free hand and hung for a moment with his feet dangling beneath him. He pulled himself up until he could lay his elbows on the roof, then heaved and kicked his legs, and walked himself up the roof by his elbows until his upper body lay flat against the tile shingles. His breath came in heavy gasps, and his heart hammered against his breastbone from the effort.

Lord, if this is a message I may need to lose some weight, you at this moment have my undivided attention. God, this would have been easier twenty years ago!

Hieronymus craned his neck to look up the steep peak of the roof, the next great obstacle of his ascent. He sighed and thumped his head against the tiles, caught his breath, and then slowly wriggled his way up in an undignified manner not unlike that of a lizard.

The roof creaked and groaned in protest at his weight, and Hieronymus gritted his teeth against the bile churning in his belly at the thought it might give way beneath him, dooming him to a fall of indeterminate height through the warehouse. He put his head down and continued shimmying upward, carefully testing each tile with his fingers and feet to be sure it would not work loose. Some rattled in a most alarming manner, but demonstrated the high quality of the roofers' craft by remaining firmly affixed in spite of the steep pitch. Nor did the exposed edges of the tiles catch upon his doublet or his belly, and with no real misadventure he soon found himself grabbing hold of the ridge.

Hieronymus hauled himself up onto his hands until his head popped up above the top of the roof. He found himself looking somewhat to the west across Leyen, with the moon just beginning its descent from its zenith. It hung like a silver disk over the western battlements, and glittered on the dark surface of the Nebel River as it rounded the bend to pass along the western side of the town. Shadows stretched across the city, not quite falling asleep as the night wore on. The distant murmuring echoes of voices filled the night air at the inns and taverns nearby, and lamps glowed in the windows of the town houses. Only the heavily commercial quarters — such as that which he now occupied

— were completely still, awaiting the return of dawn to begin their business anew.

He grunted, heaved, and strained, until he was sitting atop the ridge. Hieronymus mopped the sweat beading his brow on the back of his sleeve and sat for a moment, straddling the rooftop so he might not topple over in either direction to the ground below. The evening was warm, but a welcoming breeze danced along the rooftops, stirring his finer hairs and refreshing him from the effort of his climb. He sighed as he regarded the wall looming against the night sky ahead of him; the merlons of its crenelated battlement stood out like gray shadows in the moonlight against the dark southern sky, like the blunt teeth of some tremendous beast.

Idleness is the Dark One's tool, my lad. There will be time enough to rest while we wait for Tetty, so best get a move on.

Hieronymus eased himself to his feet and stuck his arms out to either side for balance. He deliberately placed one foot in front of the other as he made his way along the ridge, and wobbled to and fro all the way along the length of the roof. With a slight shift in his knees to lower his point of balance, he made it with not-quite-catlike grace to the end of the roof. He balanced there for a moment and considered the jump before him.

A gap of a good dozen feet spanned the distance between the end of the roof and the innermost edge of the catwalk topping the town wall half again his height overhead. A fall from his current perch would almost certainly break his legs, if not his neck. Nor did he trust his footing on the narrow ridge to back away for a running start at the gap. Not a soul was to be seen at this part of the wall;

any guards manning the battlement would likely be standing watch at the gates themselves, or from one of the towers. He had only to make this simple mad leap of faith, and he would surely be free of the town.

Hieronymus held his breath and made the sign of the Wheel.

Lord, I have trusted you this far, and you have not failed me. But should I very shortly be having words with you in person, rest assured I shall be giving you an earful!

He gathered his weight and planted his feet as best he could on the narrow ridge of the roof, and coiled his legs beneath him. His fingers twitched, and he wiped the sweat gathering on his palms on his thighs to ensure a sure grip. Hieronymus licked his lips. He tensed, and then released the tension in his limbs and sprung for all he was worth into the air. Others might have scoffed at the absurd sight of him heaving his bulk into empty space for an endeavor that even an accomplished acrobat might well refuse to attempt.

It might almost have been worth attempting the feat under the full light of day just to see their reactions.

Hieronymus swung his arms and kicked his feet against the air, and then, at the very last moment stretched out with his hands. His fingertips caught the very edge of the catwalk, and he squeezed them tight round the sharp corner of the brickwork until it nearly cut into his palms. The rest of his body swung forward and struck the side of the wall hard enough to force a grunt from his lungs. But his grip remained sure, and he did not loosen his hold.

He hung there for a moment and strained his ears for any sign the noise of him hitting the wall might have been heard. However no call of alarm went up. Nor was there any voice near at hand, or even the tread of boots upon the catwalk topping the battlement.

Satisfied, he hauled himself upwards. His arms ached in their sockets from the sudden burden placed upon them, and his middle throbbed from the force of his weight striking the wall, but otherwise he was unharmed. Hieronymus worked himself up onto the catwalk and crawled to the battlement. He peered over the side; the drop was a considerable one, and there was no convenient brush near the wall which might break his fall. The battlement overhung the wall itself, and was supported by regularly-spaced corbels. Between each was a machicolation looking down onto the base of the wall about thirty feet below.

Hieronymus looked both ways along the wall. The ground below was relatively level, and there was nowhere near at hand where it climbed higher up the wall. He sighed.

Well, one spot is as good as the next. Why did I not think of grabbing some damned rope while I was stumbling about in the dark?

Hieronymus shrugged out of his packs and slung Elsabeth's sword securely at his back. He leaned out from one of the crenels as far as he dared and released his burdens, and they struck the ground beneath the wall with a *whump* and a clatter. Then he climbed up into the crenel himself, turned around, and carefully backed himself down over the side. He slowly lowered himself as far as his arms allowed, and peered over his shoulder to find his landing point.

He released his grip, throwing his weight around to face away from the wall.

The fall ended with alarming suddenness. The moment Hieronymus's feet struck the ground, his legs collapsed under him, and he threw himself forward into a roll. He careened across the ground, arms shielding his head and neck, until he rolled to a stop on his back with his limbs splayed out in all directions. He checked himself for injury, but a quick survey revealed nothing more serious than a few bruises from the fall.

Hieronymus sat upright, and rubbed the back of his neck.

When I see that girl I shall be giving her a piece of my mind, and that is certain!

And so he picked himself up, retrieved the packs and his staff, and hurried off for the agreed-upon meeting place.

"YOU ARE LATE, GIRL," HE SAID, WHEN ELSABETH finally arrived at their rendezvous near the west bridge.

Fortunately, Hieronymus — still clad in his merchants' garb — had the good sense to choose a place somewhat out of sight of the guards patrolling the town walls and those stationed at the gate itself. Her clothes were wet, and to her consternation she was suddenly aware the white linen of her chemise was no longer entirely opaque. Her bumps and bruises ached as the excitement of her flight faded, but the night was warm and her hurts were not serious. Still, she limped slightly and was glad for an opportunity to throw herself down onto the grass and rest, if only for a moment.

"Hello to you, too," she grumbled, and mopped her face. When she looked up she noticed two quite conspicuous absences. "Where are the horses?"

"'Tis funny you should mention that. Garnerius' men are in Leyen," he said.

"I know," she said. "He visited Cuncz tonight."

"Well, they are now searching for us, and they got to the stables before I could."

"Bugger," she said, and twisted her lips. "Come on, we better be long gone from here before first light."

"Run into some trouble, then?"

"'Twas not the most graceful and subtle of escapes. The more miles we put between us and Leyen, the better." She levered herself to her feet. "We have some time at least before the search gets really persistent, I think. Cuncz should not wake from his little nap until well into tomorrow."

She limped over to her belongings, grabbed her sword, and belted it round her waist. Then she threaded her arms through her jacket, gathered up her pack, and started off.

"Well, I guess you really are that good, eh?" he said.

Elsabeth glanced over her shoulder and flashed him a mischievous smile. "Oh I am. But he was even better."

Hieronymus's step faltered at that. "That would explain your limping then."

"No, the limp is from falling off the roof. Or down the well. Or maybe I strained something climbing out of that tower window. I really have had a rather long night and would like at least a few hours' sleep at some point. So let us just get as far as we can, and find a good place to set camp. If luck is with us, the papers I found will still be legible if all the ink has not run off them first."

They turned north into the plains once the walls of Leyen were out of sight behind them, and marched for two or three hours in that direction. A rosy blush appeared on the horizon to the east as night slowly loosened its grip on the world and gave way to dawn. The stars winked out and faded, and the sky brightened. The flat land northwest of the town left them with no cover, so they were obliged to stop and set up camp out in the open. They made no fire, and Elsabeth merely laid out her bedroll, threw herself down, and fell right to sleep.

She awoke again only a few hours later. Hieronymus, snoring in his bedroll nearby, gave Elsabeth time to slip a short ways away and change into her traveling clothes. She adjusted the hang of her sword at her hip and the rondel at her back, and arrived to find her companion dressed once more in his woolen mantle and watching her with a smirk.

"Lech," she said, as she returned to her bedroll and threw herself down on her backside.

"I was just admiring what the Lord of All saw fit to grace the world with when you slipped from the womb. There is no harm at all in taking just a peak," he said. "I certainly hope last night was worth all the trouble. Especially what I went through sneaking around half of Garnerius' men to escape that wretched city!"

She flashed him a wicked smile. "Oh, it was. We went for hours and hours. In fact the first time we did not even make it to the bed and he took me right there on the floor."

Hieronymus spit her with a glare. "Now that is just being cruel, Tetty."

Elsabeth did not let him off so easily. "It really was amazing, perhaps the best I ever had. I might still be there now if we did not have a job to do."

"I am sure with your impressive history you will find someone to make you forget about him soon enough," he said. "The body is a sacred temple crafted by the Lord himself. You have turned yours into the village fair."

"And I daren't wonder what the Lord of All must think of the sewer you have turned yours into," she said. Elsabeth opened the papers — actually, seven sheets of vellum — taken from Cuncz's desk, unfolded them, and spread them out so she could examine them.

Fortunately, the damage caused by her unexpected fall into the well was not serious, and the text was still clearly legible. It was written in a bold and elegant hand with black ink only slightly faded from age. She skimmed over the first, then the second, with an ever-increasing arch of her eyebrow.

"These are the papers of legitimation for Cuncz, drawn up at Rupertus von Leyen's orders. Father Garnerius was a signatory and witness to all of them," she said.

Hieronymus frowned. "Curious. I questioned some of the locals over a few rounds of Karnöffel while you were engaged in all manner of undignified debaucheries with Cuncz. 'Tis said rather quietly — idle gossip, as it were — but there are rumors nonetheless in Leyen that Father Garnerius was a frequent visitor of Rupertus' wife."

Elsabeth regarded him with a raised eyebrow. "Really?"

He nodded, and stroked his beard while he looked over the documents himself. "'Tis what was said around the inns and alehouses, at least."

She clicked her tongue. "And here you complain about my debaucheries."

Hieronymus harrumphed indignantly. "Now look here, my dear Tetty: You might be indisposed to consider my counsel, sincerely as 'tis given. But at least have the good sense to learn from my long experience, for I have been at this business since you were naught but a mischievous gleam in your father's eye. There is no better place to part a man from his secrets than in a well-stocked common room."

"Oh spare me the dramatics, love, and get to the point. You think Cuncz is a bastard?"

He shuffled through the documents and considered them carefully. "Possibly. That may be why it took so long for Cuncz to be presented; an affair between the Abbot and Rupertus' wife would make for quite the scandal if 'twere known. Perhaps she revealed it on her death bed if she died in childbirth."

She considered the implications. "But why wait so long to announce it? And why would Rupertus take him as his own regardless? More to the point: If 'twere thought he was Rupertus' own, then bastard or not, why go through all of this?"

Elsabeth motioned at the papers in Hieronymus' hand to emphasize her point.

"Hmm, that is the rather vexing bit. But it may have taken time to silence any other witnesses, and perhaps some politicking between Rupertus and the Abbot. Rupertus would have been in something of a tight spot; a Lord needs an heir, after all. Of course, there is another possibility."

"And what is that?"

"'Twas not Rupertus' wife that Garnerius was seeking out after all. Perhaps 'twas Rupertus himself all along. Perhaps 'twas merely a ruse to distract folk from a conspiracy between them."

"Well, that certainly fits with why we were sent here to investigate." She took back the papers again, and sat back on her heels with a frown directed at two particular sheets of vellum.

"Cuncz left me alone in bed in the middle of the night to meet with Garnerius in secret. And if I need to make the connection for you, this would be that mysterious visitor those fellows at the inn mentioned."

The friar harrumphed, and fixed her with a particularly indignant look. "My mental faculties are quite up to the task of coming to such a conclusion without your assistance, you irreverent harpy."

She tapped the top sheet against the others thoughtfully. "Oh good, and here I thought you would only slow me down. Well, Cuncz thought I was still asleep and did not realize I followed him to his meeting. Father Garnerius certainly seemed insistent that these documents be removed to somewhere more secure before something happened to them." Elsabeth smirked at Hieronymus. "'Tis a pity Cuncz was a bit preoccupied last night."

"Yes," he said. "Quite the pity. If you are finished with your fond reminiscences over your unseemly nocturnal escapades, we are rather exposed out here. If you have some idea of where to go next, I would rather love to hear it."

"A moment," she said, and looked over the documents once more. Elsabeth frowned as one detail in particular caught her eye.

"These dates seem odd. I would venture Cuncz was born no later than perhaps 1416 or thereabouts, if I were to judge his age by looks. 'Twas not a topic of conversation that came up last night. But look at this," She held them out for Hieronymus' inspection, and he leaned over her shoulder for a closer look. "'Tis dated 1420. There is also a second witness on all of these documents — a Father Ehrhart. Do you know him?"

Hieronymus twisted his mouth in a scowl. "Ah, yes, because all of the clergy clearly took their vows together and all know one another personally. No, I don't know him, though I can say at least I do know *of* him. As I recall, Ehrhart is prior of Alsfeld Monastery. 'Tis about a two day walk east of Leyen, on the north bank of the river."

Elsabeth folded the documents again and stuffed them into a pouch on her pack. "Well, that sounds as good a place as any to turn next."

"You are forgetting that means we must walk right past Leyen. And while 'tis a two-day march on foot, even the Right Reverend Garnerius's fat arse can beat us there by horse with plenty of time to hold communion for all the brothers while he waited."

She shook her head. "Even if Garnerius is not well on his way back to Friuli Abbey by now, they may be distracted scouring Leyen for us. And they may not know about the theft of those papers until after Cuncz wakes. Garnerius has no authority in Leyen, so I think Cuncz's chamberlain would be in charge of any search until he finishes sleeping off the drug I gave him, and that may delay a serious one until he does. I suspect that buys us some time, and they would not be expecting us to double back and head that way."

Elsabeth got back to her feet and packed up her bedroll. "That gives us a small head start, at least. I think we should hurry and take advantage of it while we have the time."

Hieronymus grumbled his dissent while they hurriedly packed up their camp, but reluctantly accepted her decision. Soon they were off again, turning east but keeping away from the river until well after they passed Leyen again to their right. They saw no one as they cut across the fields, or when they finally rejoined the river and stepped out onto the road.

It was little more than a flattened, hard, and badly-rutted dirt track with ill-defined grassy edges. It followed the course of the Nebel as it wound out of the east on its journey past Leyen. East of Leyen the cleared fields on the north side of the road gave way to woodland. The hiss of wind through the trees and the singing of birds was a lively change from the still land outside the forest. Unfortunately, it made listening for pursuit on the road a challenge, and the thickening stands of trees and the surrounding undergrowth greatly diminished their ability to spot trouble approaching.

Nonetheless, the two days of travel passed uneventfully, and by the end of the second day they reached a fork in the road. Hieronymus led her on the southern branch, which climbed a rise to a bluff overlooking the water that lay fifty or so feet below. Perched atop this bluff, behind a thick and low wall of stone, stood Alsfeld Monastery.

"Well, fortune has been with us this far, it seems," Hieronymus said, and craned his neck to look up at the complex. "Now much as I am sure it pains you, I suggest you let me do the talking lest your tongue land us in more trouble than we have time for."

Elsabeth glowered at him, but quickly decided for expedience's sake not to argue the point. Instead, she heaved a sigh and rolled her eyes.

"Well, lead on then, and do try not to get into any quarrels on the finer points of scripture. Again."

Hieronymus twisted his lip as he waddled up the hill, supported by his staff. Elsabeth easily paced him on her long legs. "That fellow was preaching blasphemy, and someone had to put an end to it!"

"What he did not need was a few lumps from your staff. Do try to be on your best behavior."

"My dear Tetty, you worry too much. We'll be gone before Garnerius is the wiser!"

21

"ORGIVE ME, FATHER," THE CHAMBERLAIN said, "but Herr Baron has still not awakened!"

Garnerius scowled, and felt the blood surging into his cheeks. He balled his meaty hands into fists and straightened over poor, hapless Conrat cringing before him, as if he was cowering in the presence of the Lord of All himself.

"Then wake him!" he roared, caring not the least whether his voice carried through the whole of the castle.

"We have tried, Father! The apothecary has administered a number of remedies already, but whatever he was given last night is potent. I fear all there is for it is to let him sleep it off."

Garnerius fumed and stomped around the great hall of Leyen, tearing at his hair. Cuncz's three favorite guards — Garnerius never bothered to learn their names — watched him closely. Their distress over their master's condition was clearly evident on their faces.

"I cannot begin to stress the urgency of this matter. I need him now!"

The chamberlain's features twitched. "I beg the Father's forgiveness, but there is nothing I can do to rouse him. We have been trying all night long; I myself have hardly slept a wink while tending to him."

Garnerius rounded on him. He was unaccustomed to such back-talk from a lowly functionary. Again, the chamberlain blanched when his glare settled upon him, as if his eyes blazed with the light of the Almighty. And yet he still did not budge from his place in the middle of the hall.

No sooner had he left his meeting with Cuncz the night before, had the captain of his escort arrived with news that the horses of the friar and his companion had been found in Leyen's stables. Though a thorough sweep was made of the town, both fugitives had vanished without a trace. Not a single innkeeper spoke of having seen them. Of that Garnerius chided himself; almost certainly they would have arrived in disguise, and he cursed the souls of Dietrich and Michel to an eternity of torment in the Dark One's deepest pits for their sloppiness.

He had rushed back to the castle upon hearing the news, only to be met by the chamberlain in the hall telling him that Cuncz had been drugged and could not be roused.

"Tell me about the woman he entertained last night," he demanded. "Who was she?"

A hint of indignation appeared on the fellow's features. "I beg the Father's pardon, but 'tis not my place to discuss Herr Baron's private affairs in this manner."

"'Tis very likely the woman poisoned him!"

"I am aware of it, and I assure you I am having the city swept for her as we speak."

Garnerius stomped towards him. "Who. Is. She."

The chamberlain flinched at the threat in his voice.

"She presented herself as a merchant's daughter. Herr Baron took a fancy to her when he spied her while on a ride and had her brought here."

"What was her name?"

"'Twas not my place to ask such questions. I was only bidden to issue a summons."

"What did she look like?"

His face colored momentarily in embarrassment at the pointedness of the question.

"If the Father must know, I must admit she was quite the striking beauty, and I can hardly fault Herr Baron's interest in her. Were I twenty years younger and unwed, I might have considered a dalliance myself."

"I don't want to hear such vagaries, nor do I care where you would stick your cock if you were wont!" Garnerius snapped. The chamberlain nearly jumped out of his shoes, and his face turned a brilliant shade of crimson at the unexpected vulgarity of his remarks. "What did she look like?"

"She was quite unusually tall," he sputtered. "And I suppose she must have an active life, which would make some sense if she travels often and aids her father in his work. She had a woman's figure, but 'twas not soft from idleness like I see in most women of breeding. But 'twas her hair that truly caught the eye."

Garnerius narrowed his eyes with suspicion. "Her hair?"

The chamberlain nodded. "Aye, her hair. 'Twas like polished copper. Altogether uncommon, I am sure."

Garnerius grabbed fistfuls of his hair as the chamberlain spoke and stomped around the room once more. Cuncz's guards watched him with bemusement, but fortunately thought better of opening their mouths. He strangled a curse as that *woman's* face popped unbidden to mind; her burnished copper hair spilling down her back with utter disregard to propriety, the mischievous sparkle in her green eyes when she caught his straying over her figure, as if it were something she not only anticipated, but a reflex she actively cultivated in her dress and manner.

But beneath his barely-contained wrath, Garnerius' heart climbed up into his throat, and fear gnawed at his belly.

Get hold of yourself! You knew even before he opened his mouth it was her. And if she was indeed here while you met with Cuncz, then 'tis altogether likely she was here for a purpose. She almost certainly knew...

Garnerius spun on his heel, and stomped purposefully towards the chamberlain.

"Take me to Cuncz's private study at once," he demanded.

The chamberlain blinked in astonishment at the sudden command, and stood for a moment taken aback.

"I beg the Father's pardon?"

"You heard me! Take me to Cuncz's study immediately. That woman is a spy, and if she was here and responsible for Cuncz's current state then I must see to it that certain documents in his possession are secure."

"I am afraid I cannot allow you into Herr Baron's private offices until he has awakened," the chamberlain said, and this time it was Garnerius' turn to stand blinking stupidly in disbelief.

"What did you say?"

As if taking courage from Garnerius' amazement at being refused such a request, the chamberlain straightened to his full height and gazed levelly at him.

"I cannot allow you into Her Baron's private offices until he has awakened. They are, after all, his *private* offices, and I'll allow no one to intrude upon his personal affairs without his express permission."

Garnerius stretched up until he was all but bending the smaller man over backwards in his efforts to meet his gaze, and yet the chamberlain still did not break.

"Don't make the mistake of dismissing me for some meek village priest," he snapped, and his voice shook the hall.

The rattle of armor and the soft tread of boots on the floor behind him was his only warning that Cuncz's guards were in motion, and a dangerous, brittle silence hung over the hall as his voice died away.

"Rest assured, Father, I don't mistake you for anything. But with all due respects to your station: This is not Friuli, nor is Leyen held in fealty to you. You have no authority within these walls. If there is a threat to the security of Herr Baron's dominion, it falls upon Herr Baron to address it. I will permit no man to search his private papers unless he himself should so command it, or his Grace the Prince-Bishop himself were to issue such a warrant."

The chamberlain gave a small nod, and Garnerius glanced over his shoulder. The three guards stepped back from him a pace, and planted the ends of their tall halberds in front of them; relaxed, but ready to take them up at the slightest hint of danger. Garnerius' face heated, but the chamberlain spoke the truth about one thing: he held no real authority here, and even his ecclesiastical station would avail him nothing.

Instead he clenched his teeth and speared Cuncz's man with his most venomous glare.

"Obstinate, obstructionist fool! Every moment's delay gives that woman and her accomplice more of a head start, and you stand here barring me from ascertaining just what disaster your Lord has brought upon himself with his wayward eye and ill-considered lust!"

The chamberlain squared his shoulders and curled his lips indignantly. "Perhaps, Father, had your own men not allowed her to escape your clutches in the first place, then this would never have happened! Mark my words, I am no less eager to see her punished for her assault upon Herr Baron, but I am quite clear on my duties here, and until Herr Baron has awakened, no one shall intrude on the privacy of his offices.

"I have already dispatched men to scour the road along any direction she might have taken. Rest assured, she will be found."

IT WAS WELL INTO THE DAY BEFORE CUNCZ FINALLY awakened from whatever drug Elsabeth Soesten had administered to him. Garnerius spent his time alternately lost in prayer in the guest quarters prepared for him at the chamberlain's orders — the only concession the damned fool would make over the seriousness of these circumstances — and pacing in frustration around his rooms. The scouts searching the roads returned empty-handed. He fumed that two travelers on foot — their horses were still secure in the stables where his escort discovered them, and none were missing from Cuncz's stables — could so easily slip through a concerted search of the countryside.

Garnerius stormed through the passages of the castle under escort of the chamberlain and one of Cuncz's bodyguards. He quietly mulled over the well-earned chastisement he would deliver to his co-conspirator when he was finally in his presence. He only hoped they would be left alone so he would not have the burly guardsmen interfering when he wrapped his meaty hands round Cuncz's neck!

The chamberlain led him up a flight of stairs, and exited along the corridor leading to the private dining hall above the main hall. Servants scrubbed the floors and windows, and tended to the hangings decorating the interior walls. They gave way promptly upon their approach, and bowed their heads in deference. Garnerius passed them without offering so much as a blessing or a kind word.

They arrived at the entrance to the dining hall. The chamberlain stopped beside the open door and motioned for him to enter. Garnerius skewered him with his glare.

"Leave us. I'll speak with Freiherr von Leyen alone and wish not to be disturbed," he said.

The chamberlain screwed up his features as if to protest, but after a glance into the chamber, inclined his head and made room for him to pass. Garnerius swept through the doorway, and the chamberlain closed it behind him.

Upon entry he found the dining hall empty, and a frown crossed his features.

Where is that damned fool hiding?

Garnerius picked his way across the hall and through the open door leading into Cuncz's darkened private office. Curtains hung over the windows along the north wall, and all of the lamps were extinguished, leaving the room rather dark. Only the light spilling across the doorway from the dining hall provided him with enough illumination to see by. Cuncz lay on a couch in one corner, stripped down to his undershirt, and pinching his brows. Garnerius heaved a sigh and started across the floor. The other made no move to rise for a proper greeting.

"Good morning, Father," Cuncz said, and his voice tremored weakly. "Do forgive me for not standing to greet you."

"Don't 'Good morning, Father,' me," Garnerius said, loud enough to enjoy some satisfaction in the pained expression upon Cuncz's features. "'Twas your own foolishness that brought you to this end!"

"Oh don't lecture me! How was I to know the girl intended to drug me?"

"I warned you to be cautious, did I not?"

"I don't recall you warning me that any maid I might bring to my bed might be an assassin. In fact 'twas not until I awoke and poor Conrat told me of your pique that I even might have suspected anything of the sort."

Garnerius' face heated in chagrin.

"That was my error," he said, and the admission of his failure twisted like a dagger in his belly. "I never anticipated they would come all the way here."

Cuncz winced as he sat up on the couch and buried his face in his hands. Garnerius at least consoled himself with watching the younger man pay dearly for his dalliance.

"Maybe had you taken more discretion in managing this affair, things might have turned out differently," Cuncz said. "I seem to recall suggesting you ought to have contented yourself with rewarding them for a job well done. They might have even been useful in the future had they not been crossed."

Cuncz chuckled softly, and the sudden pain in his countenance told Garnerius he instantly regretted it.

"I rather admire their cunning and boldness, I must confess. Not only did they manage to gain entry to your abbey, but with naught but a wink and a smile she slips into Leyen, drugs me, and manages to slip your grasp again."

Garnerius' face heated, and it was all he could do to restrain himself from flying across the floor and finishing the task the woman's poison failed.

"You do realize that she was here for a reason," he said instead. "She was almost certainly looking for the connection between us!"

Cuncz nodded into his hands.

"Yes, I had considered that point after I woke," he said.

Garnerius stared at him for a long moment. Cuncz did not so much as raise his head from his hands, or even stir on the couch. The silence stretched out uncomfortably, and he shifted on his feet. No one moved in the dining hall outside, and the shuttered windows muted the singing of birds and the activity in the courtyard beyond.

His impatience swiftly got the better of him. "And?"

Cuncz peered up at him from between his fingers. He heaved a sigh, and raked his hands back through his hair. His face was pale and drawn, and had a decidedly unhealthy pallor. Whatever drug the woman used had clearly taken its toll.

"And what?" Cuncz asked, his voice colored in what sounded suspiciously like callous indifference.

He sneered down on the younger man. "And what do you intend to do about it?"

"Father, right now 'tis taking all my will to remain upright. I have not been able to keep a scrap of food down since I crawled out of bed, God forbid something to drink! I assure you that has taken rather much of the focus of my attention thus far, and this conversation certainly does not help."

"I'll remind you, boy, that there is a good bit more at stake now than the condition of your bowels! 'Tis my neck hovering over the block, and yours with it, if you have a care!"

Something dangerous flashed in Cuncz's eyes, and Garnerius flinched in spite of himself.

"I'll thank you, Father, not to call me that! And I assure you, I have not forgotten the precariousness of our circumstances."

Garnerius clenched his teeth to cut off the retort forming on his lips, and balled his hands into fists. His body trembled from head to toe in exasperation. "I don't know how you can remain so damned calm at a time like this!"

"By accepting what is out of my control, for a start," Cuncz said.

"So you intend to just sit there, and let her run all the way to his Grace?"

Cuncz shook his head. "Of course not, but 'twas your rashness that drew her and her companion back into it, and I would rather not make the same mistake."

His face heated again, but he held his tongue out of chagrin. Cuncz was right, of course, though he was loath to admit it, and certainly would not to his face.

"So she has the documents in your keeping?"

He shrugged. "I don't know. I have not yet had the opportunity to check."

Garnerius buried his face in his hands.

"Good God, man! Why not? Doing so would certainly be something within your control. I would have done so myself had that damned chamberlain of yours not barred me."

Cuncz impaled him on his glare. Frail though he seemed in his present condition, Garnerius recognized the threat in his eyes.

"I'll also thank you not to speak so disparagingly of my men. Conrat was carrying out the duty that I set for him. Leyen is mine, Father, and I'll have no one intrude upon my domain."

Devious bastard. How quickly you forget just who put you in this seat in the first place. I think perhaps your own usefulness may be drawing to an end.

"Well, you are awake now. I want to know whether those papers are safe, because if not and she was able to find them, this matter will become much more dangerous."

With an effort, Cuncz levered himself to his feet. He swayed unsteadily for a moment, but Garnerius made no effort to aid him. Instead, Cuncz swept his arm in a mocking gesture directing him towards the desk. He rolled his eyes at the younger man's pique, but hitched up his robes of office nonetheless, and stumped in that direction. Cuncz followed after with carefully measured steps. When he reached the desk, he laid a hand on it to help support him as he circled round to the far side and dropped heavily into his office chair.

Garnerius stuffed his arms into opposite sleeves of his robe to still his impatient fidgeting and waited. Cuncz opened the locked drawer of his desk with deliberate slowness, and walked his fingers through the papers within until he found what he was looking for: a nondescript leather dispatch case. He removed the case from the drawer and casually flipped it open. Garnerius could no longer mask his pique, and rocked from foot to foot while Cuncz thumbed through the documents within. The other paid him no mind, however, and methodically checked each paper until he reached the very end.

Cuncz's expression did not change as he snapped the case closed again, and returned it to the desk drawer. The drawer thumped shut, and he leaned his elbows on his desk and tapped a finger against his lip thoughtfully.

Garnerius watched and waited and shifted his weight. And still Cuncz said nothing. He ground his teeth until he thought they might explode into dust.

"Well?" He finally asked after an interminable pause.

"Well," Cuncz said, with almost casual disregard. "I have a thought where she might be heading next."

Bile churned in his belly at Cuncz's words, and his face heated in frustration when the other still did not continue. "And that is?"

He shrugged. "I would imagine she is well on her way to Alsfeld by now."

Garnerius threw his hands up into the air in aggravation and stomped away from the desk. "How can you sit there so calmly!" he shouted, and his voice practically shook the office. He finally had the satisfaction of seeing Cuncz react, a slight tightening of the corners of his eyes.

"Please, Father, not so loud," he grumbled, and nursed his temples.

"Not so loud? You damned irresponsible child! If she has those papers—"

"I know what it means, Father," Cuncz said. He narrowed his eyes to warning slits, and Garnerius flinched back in spite of himself. "I am quite capable of considering the implications without you to point them out for me."

Garnerius rounded on him, and returned to the desk. He planted his fists and leaned over until his face was so close to the younger man's he could practically smell the sweat and vomit from his drugging.

"I have not labored this long on your behalf only to see everything I have worked towards compromised by your insatiable desire to bed any woman with a pretty smile who crosses your path, and certainly not your complete disregard for the seriousness of this matter!"

Cuncz rose slowly and matched his posture. Weakened though he was, he nonetheless presented a formidable presence that left Garnerius feeling quite small.

"And what would you have me do, Father? Storm around the room carrying on like the child you accuse me of being? We know where she is headed; like as not to follow up on those papers in Alsfeld. 'Tis a two day journey by foot. Neither your people nor mine have reported any horses missing and we have theirs, so they will almost certainly be walking. 'Twill be no great undertaking to catch them up, either on the road, or at the monastery itself.

"I'll have our horses saddled at once, and we can be off immediately."

Garnerius stabbed a finger at him.

"That had best be the case! And when this matter is settled, I intend to see to it that every loose end is tied up. There will be no more mistakes."

Cuncz quirked a smile that sent a shiver down his spine. "I am sure you will, Father, and you can certainly trust me to do my own part."

He spit the younger man on his glare, but Cuncz's features did not as much as twitch.

I think your part has long since ceased being of any use to me. When this is over, I shall see to that as well.

22

IERONYMUS LEANED ON HIS STAFF WITH A pendant of the Wheel displayed prominently around his neck as they approached the gate and awaited the guard to clear them for entry into Alsfeld.

The gatehouse of the complex was a two-level structure that gave the impression of fortification, however the outer wall was merely for purposes of privacy and would never stand against even a half-hearted assault. The guard on duty was a rather short and scrawny older man with a weathered face, dressed in a faded linen gambeson under a well-worn brigandine. He wore a dagger at his back, and a crude-looking axe with a short haft at his belt. He regarded Hieronymus with bored indifference upon their approach, but his eyes then wandered Elsabeth's body for a moment longer than proper, and he scowled at the sword at her hip.

"By command of Father Ehrhart, your arms must be surrendered at the gate before I can admit you," he said in a very official and automatic tone.

Hieronymus gave up his sword and buckler, and handed both over to another guard who appeared from a staircase leading up to the second level overhead. He inclined his head slightly to consider the gatehouse on his way through. There was no sign of murder-holes or a portcullis; only the timber gate denied entrance to or from the monastery.

Elsabeth handed her sword over to the second guard with visible reluctance.

"Do be careful with that," she said with a note of warning in her voice. "If I don't find it again when I return, the good prior will need to find two new guards."

Elsabeth started to follow Hieronymus through, but the gate guard stopped her.

"Half a moment," he said, and stepped into her path. Irritation over her threat colored his voice, and Hieronymus heaved a sigh at the brewing confrontation.

Elsabeth stood a good head taller than the fellow and, despite her lithe build, he suspected she still outweighed him. The guard casually strolled up to her and soon had his hands on her, running them the length of her body and groping her with an excuse of seeking hidden weapons. Elsabeth tired of the game when his searching fingers went to her backside, and in one smooth motion twisted his arm around, flung him up against the gate, and pinned him there by the sleeve of his gambeson with her rondel.

"I trust you are satisfied?" she asked with a glare.

The guard removed her dagger from the gate and freed himself, and with a huff strode over and handed it to his companion before angrily waving her through. Elsabeth nodded curtly and joined Hieronymus inside, with a glance over her shoulder to watch their weapons taken up to the second floor of the gatehouse.

"Charming as always," Hieronymus muttered as he led her along the path through the outer court.

Elsabeth scowled at him. "Oh don't give me that. You saw how he had his hands on me."

"I thought you enjoyed being pawed by every strange man you came across."

"Only by invitation."

"You did threaten him."

"I merely wished to make it clear how unhappy I will be if my sword is not where I left it when we come back."

"Yes, two guards are completely worth a sword."

She spit him with a warning glare. "That one is to me, and you know better than to say anything more about it."

Hieronymus merely shrugged, and they continued the rest of the way in silence.

Beyond the wall was an outer court with guest houses, servants' quarters, and a few other storage buildings and workshops, along with ponds, gardens, and a dairy. Separated from this by a hedge was the inner court and its laundries, infirmaries, bakehouses, a brewery, granaries, and stables. The monastery itself dominated the heart of the inner court. The church rose prominently at the north end, with ranges on the east, west and southern faces to enclose the cloister.

There were a few lay people in the outer court, most of them servants running errands for the complex up ahead or tending to the grounds, gardens, and workshops. All of them ignored the pair as they made their way along a path paved with white cobblestones, and bordered with beds of yellow and white flowers. Hieronymus saw no sign of guards other than those at the gate, and the outer court was silent.

The inner court was another matter entirely. Children darted to and fro through the court. All were boys, ranging in age from a few years old to nearly early manhood. The eldest helped watch over the youngest under the close eye of the brothers of the monastery, though the boys all appeared to be laity and dressed in simple and at times worn and well-used clothing.

Some sat in circles around the brothers as they lectured on diverse subjects; in one corner of the court Hieronymus even caught a glimpse of a brother giving lessons on the sword and buckler, while another wielded a staff in what looked to be a variation on the teachings of Russdorffer (at which Elsabeth rolled her eyes when she spotted him). Others were engaged in a variety of exercise, particularly games of chase and other sports. Hieronymus chuckled warmly in greeting whenever such games spilled over onto the path, and the children greeted him with solemn nods and "beg your pardons" before rushing off to begin their games all over again. Elsabeth quickly became a subject of intense scrutiny and speculation, and many stopped what they were doing to stare as she passed.

"It reminds me much of Pruck," Elsabeth said as they made their way through the chaos.

Hieronymus eyed her closely at the sudden hollowness in her voice.

"One of these days you must tell me whatever led you to such a place, much less how you convinced Father Ottin to sponsor that letter of dispensation from his Grace."

"As I have said on many an occasion, I don't want to talk about it," she said, and her face tightened with some distantly-remembered pain.

"You know that only piques my curiosity more."

Elsabeth speared him with as dangerous a warning glare as he had ever seen, and Hieronymus flinched under its withering heat. "I'll warn you one last time: Don't press me about it."

He harrumphed, and resumed his waddling pace along the walkway through the grounds. "Fair enough, though I don't know what there is to be so testy about."

"Just don't," she said. "I have done you the courtesy of never asking how you came to leave the service of the Baron of Godra. The least you could do is respect my silence on this."

Hieronymus looked at her again in amazement at the deep melancholy in her voice. Her features were drawn as if she had been struck, and her head and shoulders slumped. Elsabeth said nothing more, however, and he let the matter drop for the moment.

She followed along behind him in silence as they approached the church. It was a modest structure two stories in height, and not nearly as lofty as the church in Friuli. However, outwardly it was not dissimilar in its arrangement: The eastern end was a round structure with a domed roof, and a long axis stretched toward the façade at the west end. The east range met the church at the center of that chamber, with a small side door exiting into the courtyard to the north directly opposite. The façade extended a few dozen feet beyond the wall of the west range. At each corner of the façade stood a tower four stories in height, framing a porch mounted by a short flight of three steps. Most of the building was in the ubiquitous red brick, but the façade was made of white stone, with its three processional doors mounted in marble archways, all carved and decorated with sculpture.

Hieronymus climbed the stairs onto the porch and made his way to the middle door, which stood open to let in light and the summer breeze. They passed through and entered a vestibule with a floor of colored tiles and plastered walls. Doors at either hand led to the towers, and marble fonts stood at either side of the doors leading into the nave. Hieronymus stopped, dipped his fore and middle fingers into the water, and made the sign of the Wheel before proceeding. Elsabeth doffed her hat and did likewise.

"I am rather surprised you did not burst into flames just now," Hieronymus murmured upon entering the nave.

She did not turn her eyes on him after his remark, and instead swept her gaze across the church on her way down the carpet running along the nave. A young novice tending to the church spotted them upon entering and started toward them.

"This is hardly the place to hound me about my sins, considering you have a list long enough the Lord of All himself would blanch upon reading it," she muttered back.

Even with her lowered voice, her words were amplified much more than Hieronymus cared for, but if the novice heard her he did not show it when he reached them and bowed in greeting. He eyed Elsabeth somewhat uncertainly, and his face colored slightly in what Hieronymus had determined was quite the common reaction to his companion's appearance. His features were boyish, and his head was topped by an unruly mop of sandy hair.

"Welcome to Alsfeld, and may the blessings of the Lord be upon you. Is there anything I may do to assist you, Brother?" he said pleasantly to Hieronymus, then almost as an afterthought turned to Elsabeth and inclined his head. "Gnädige Frau?"

Hieronymus stretched to his full height, and twisted his features into his most righteously commanding glower.

"Yes, there is, my son," he said. "I have a need to speak with Father Ehrhart. Do run along and fetch him for me."

The novice stumbled a moment at the rather brusque request, and he hesitated to find his voice. "I am sorry, Brother, but Father Ehrhart is in private prayer and asked not to be disturbed."

He skewered the lad with a glare, and a hint of authoritative anger slipped into his voice. "Now look here, my son, I have not traveled all this way from my province to be thrown out on my backside by a novice who only just received his habit."

Elsabeth struggled to keep the smirk from her lips, and the youth broke down into a fit of stuttering.

"I shall have a meal and a place to rest from your journey prepared for yourself and your companion while you wait, but Father Ehrhart is simply unable to see you—"

Hieronymus cut him off. "Oh enough of this," he said, and started off down the nave. "I will go and see him myself. The dormitories are in the east range, as I recall? And I shall have a word with the good Father about his brothers keeping important business from him."

The novice followed after Hieronymus shouldering his way along the aisle, babbling and practically tripping over his habit in an effort to cut the friar off.

"Wait. Wait! Please, just a moment! I will see if he has a moment he can spare, but I must insist you wait here!"

Hieronymus stopped and regarded the novice, somehow managing to look down his nose at the younger man, though the latter towered over him. "Very well, but I have little time to waste. This matter is of the utmost urgency and needs his attention immediately."

"Yes, Brother, I will go at once. Lord be with you," he said, bowing fervently and hurrying from the church. Elsabeth watched him go, then shook her head and rolled her eyes.

"You do know they are building a special hall in the Underworld for you," she said.

Hieronymus merely shrugged. "Just remember coming here was your idea, Tetty. And besides, we do have little time. Your dearest love can still catch us here before we can leave. Or he might be here already and that rascal could have been told to keep us busy."

"Well, if he is, I promise we will wait until we are out of the church to tear each other's clothes off."

"At least now you are thinking sensibly."

"One of us has to. Just remember I blame you for all of this."

After several minutes the novice returned, trailing behind an older figure who Hieronymus reasoned from the belt of braided gold and red cords cinching the habit of brown wool about his waist was Father Ehrhart. He was a tall man with a short and neatly-trimmed silver beard and silver hair cropped similarly short, but otherwise was of unremarkable appearance.

Father Ehrhart turned down the nave with a purposeful stride. The novice following in his wake struggled to keep pace. He slowed upon his approach and stuffed his hands into the opposite sleeves of his habit. Hieronymus inclined his head respectfully in greeting, and Elsabeth followed suit.

"Well?" Ehrhart said, his voice a blend of curiosity over the urgency of the summons and mild annoyance over the disruption of his church.

"Greetings, Father Ehrhart, and thank you for seeing us on such sudden notice," Hieronymus said. "I am Hieronymus, a brother of the Order of St. Olivus and I am here on a matter of some urgency."

"Yes, so Brother Auberlin has said. You certainly gave him quite a fright, Brother Hieronymus. Perhaps this has become common among the Olivians, but our novices here are not accustomed to such...fire. Nor of having to interrupt the private prayers of their superiors." The last he added with a pointed glare, which Hieronymus ignored.

"I beg your pardon, Father, but as I said, the matter is something of an urgent one. May we speak in private?"

Ehrhart heaved an impatient sigh and waved toward a door in the middle of the nave on the south wall. "Brother Auberlin, see to it that we are not disturbed. I trust that this time you will not have difficulties obeying my instructions?"

Auberlin swallowed visibly and his face paled. "Yes, Father. I mean, no, Father. I mean..."

"Yes, yes, I know what you mean." He rolled his eyes and motioned for Hieronymus to follow, but when his eyes fell on Elsabeth he frowned and hesitated. "'Tis not our practice to permit women to set foot in the cloister."

She opened her mouth to protest, but Hieronymus spoke first before she might say something unfortunate.

"My companion, Elsabeth Soesten," he said in introduction. Elsabeth inclined her head again in greeting. "She is assisting me with the matter on which I have come, and will be quite necessary in our discussion. I will take full responsibility for her if you require it of me."

Ehrhart regarded the pair for a moment, then heaved another sigh and nodded. "Very well. Come."

Ehrhart led them through the door, and they stepped into the cloister itself. An arcaded walkway encircled the garth — a lawn of green grass with a pool at its center — and separated it from the walls of the church and ranges enclosing it. The sun hung high overhead in a clear blue sky, dotted here and there with the occasional cloud. Hieronymus could hear the laughter of the children playing in the inner court beyond the cloister, and his thoughts momentarily returned to Elsabeth's curious reaction and remarks. There was no one else about, and they followed Ehrhart as he made his way to the pool, where he waited for them to speak.

"I have noticed, Father, quite a large number of children seem to reside here at Alsfeld," Hieronymus began, returning to the business at hand, and pushing aside other concerns for future musing. "Are they here to devote themselves to the Lord of All?"

"No," Ehrhart said, "Not all. Some will eventually choose this path, as poor Brother Auberlin did. The others we keep here because they have no one else to care for them."

"Alsfeld is an orphanage then," Elsabeth said, and made it a statement of fact.

"That is one of the services we offer here, yes. Aside from our own studies and devotion to the Lord. And if you have intruded on my private prayers only to prattle on about the unfortunates in our care, then I must kindly ask you to leave."

Elsabeth set her pack down on the grass and removed the documents.

"We are here at the request of an agent of his Grace, the Prince-Bishop," Hieronymus said. "The trail has led us to your gates, and we wished to ask about something rather curious."

Elsabeth handed the stack of vellum over to the prior who studied them with a frown.

"Where did you get these?"

"Under the circumstances, 'twould be better if you did not know," Elsabeth said. "But you do recognize them?"

"I do. These are documents of adoption and legitimation drawn up by Rupertus von Leyen when he adopted a son here."

Elsabeth frowned. "Cuncz von Leyen was adopted from Alsfeld?"

Ehrhart glanced up from one of the pages at her. "That is what I said, is it not?"

"Forgive us, Father," Hieronymus interjected upon recognizing the irritation in the other's voice. *The fool girl will get us both thrown out on our backsides before we learn anything of use!* "But we were given to understanding Cuncz was born to the Baroness. And if I may say, we have heard considerable rumor that Father Garnerius of Friuli Abbey may have had a closer relationship with her than would have been proper for a man of his station."

"You, Brother, I thought would be above listening to such mindless gossip among the laity. I witnessed the adoption myself, accounting for my signature. Father Garnerius was present as well."

Hieronymus leaned on his staff and watched the prior carefully. "Quite a ways for a man of Father Garnerius' stature to come to witness an adoption, then, was it not?"

The other shuffled through the documents page by page with a dismissive grunt, before returning them to

Elsabeth. She in turn slipped them back into her pack and slung it over her shoulder once again.

"Father Garnerius has had a personal interest in Freiherr von Leyen from the start. 'Twas he who delivered him as a babe to Alsfeld, and personally arranged for his care and education. He visited from time to time to check in on his health and the progress of his education. And then to arrange his adoption and legitimation by the old Baron."

Elsabeth raised an eyebrow. "That does not strike you as unusual?"

Ehrhart sighed. "Less so than you might think. I have seen many boys come through here of uncertain parentage who, I suspect, have family nearer at hand than they realize. There are simply some among the clergy who do not take their vows as seriously as they ought, while the Bishops turn a blind eye or indulge in it themselves."

Elsabeth suppressed a laugh in Hieronymus's direction. He glared at her in silent warning, but Ehrhart showed no sign of noticing either of their reactions.

"What can you tell us of Cuncz's provenance?" she asked instead.

"Almost nothing aside that his mother was an unwed laywoman, I am afraid. Father Garnerius brought him here personally, and of his mother I was given no name."

Elsabeth frowned. "So he could still be Father Garnerius' son?"

Ehrhart grunted. "Perhaps. As I said, 'twould not be unusual."

"But clearly the official tale — and even the tales round Leyen's alehouses — is false," Hieronymus said.

"Oh, the fate of the late Baroness is certainly true," Ehrhart said. "She did indeed die of complications during childbirth, but the babe I am sorry to say died with her."

Elsabeth's face turned thoughtful, but whatever was on her mind she did not see fit to share, and left Hieronymus to continue the interrogation. *Not that I need her to say a word, I believe I have a thought of just what wheels are turning in that head of hers.*

"So what of Cuncz's true mother?" he asked. "Do you know where she could be found?"

"The churchyard of Friuli Abbey," Ehrhart said. "That his mother died in childbirth at least is true, and if she were buried in a common grave then I suspect there is no purpose in searching further for her."

"When was Cuncz brought here?"

Ehrhart considered for a moment. "'Twould have been the spring of 1414, as I recall."

Elsabeth folded her arms across her chest and glanced at Hieronymus.

"Well, I do think 'tis rather odd Father Garnerius would take such a personal interest in this babe, would you agree?" she said.

Hieronymus nodded his agreement. "Most unusual, Tetty. One might almost say suspiciously so."

Ehrhart looked between the two of them, and a frown of disapproval creased his features.

"What is the meaning of this? You say you are here in the name of his Grace the Bishop, yet all you do is pry into the private affairs of the Baron. And do I miss my guess in suggesting those documents you brought were stolen?"

"What his Grace knows of all this is beyond me to say," Elsabeth said, "only that we are acting under the instruction of an agent in his employ. Now perhaps Father Garnerius is merely a dirty old monk who could not keep his crosier under his habit—"

"Elsabeth!" Hieronymus said, mortified.

"—but I do know for certain that I have woken to an assassin standing over my bed, and I have fallen down a privy shaft, off a roof, down a well, and jumped out of a tower, and I am bloody well wanting to know what all of this is about. So forgive me for my sins, Father, but I think a little bit of thievery at this point might be a slight bit justifiable."

The prior opened his mouth as if to issue a retort, when a sudden commotion from behind spun them both around. Elsabeth by force of habit reached for the sword that was not at her hip, but Hieronymus maintained his composure (though also took a more secure hold of his staff). Brother Auberlin ran as swiftly as his long habit allowed him, crying, "Father Ehrhart! Father Ehrhart!" with an alarmed expression twisting his features. He stopped and doubled over to catch his breath. "Father Ehrhart!" he gasped again.

Ehrhart sighed patiently. "Yes, Brother Auberlin? I thought I asked we not be disturbed?"

"Yes, Father." Auberlin's face colored abruptly at the rebuke, "But Father Garnerius is here with Freiherr von Leyen, and they demand to speak with you."

Hieronymus's face drained of color, and Elsabeth muttered a subdued "bollocks," after which she quickly made the sign of the Wheel.

"And what is the purpose of their visit?" Ehrhart said, his voice was calm, but Hieronymus watched the corners of his eyes tighten.

"Them, Father." Auberlin needlessly raised a hand to indicate her and Hieronymus. "He said two thieves might be headed this direction to hide in the monastery. Thieves, Father!" Auberlin leveled a suspicious glare on them, which Hieronymus found almost comically misplaced on his youthful features.

"And what did you tell them?"

"That you were attending to a private meeting, and requested not to be disturbed, but 'tis Father Garnerius and the Baron, Father. They insisted. And rather officially, at that."

"The Baron bears no authority within these walls and he well knows it." Ehrhart sighed. "Father Garnerius, however, is another and more complicated matter. Tell them I will join them shortly. Take them to my office in the south tower and see that they are comfortable."

Auberlin shifted uncomfortably at the thought of going back in to address the Abbot, but nodded. "Yes, Father."

"And say nothing of our guests, understood?"

"Yes, Father!"

"Good. Now go."

Auberlin bowed stiffly at the waist, and hurried back to the church. Hieronymus muttered a quick prayer that Garnerius and Cuncz neither chose to follow him, nor heard the racket made by the young novice in his panic. Ehrhart turned to them and studied them sternly for a moment.

"Now, what to actually do with you two," he said.

Hieronymus drew himself up to his full height and gazed back at the prior. "We have reason to believe that Father Garnerius may be plotting something against the wishes of his Grace, though what that may be we cannot say. Part of the proof is already in the hands of our contact. It may be nothing, but I trust this man speaks the truth as to his association, and we have seen first-hand that there is some sinister game the Abbot is playing. If the Right Reverend has committed a crime, his Grace will wish to see all of the evidence we have found."

"It may take some time to sort out all that you are telling me, with what I am sure will be a wildly different tale that Father Garnerius will tell. The south range is often empty this time of day, and its door is always open to guests to come and go as they please. You might enjoy the privacy there while I meet with The Baron and Garnerius."

Hieronymus bowed low. "Blessings of the Lord be upon you, Father, for your time. Come, Tetty, let us see what refreshment we may find there."

He started off toward the south range. Elsabeth bowed to Ehrhart, and excused herself politely before following after him.

F ATHER EHRHART'S OFFICE ON THE TOP FLOOR of the south tower of the church's façade was austere and functional, with nothing in the way of comforts, and little more in decoration. A desk occupied the west wall beneath the windows looking out across Alsfeld, with only a thick white candle in a heavy lead candlestick for illumination at night. A simple bookshelf filled much of the north wall, opposite more windows gazing southward across the grounds. A doorway in the southeast corner led to a landing, and from there the stairwell descended to the level below. There was nothing else to distract one's attention — no tapestry, no artwork of ecclesiastic nor even secular merit — from the tedium of waiting, and Garnerius fumed silently in the hard-backed chair.

Cuncz sat at ease in another chair beside him nursing a glass of wine (Garnerius had refused the offer of refreshment from the novice sent to entertain them). His normal color had returned since they set out for Alsfeld, pushing their horses as hard as they dared in the hope of running down their quarry on the road. But there had been no such luck; they encountered no one on the journey and had only the word of the guard at the gate that the pair had entered the monastery grounds and not slipped out again.

"The nerve of the man to keep us waiting like this!" Garnerius grumbled. "By God if they should slip my grasp again on account of his delay ..."

"You will what?" Cuncz said with a chuckle into his goblet. "Excommunicate him? Have him flayed alive? Perhaps hang his corpse from the tower?"

Garnerius narrowed his eyes in warning at the other's mocking tone.

"Perhaps you find this amusing now, but it won't be when that is what the Prince-Bishop does to us if he gets his hands on those papers!"

Cuncz sighed. "'Tis all well in hand, Father; the grounds are being searched, and I have men camped right outside the gates. They shan't escape this time."

"They had best not! I wish you had taken this matter seriously enough to not dull your wits with drink now. 'Tis what allowed the girl to slip your grasp in the first damned place."

"I assure you, Father, my wits are far from addled. 'Twas only what she added to my drink before that put me down, unless you think your colleagues would be so treacherous."

Garnerius heated at the accusatorial tone in Cuncz' voice, but practicality in such matters won out over the irreverence of suspecting a fellow man of the cloth, and he held his tongue.

"Under the circumstances, I am not of the mind to be taking chances, especially given the profound affect that woman seems to have on every man she comes within sight of."

"Why Father, you did notice," Cuncz chuckled delightedly. "I imagine your vows must be torture when presented with such a fine example of the Lord of All's eye for creation. 'Twill surely be a pity if we have to remove that pretty head from her shoulders."

"And that is why you shall not have a say in the matter. This woman and her companion have already caused enough trouble, and I'll not have your ill-considered lust complicating things further than it already has!"

"Tch. 'Twill surely be a pity indeed."

Any further retort was interrupted by the creaking of the wooden steps in the stairwell beyond the office door. The hinges squeaked as someone entered, and Garnerius craned his neck to fix his eyes upon Father Ehrhart slipping into the office. He glided with practiced solemnity across the floor and round to the opposite side of the desk, then lowered himself gently into his chair. It, like the two Garnerius and Cuncz occupied, was a plain wooden seat without so much as a leather cushion, much less any ornamentation, and one well-suited to the plain and simple figure of the prior of Alsfeld.

"Freiherr von Leyen, Father," Ehrhart said, offering them each a nod in turn. "I apologize for keeping you waiting. Brother Auberlin says you are here on a matter of some urgency?"

Cuncz chuckled into his wine, but Garnerius's face heated at the dispassionate tone of the prior's voice.

"Yes, Father Ehrhart," he said, and allowed the full weight of his impatience to creep into his voice. "And I am rather concerned that this is how you would treat matters of urgency."

Ehrhart raised an eyebrow at his show of indignation, but any hopes Garnerius held it would elicit some reaction were swiftly quashed.

"Yours is not the only matter with which I need to attend, Father. Alsfeld is perhaps not so large as Friuli, but nonetheless has its own concerns which need addressing."

Cuncz quirked a grin. "He does have you there, Father."

Garnerius skewered the younger man with a glare. "Be quiet! You have caused enough trouble as it is." He then turned his glower on Ehrhart, but neither of the two men was much impressed. Cuncz merely shrugged and took another pull of his wine, and the prior simply watched and waited for him to continue. "As I told your novice ere we were unceremoniously left here for whatever business was so important to conclude, two fugitives and thieves were seen heading this way from Leyen."

He stood and leaned his fists into the prior's desk. "Your guards at the gate have already confirmed they have entered the grounds and did not yet depart. I want them. Now!"

Ehrhart settled back into his chair and steepled his fingers. "And you are certain they are within the cloister itself?"

"Our men are already sweeping the outer and inner courts for them, but I intend to be thorough. One is a man who styles himself as an Olivian Friar, and 'twould be a simple matter for him to bluff his way inside."

"And the other?"

"Quite a striking woman," Cuncz said wistfully, waving his wine glass for emphasis. Garnerius gritted his teeth. "I can honestly say if you had seen her you would not soon forget her, vows or not."

"'Tis not our practice to permit women within the cloister."

"The woman is a guileful creature," Garnerius interceded when Cuncz opened his mouth for a smart retort. "I would not be surprised if she had gained entry under a false guise, as well."

Ehrhart leaned his elbows over his desk and considered his words carefully.

"I wonder, what might they have stolen that would bring you all the way here from Friuli, Father? And why would Freiherr von Leyen himself personally lead the hunt for them?"

"I have reason to believe they stole a reliquary from the church in Friuli," Garnerius said. *And that is true enough for the Lord of All.* "They were spotted fleeing the town after the theft and making for Leyen. I came to warn Freiherr von Leyen, but by the time I arrived, it appeared they had already struck again."

Cuncz grunted.

"Indeed they had," he said. "Oh, the woman is indeed a guileful one as the good Father said." A smile crept onto the Baron's lips, and Garnerius rolled his eyes. "She guiled her way right into my bed, drugged me, and then made off with some rather important personal documents."

Ehrhart blinked at Cuncz's frank confession, but if he was discomfited, it did not show on his infuriatingly placid features.

"I see," he said, his voice never rising. "I do believe there are things to be said for chastity and temperance. What is written was written for good reason, after all."

"As I intimated before, Father, had you seen her for yourself, I am sure you would understand."

Garnerius heaved an exasperated sigh and rolled his eyes.

"This repartee is pointless and only wasting time!" he groused. "Every moment of delay just gives them time to slip through our grasp again."

"Of course," Cuncz said. "That is why he is stalling us."

"Stall—"

Garnerius looked sharply at Ehrhart, and there was no mistaking the slight and amused tugging at the corner of his lips.

"Freiherr von Leyen is certainly quite observant," he said, wholly nonplussed at having been so exposed. Garnerius' face heated, and he balled his hands into fists. "They actually came to see me directly about some rather curious information in their possession, and wanted to inquire into your provenance."

Garnerius' face drained of color, and were it not for the desk near at hand his knees might have collapsed beneath him entirely. "Then they know ..."

"That Rupertus adopted Cuncz from Alsfeld, and legitimated him under your counsel? Of course! I serve the Lord of All, Father, and if I owe fealty to any other lord 'tis to his Grace the Prince-Bishop. I don't know what this politicking is about, nor do I care. They came to me claiming to be investigating a matter on his Grace's behalf, and so I told them what I know."

"Damn them," he murmured. He slammed both fists down on the prior's desk as his temper got the better of him. "Damn them!"

"Language, Father!" Cuncz said, and affected an insincere expression of outrage. "What would the Lord of All think?"

"Where are they?" Garnerius demanded, rounding on Ehrhart rather than take Cuncz's bait.

"The last I saw of them I was having them taken to the south range for refreshment after their journey," Ehrhart said. "This was right before I was summoned away for this meeting."

Cuncz's chair squeaked as he pushed away from the desk and rose in one smooth motion. Garnerius kept his eyes locked on Ehrhart while the younger man circled round him, casually swirling his wine on his way to the windows in the south face of the office.

"If they should escape—"

"You will what?" Ehrhart asked, and rose from his own chair in challenge. "Have an assassin waiting to cut my throat in my bed? Oh, she did not make the accusation openly, but I can piece together the insinuation myself. And though you may be my superior in the Church, Alsfeld does not answer to you. Not directly. 'Tis mine to administer, and his Grace will certainly be intrigued to hear my report."

Garnerius' throat went dry, and ice formed in his belly. For a moment he entertained the thought of seizing the candlestick and bringing it down on Ehrhart's head, but before his hand could stray towards it, Cuncz's voice drew his attention to the windows.

"Father, I do believe we ought to conclude our business quickly if we have a mind of catching our prey," he said.

Garnerius rounded on him and rushed to the window. Cuncz motioned lazily with his wine goblet towards the lawn of green grass stretching out from the south range and towards the hedge separating the inner and outer courts. Two figures — one clad in a brown woolen habit much like that worn by Ehrhart, and the other in the distinctive black mantle of an Olivian Friar — hurried away from the cloister.

"Damn!" he snarled, and smacked his fist against the window frame. "Another distraction?"

"Oh, almost certainly," Cuncz said. "You must admit, Father, he played his hand quite well."

Garnerius glared at him, then rounded on Ehrhart and thrust a finger at him.

"This matter is not over between us, I warn you!"

Ehrhart merely grunted dismissively. "Oh, I believe it is. You have no authority over Alsfeld. You may, perhaps, bring this matter up with his Grace, though I do wonder how he will receive you. Now, if there is nothing else I do have other matters to attend to. Do give my regards to his Grace when next you see him."

His mind reeled at the dismissal and the thought of his quarry slipping his grasp once again. *If she makes it through to his Grace, I am finished!*

"Come on!" he snapped at Cuncz, and hurried for the stairwell.

"'Twas a pleasure to meet you again, Father Ehrhart," Cuncz said casually as he drained his wine and left his glass on the windowsill. "I do hope our next meeting is more pleasant!"

WELL, YOU ARE JUST CARRYING OUT ONE sacrilege after another today," she said as she stepped out of the range and into the inner court. Elsabeth had wrapped herself in the woolen habit of a monk over the rest of her clothes, with her long copper tresses tucked away inside a cowl.

"Oh pipe down, Tetty," Hieronymus hissed from within his own hood. "You have taken a vow of silence, remember? Lord of All knows having that tongue of yours still for a time will be as much a miracle as us getting out of here without being spotted, but at least try to make it to the gates without it wagging."

Elsabeth glared at him but did not respond. True to Ehrhart's word the south range had been deserted, and in a storage room at the end of the hall they had found stacks of folded habits and cowls, all voluminous enough to disguise the telltale feminine curve of her figure.

The hedge separating the inner and outer courts was broken on all four sides with open archways, and when they stepped out of the south range they found one of these passages directly across from them. With a cautious look up and down the inner court, Elsabeth and Hieronymus hurried through, before cutting to their left and making their way eastward along the hedge. They saw only a few servants tending the hedge and gardens in this part of the outer court, and no one stopped them. On rounding the corner to head north, they saw the first sign of trouble; several armored men bearing halberds were scouring the grounds, stopping passersby and questioning them intently.

"Just keep walking, Tetty," Hieronymus muttered. "And keep quiet."

They ignored the soldiers and continued along their way, with Hieronymus setting a carefully measured pace to pass them as quickly as possible without arousing suspicion. Fortunately, the soldiers seemed more interested in intimidating the laypeople and paid them no mind. Elsabeth and Hieronymus soon passed them by, and wove between buildings to avoid knots of other soldiers searching the grounds on their way across the rest of the inner court to the main gate. They made it without incident, and upon their approach the gatekeeper met them with a reverent bow.

"Good day to you, Brothers," he said pleasantly. "There are some mighty strange goings on today.

Elsabeth cast back her cowl. "Yes, quite odd. Now then, I believe you have something that belongs to me."

The guard jumped in surprise. "Blasphemous wench—" he started, before seeing Hieronymus throw back his own hood. "What is the meaning of this?"

"We are cutting our visit to Alsfeld short," Hieronymus said. "Do be a good lad and fetch our weapons. Quickly and quietly, now, we would rather like to avoid a scene."

He nodded, his eyes still bewildered, and called up to his companion in the level above through a cleverly-concealed grate. A moment later the younger guard returned with their weapons cradled in his arms. Elsabeth snatched away her rondel and stuffed it through the cord belt of her habit, and reverently retrieved her sword and slung it over one shoulder. Hieronymus reclaimed his sword and buckler.

Hieronymus made the sign of the Wheel between him and the guard, and said, "Blessings of the Lord be upon you, my son," then he took off briskly with Elsabeth close behind him.

In the field just outside the gate they ran right into a hastily constructed encampment. The standard of Leyen fluttered at the end of the poles marking the boundary of the camp. Horses were picketed neatly along one side away from the road where plenty of grass was to be had, while a few of the soldiers milled about tending to the animals and gear. One or two stood guard, but leaned casually on their spears and showed little interest in their surroundings. Elsabeth supposed the rest were accompanying Cuncz and Garnerius into the monastery to search for the two fugitives.

"Well, that could be trouble in the near future," Elsabeth said as they made their way along the road. The soldiers in the camp showed no sign of making a move to stop them. "Even if they let us pass, they can overtake us easily once Garnerius and Cuncz realize we have slipped away."

"Hm, yes. We can always find a place for you to strip down and offer them a distraction, seeing as it worked so well against Cuncz."

"Oh, very funny. Do you remember that bit of trouble we ran into in Erfurt?"

Hieronymus scowled. "Yes, quite well. As I recall I ended up naked in the town square tied to a lamppost."

"No! No, no, no, no, no, after that. Never, ever, speak of that again. The sight of it still gives me nightmares."

"Ah, yes, I see what you are getting at. I think it might work."

Hieronymus turned away from the road and made his way toward the camp. Elsabeth raised her cowl again and pulled it low over her features, and followed him right up to the guards, who did not even straighten when they approached.

"Greetings, my sons," Hieronymus said, "and the blessings of the Lord be upon you."

"Good day, Father," one drawled. He leaned heavily on his spear. "What brings you out of your walls?"

"Thank you, but I am a humble Brother only. Father Ehrhart asked that we see if anyone in your camp might need the services of a priest this day. My companion and I would be glad to take confession for you and your comrades."

"Kind of you to offer, Father," the soldier said, ignoring Hieronymus's correction of his office. He glanced at Elsabeth, but gave her no more than a cursory look. "You two expecting trouble or something? Tend not to see your sort bearing arms."

"Our teachings do extend to the noble art of defense, my son, and we were just on our way to Waldeck up the road at the request of one of the tradesmen to instruct his son. My companion is quite well versed in the style of Paulus von Soest, though I myself was a student of the great Leonardus in my youth. And as we were already due to be about, Father Ehrhart asked that we offer our services before we departed."

"We do appreciate it, Father. Some of us have not had a good confession in a stretch."

"Ah, then we shall begin right away! Brother Clement, do see about those good men tending to the horses, while I take confession here." Elsabeth bowed solemnly and made her way toward the picketed horses. "You will need to pardon Brother Clement, he has taken a vow of silence so does not speak, but he can listen nonetheless," she heard Hieronymus explain as she slipped away in silence.

Though hastily set, and designed for quick abandonment at need, Elsabeth found the camp to be neatly arranged in quite an orderly fashion, with a clear demarcation between sleeping areas, latrines, and cooking fires. She easily threaded her way among the packs and bedrolls, and headed unerringly towards the lines of horses picketed at the edge of the camp. She reached them without interruption and made a quick survey: The horses stood side by side in two groups, with each picket line tied between a pair of tall wooden stakes driven into the ground. The men left behind to tend the animals worked at the far end of the lines, and Elsabeth found herself left alone. The horses nearest her were still saddled and ready for riding, while the men at the far side worked their way down the line to remove their harnesses one by one. She smiled, and after a quick look about to make sure no one was near enough to see, ducked down and pulled both stakes at her end from the ground.

Elsabeth chose the two nearest horses — both fine, swift coursers — on the rear picket line and quickly untied them. She lead them both a little ways away, drew her sword, and swatted one of the other animals on the hindquarters with the flats and gave a sharp yell. The horse bellowed in surprise and bolted, taking the rest of the picket line with it. The other line startled as well, and soon the entire herd was stampeding away. A shout of alarm filled the camp as the soldiers took off after them or sprung out of the way to avoid the crushing weight of the panicked animals, and Elsabeth used the time to cast off her habit and hook her sword to her belt before swinging up into the saddle.

She spurred the animal forward and charged through the living areas of the camp leading the second horse behind her, scattering tents, packs, and bedrolls, and nearly rode down the two guards, now standing dumbstruck at the confusion erupting behind them. One spotted her and charged, but Hieronymus stuck his staff between his legs, and he tripped and tumbled to the ground in a heap. His companion went down from a quick blow to the teeth when Hieronymus spun around to face him.

Elsabeth tossed the reins of the second horse to him, and he clambered up with an effort.

"Well timed, Tetty," he said. "I don't think I could stomach another moment of their whining. You would think the Lord of All actually cared about every little impure thought that runs through a man's mind when a pretty girl walks by. Where to?"

"Back to Friuli," she said, and spurred her appropriated horse, with Hieronymus close behind. "If Cuncz was born there, there is sure to be a record of it, and maybe that will be enough to satisfy the Bishop and get us out of this mess."

She turned her horse up the road and they left Alsfeld behind them.

THEY ARRIVED AT THE CAMP TO FIND EVERYTHING in chaos. Panicked horses darted this way and that, pursued by their scrambling handlers. A few men were battered and bloodied from their efforts, or simply from standing in the path of the horses when they bolted. Baggage was trampled, cook fires were scattered, and tents were ripped apart.

Garnerius numbly surveyed the damage. He did not even need to ask what had happened; the bedlam spoke for itself. And yet he found himself pulling aside one of the scrambling guards anyway.

"What in God's name happened here!" he shouted over the cries of the horses and the yells of the men wrestling to calm them.

"Father! Herr Baron!" the fellow stammered, and straightened upon realizing whom he was addressing. "I don't quite know what happened. Two priests came out from the monastery to take our confessions on their way to Waldeck, and the next I know they have made off with two of the horses and scattered the rest to the winds! We are chasing down the runaways now, but 'tis as if the Lord of the Underworld himself is driving them."

"Which way did they go?" Garnerius said.

"'Twas not towards Waldeck, I know that much," the guard said, and waved his arm down the road away from the monastery. "They rode off to the west."

Garnerius gritted his teeth.

"Friuli," he said.

"What?" Cuncz said, his features bunched in confusion.

"They are headed back to Friuli."

"Surely they can't be that foolish; their faces are known by every man in the town by now. And that way leads to Bremen, as well, if they turn north."

Garnerius rounded on him, seizing him by his doublet. Cuncz's men all sprung forward in defense of their Lord, and Garnerius' responded in fear that they might make a move against the Abbot. Tension so thick it could be cut with a knife hung over the wreckage of the camp as the two sides stared each other down.

"They have thrice slipped my grasp, and I'll not underestimate them again! If they are headed west they must be returning to Friuli."

"But why?" Cuncz said. "Don't they have everything they need already?"

"Not everything," Garnerius said. He released him, and cradled his head in shaking hands. "Not everything. There is one more piece to the puzzle, and that is in Friuli!"

Cuncz straightened his doublet with an indignant tug. His guards stood down, and Garnerius' own men with them. "Very well. As soon as we have enough horses rounded up, we—"

Garnerius glared at him. "No. I. You, I suggest, return to Leyen."

Cuncz stiffened, glowering at him. "I should think—"

"No! You have already caused enough damage. Friuli is my concern. Go back to Leyen, and I will contact you once this matter is settled!"

LSABETH AND HIERONYMUS PUSHED THE horses as hard as they dared, and stopped only well into the night to catch a few hours of sleep before resuming their ride just before daybreak. They reached Friuli a little after midmorning with no sign of pursuit on the road behind them, and left the horses in the care of a communal stable just inside the gate before making the rest of the trip to the Abbey on foot. They now stood watching the gate from a corner across the street.

"Well, here we are again," Hieronymus said as he stared up at the Abbey frowning down upon the town. "Are you sure this is a good idea?"

"No," she said. "But I think I am rather out of good ideas at the moment."

"I have always wanted to visit Navarre."

"Somehow I doubt the Bishop's man will let us off so easily. There is always something to get us re-interested." Elsabeth folded her arms across her chest and watched the gate with a sigh. "Well, how do you want to do this? I for one, would rather like to avoid another climb up the privy shaft, especially in the middle of the day when 'tis more likely for someone to use it. And without knowing how long Garnerius and Cuncz will be delayed rounding up their horses, I think it best we not try to wait until dark."

"Well, I suppose that just leaves us the front door this time."

Hieronymus stepped around the corner and started across the street. Elsabeth quickly rearranged her sword to hang beneath her jacket, then hurried after to catch up and walk beside him. He regarded her with a slight roll of the eyes, but said nothing as they approached the gates. Elsabeth fidgeted with her sword to better hide it from view. Hieronymus did not even bother; the guards waved them through with only a cursory looking over.

I suppose with the Abbot not in residence they are off their guard, and no one has warned them to be on the lookout for us.

The Abbey's layout was much the same as Alsfeld, though the church was larger, and with an even more opulent façade of imported white marble. The chapter house stood out notably on the east range with its peaked roof. The second level, housing the Abbot's private chambers, rose high above the rest of the range. Surrounding the complex were a large hospital, workshops, bakeries, guest houses, and storehouses. All were built in the same combination of brick and half-timbered construction common throughout this part of Boehm, with tiled, peaked roofs.

Hieronymus made for the west range, and upon entry they were met by the cellarer, an older man with thin graying hair in a black habit. He bowed politely in greeting.

"Good morning, Brother," he said. "Blessings of the Lord be upon you. Is there something I may assist you with?"

"Yes," Hieronymus said after bowing in return. "My companion has a need to review the Abbey's records of births and deaths over the last thirty years."

The cellarer looked at Elsabeth uncertainly for a moment. "May I ask the purpose?"

"'Tis a personal matter," Elsabeth said.

"Ah," he said. "We typically don't allow the laity to view the Abbey records without the permission of Father Garnerius, who I regret has been called away from Friuli on business. However, he should return within the next few days..."

"Forgive me, Brother," Hieronymus said, "but I am afraid we don't have time for that." He glanced up at the ceiling and muttered, "Lord of All please forgive me for what I am about to do." Then he drew his sword and placed it at the throat of the cellarer. His gray eyes widened in shock, but he admirably maintained his composure.

"If you will follow me, please," he said.

Elsabeth drew her rondel and placed it at the cellarer's back, so Hieronymus could return his sword to its scabbard. He led them out to the arcaded cloister, where a few brothers of the Abbey gathered and spoke quietly among themselves. Elsabeth adjusted the sleeve of her jacket to cover her hand and weapon and shifted around to the cellarer's side, while Hieronymus flanked him on the other. For his part, the man did not make a sound or give any indication to his brothers of anything out of sorts happening, and they passed without incident through the cloister and into the deserted east range. He turned to his left, past the chapter house, and stopped before a door.

"The library is through here," he said calmly, with the tip of the rondel still leveled at his side.

"Open it," Elsabeth said firmly, and the cellarer did as instructed.

The library was a large room extending well back from the outer wall of the east range, though not quite as large as the chapter house. Volumes of manuscripts lined the shelves, with a stepladder near at hand to reach the highest ones. Other books sat stacked on tables in the center of the room. A large and beautifully illuminated bible lay open on a pedestal near the door on their right as they entered, and there were also a few glass cases containing a wide array of artifacts. Along the wall on one side were a series of desks that served as workplaces, where a few scribes worked copying manuscripts. The *armarius* noticed their entrance and started toward them.

"Clear the room," Elsabeth ordered the cellarer quietly.

"Good morning, Brother," the *armarius* said in turn to Hieronymus and the cellarer when he reached them. "What may I do for you?"

"These good people have need of privacy while they consult our records," the cellarer said. If he gave any indication of his predicament, Elsabeth did not catch it.

The *armarius* frowned at Elsabeth and Hieronymus. "I was not aware anyone had been granted access to them. Has Father Garnerius returned already?"

"I'll discuss the matter with Father Garnerius when he returns," the cellarer said. "For the moment, I am convinced that these good people have need to view them, and they have requested privacy while they do."

The other regarded the cellarer for a moment, then sighed and nodded. "Very well, Brother." He turned to the scribes, who had paused in their work to watch the commotion, and motioned them out. Elsabeth kept close to the cellarer, concealing her rondel between them, and when the last filed out Hieronymus closed the door behind them. There was no bolt or lock.

Elsabeth stepped away from the cellarer and returned her weapon to its sheath at her back. "We do apologize for this, but we really don't have much time." She swept her eyes around the shelves, and frowned when a system of organization was not readily apparent. "We need information on births and deaths recorded by the Abbey in the Spring of 1414," she said. "Where are they?"

"This way," the cellarer said, and led her to a shelf in the middle of the wall. He pulled the stepladder over, climbed up, checked the spines of the books, and then pulled down a large leather-bound volume. "Here it is. May I ask what this is all about, and why 'tis so important you would threaten violence in a house of the Lord?"

"I am sure the Lord of All will find it in His heart to forgive us if what we need is here," she said, but did not answer his question. She led the cellarer to a table, where he laid down the volume and opened it. "I presume 'twould be chronological by month?"

He nodded. "Yes, but the *armarius* would have better knowledge, I should go—"

Elsabeth's hand shot out and snatched his robe when he tried to slip away. "No, you shall stay right here. We can find it without his help." Elsabeth began paging through the entries line-by-line, each written in the same firm hand. The ink was somewhat faded, but the vellum pages were still clear. Most of the births and deaths were fairly ordinary; deaths from disease, age, conflict, or mishap, young children who passed after tragically short lives leaving grieving mothers and fathers, but then three entries all in a row caught her eye.

"Hieronymus," she said.

"What is it, Tetty?" he said, and approached to look over her shoulder. "You have something?"

"I think I might." She felt the cellarer lean in as well when she laid a finger on the entries. "Two women were brought to the Abbey's infirmary due to difficult childbirths. Both died, as did one of the babies. The other survived."

"Hm. Is it him, do you think?"

"It could be, but that is not the most interesting thing about it: There is no information recorded about the woman whose child survived, but the other was a common woman by the name of Katherin, from Dener, though what name her child was given is not recorded here."

"Dener is not far from Ortenau."

"Yes, and according to this, Emrich von Ortenau himself arranged the burial for both her and the child. Now why do you suppose would the Margrave personally pay for the burial of a common woman and her child?"

Hieronymus considered. "His mistress and bastard?"

Elsabeth nodded. "He must have felt some attachment to her. If she were a mere prostitute she would not even be a name in a book," she said, and tapped her finger pointedly on the other entry.

The cellarer leaned in over her shoulder to read the entry for himself and shook his head. "That cannot be right," he said suddenly, and Elsabeth and Hieronymus both turned to him in surprise.

"What do you mean?" she asked.

He studied the entry a moment longer. "I helped attend to Katherin Deners during the birth. 'Twas indeed a difficult one and she did not survive, but her child did."

Elsabeth's eyes widened. "Are you certain?"

The cellarer gave her an irritated look. "As God is my witness, I swear it to be true. The son of Katherin Deners survived. And as I recall, the other woman arrived perhaps a week later and bore a girl."

"Who made these entries?" Hieronymus asked.

"Father Garnerius always took it upon himself to enter the births and deaths."

"Bugger," Elsabeth breathed, and her eyes grew wide as saucers. "If I am right about this, he switched the children. If 'tis the same babe Garnerius brought to Alsfeld, then that means Cuncz would be Emrich's bastard." She frowned thoughtfully. "But what would Father Garnerius have to gain in hiding this, or better yet, arranging for Rupertus to adopt him?"

"Tetty, do you remember what land the Abbot had been buying up for Cuncz?"

She shook her head. "Nothing particularly stands out, no."

"One was a small township not far west from here. Friuli sits astride the border of the territories controlled by Ortenau to the west, and Leyen to the east. I think he was buying up land under Ortenau's influence adjacent to Friuli."

"But why?"

The cellarer cleared his throat. "Perhaps I can answer that. Mind you this is strictly idle gossip — and yes, even we at times fall victim to wagging tongues — but Father Garnerius and Emrich von Ortenau have had a strained relationship at best. They have had a number of political disagreements in the past, particularly where the extent of Friuli's influence has been concerned."

Elsabeth considered for a moment. "What would have happened had the Rupertus von Leyen died without issue?"

He shrugged. "Rupertus had no other kin to the best of my knowledge. I suppose the land would have reverted to his Grace the Prince-Bishop in Bremen in the absence of an heir."

"And Bishop Augustin would likely redistribute the land as he saw fit. Possibly even to Emrich von Ortenau. Oh, that is clever. Father Garnerius lets Emrich believe his child died during birth, and uses that same bastard to provide Rupertus an heir to his lands and head off any attempt by Emrich to encircle Friuli. Any child might have done the trick, but using Emrich's own bastard would be just the petty act I would expect of a man who would reward a good deed with assassins in the middle of the night."

Hieronymus nodded his agreement. "And if Emrich were to gain control of Leyen, it would make it rather difficult for Father Garnerius to expand his own political power as he would now be encircled. I suspect his Grace will wish to see this as well."

"Right," Elsabeth said, and despite the cry of protest from the cellarer tore the page from the book, folded it neatly, and stuffed it away inside her doublet. "Come on, best we not be here when the Abbot returns."

The words were no sooner from her mouth when the door to the library burst open and four guards, armed with halberds, rushed in. Elsabeth's sword flashed as it cleared her scabbard, but she found herself trapped between the rows of tables running along the library floor and with no room to position herself for a fight. The *armarius* trailed after the guards, followed by Garnerius himself. The cellarer showed deference immediately, but Elsabeth merely gripped her sword tighter and swept her gaze toward the guards, seeking for some means of escape.

"Well, you two have proven to be quite a bit of trouble," Garnerius said. He looked at her sword. "Drop it. I would much prefer to not have to shed blood here."

Elsabeth ignored the threat. The reach of the halberds worked against them in such close quarters, though she doubted the tables would prove much of a barrier. "But you have no trouble with it in an inn at night if 'tis not by your hand," she said.

Garnerius chuckled. "Quite true, my child. There are, nonetheless, precedents we must now follow. You have assaulted the Freiherr of Leyen and his guards, stolen two horses, and forced entry into the Abbey. His Grace the Bishop will wish to have you tried before you are hanged. But, by all means, resist arrest and die here. One way or another you will turn over everything you have found so this unfortunate mistake does not recur."

He motioned for the guards to advance. Elsabeth took up a guard position and backed out from between the two tables on either side, and tried circling around to the north wall of the Library. Hieronymus's sword rasped from its scabbard, and he did the same, moving to the south in an effort to split the guards so they could engage them one at a time. The guards advanced with care, however, and moved carefully to keep the pair from separating them.

Then a throaty chuckle filled the room as a familiar gravelly voice broke the building tension. "Well, what have we here? A whore, a friar, and an abbot all walk into an abbey. Hmm, I am sure you all have heard that one before, so let us forget the jokes." Out of the corner of her eye she spied a cloaked and hooded figure stepping through the doorway, followed by three guards bearing the livery of

Leyen. Three guards with very familiar faces. Elsabeth blinked in confusion when she recognized the helpful merchants from Leyen: Jacobus, Clement, and Thadeus.

"Call them off!" he said sharply to Garnerius, with a wave at the Abbot's men.

Garnerius turned and glared at the hooded man approaching him from behind.

"I beg your pardon? Have you any idea who you are addressing, my son?"

The man's voice changed, and suddenly became very smooth, cultured, and equally familiar. "Have you?" he said and cast back his hood. Elsabeth's breath caught in her throat when she found herself gazing on Baron Cuncz.

Cuncz turned his eyes on the Abbot's guards, who halted their advancement at his entry, and now watched him uncertainly. "By order of his Grace the Bishop, Father Garnerius is to be arrested at once."

Garnerius's mouth dropped open in shock. Elsabeth lowered her sword, equally perplexed, and the guards eyed each other in shared confusion.

"What is the meaning of this?" the Abbot said.

Cuncz flashed his lopsided smile. "Shall we start with attempted murder? Conspiracy? Or perhaps fraud? Really, Father, do you think you could have coerced the sale of all that land and someone would not notice?"

"You treacherous bastard! Everything I have done for you—"

"Was for your own advancement, Father," Cuncz finished for him, and his voice turned almost bored. "Did you really think my father would brook a fool for an heir?" He clicked his tongue in a most patronizing manner, and Garnerius' face turned a brilliant shade of crimson. "The hardest part about this whole charade was playing your unwitting pawn against his Grace."

He motioned to the guards. "Well, what are you waiting for? Take him away."

Garnerius sputtered furiously. The guards shrugged at each other, then did as the Baron commanded. Jacobus, Clement, and Thadeus stepped forward to help escort the Abbot from the room. When the group departed, Cuncz smiled and turned to the *armarius* and cellarer.

"Leave us, if you will. And do see to it that you don't speak of what has happened in this room, thank you very much." The two did as he asked and hastily retreated from the library, leaving them alone and at the mercy of Cuncz.

Q UNCZ STROLLED CASUALLY ACROSS THE library towards her, his hands folded behind his back, and as smug and superior a smirk as she had ever seen tugging at the corner of his lips.

"Ah, Elsabeth, or is it Gwenhevare? How wonderful it is to see you again! I do apologize for all that you have endured on my account, but unlike some others, I insist on seeing you both *properly* rewarded for your trouble."

Elsabeth gawked, and it was a moment before she found her voice. "What in God's name is going on here?"

He tsked and shook his head. "I can see you are rather confused, though I suspect you have reasoned out some of this on your own. You are quite a resourceful woman, after all. Something I find quite irresistible about you. His Grace the Bishop was suspicious of the Right Reverend Garnerius, particularly when Emrich complained about the unusual amount of land he was coerced to turn over due to some financial mistakes made by his vassals, which the good Abbot took advantage of."

Cuncz stepped further into the library and headed toward her, glancing at the books piled on the tables as he strolled past them. By now Hieronymus had sheathed his sword, though Elsabeth kept hers loosely in hand.

"You are wondering why, I suppose?"

She nodded, and eyed him carefully. "That was the one question I have not exactly been able to answer."

"Father Garnerius's eye was not on von Ortenau, although he certainly had little love for the man, but on his Grace himself. You see, he thought to set me up and use me as a powerbase against the Bishop, thinking me too disinterested in actually running Leyen to be a problem. Indirectly at first, of course, but I suspect he would have taken a more overt hand once he had the ability to do so, at which point he would have found me rather expendable. I, of course, had plans of my own that did not involve being a tool in Garnerius's hand."

"So you cut a deal with the Bishop." She made it a statement of fact.

His smile broadened. "A new Abbot will need to be appointed over Friuli, and will be made a vassal of Leyen, finally addressing the question of its status once and for all. And I get to keep the property Father Garnerius so thoughtfully acquired for me. We both make out quite nicely, I would say; his Grace rids himself of an upstart and potential rival, and I gain Friuli and a bit of von Ortenau's land. I did find myself needing to improvise a tad when the two of you spoiled the theft I arranged, but no harm done in the end.

"Now then…" he extended his hand toward her. "If you would be so kind as to return my property. Oh! And also that page I believe you took from the Abbey's records, I would rather like to see that such inconvenient documents are no longer an inconvenience. All this nonsense about me being Emrich von Ortenau's bastard shall henceforth be only that: Nonsense. As far as the world is concerned, I am indeed the son of Rupertus von Leyen and his wife.

"And I promise you will not be needing that," he added with a nod at her sword.

Elsabeth watched him for a moment, sighed, and reluctantly returned her sword to its scabbard. "You mentioned a reward?" she said searchingly. She reached into her pouch, retrieved the documents she lifted from Cuncz's study and the page from the Abbey's records, and handed them over. He did not even bother disguising it when he checked to ensure they were all there.

"Yes, of course," he said absently, then folded the pages and stuffed them inside his doublet. Cuncz untied a pouch from his belt and tossed it to Hieronymus. The friar juggled it for a moment before he had it safely under control. "For your parish, Brother. Though I suspect a goodly amount will be donated to the nunneries between here and there."

"And what about Father Ehrhart?" Hieronymus said, and narrowed his eyes with suspicion. "What do you intend to do about him? He certainly knows a good bit about this matter."

"You need not worry yourself about the good Father. I had a little chat with him after Father Garnerius left me at

Alsfeld, and a generous donation to the monastery has ensured his silence. Now, if you would do me the courtesy of giving me a moment alone with your companion?"

"Tetty?" Hieronymus said while he checked the contents of the purse with no less subtlety than Cuncz's review of his documents, and slipped the coin back in again.

Elsabeth nodded toward the door. "Go on, if he has anything untoward planned, I can handle it."

They watched him go, and when he shut the door behind him Elsabeth folded her arms across her chest and gazed levelly at Cuncz.

"You knew. The entire time I was in Leyen; at dinner, in bed, you knew who I really was."

Cuncz's smile broadened, and it was as self-satisfied an expression as Elsabeth had ever seen. "Of course. I make it a point to know everything that goes on within my territory. That you and the good friar managed to thwart my previous agents actually quite impressed me."

"I could have killed you, you know. Perhaps I could have misjudged the dose when I drugged you, or that might have been poison in your wine altogether. Or I could have just cut your throat."

"Sweet Tetty, the risk was part of what made our encounter so exhilarating! Of course, no matter what you would have done, I intended to see to it you did not leave Leyen without those papers from my desk. Conrat was not the least bit pleased with the plan, but he did carry it out quite well, particularly his delay of the Abbot to give you time to reach Alsfeld ahead of us.

"All of this is assuming I had not been killed of course, in which case you would never have escaped," he added, and scooped up her hand. "And I did mean what I said that night: You are a rare beauty, and I could hardly let you pass through my walls without sampling everything your charms had to offer. And offer you did, with only a small bit of facilitation on my part."

He kissed the back of her fingertips, and Elsabeth blushed fiercely in spite of herself.

"You sly bastard," she said.

He flashed that lopsided smile again. "The only trouble I find myself in, is having had a taste, I can't resist the thought of having more. I would very much like you to come back to Leyen with me as my mistress. You would be provided for and would no longer need to scrape a living on the road in the dangerous sort of work you do now. And perhaps I could use my not inconsiderable influence to arrange to make our relationship a truly respectable one in the future. It would need to be a lesser title, perhaps, and not right away, but in time."

Elsabeth's stomach fluttered a bit, but she pushed him to arm's length and regarded him with a smirk of her own. "More to the point: It keeps me close by where you can keep an eye on me, so I cannot let it slip just what has been going on here without you knowing of it immediately. And if I should prove to be an unfortunate liability, I would be left completely in your power."

He chuckled. "That thought does occur to me, yes. But I must say, I am rather smitten with you." Cuncz heaved a sigh. "I don't think I can ever look at another woman again without comparing her to you."

She blushed and gave him a gentle peck on the lips, then slipped past him to give herself a clean line for the door in the event he did not take her rejection well.

"I shan't deny that I'll be remembering our little tryst rather fondly on many lonely nights to come, but I think 'twould be more in my interest not to be under your roof should you decide me to be an inconvenience."

Cuncz caught her hand again and pulled her back to him.

"If that is your decision I shan't think to dishonor it by giving you an ultimatum." The lopsided smile flashed across his lips again. He kissed her long and deeply. Elsabeth closed her eyes and let a soft moan escape her throat.

Just before she pulled away, she felt something pressed into her palm. They parted, and in her hand was a gold ring set with a faceted red stone. "For you, Tetty, along with a part of the coin I have already given to your comrade. And I shall be reclaiming the horses you borrowed, of course. You need not worry about your road, however; I brought yours and the good friar's along, and they are waiting for you outside." He stroked her chin with his thumb. "Do take care of yourself; I expect to see you again."

Elsabeth let out a giddy laugh as she backed away from him, and slipped the ring into a pouch on her belt. "Oh, I shall. But I think I best be on my way before Hieronymus leaves me behind, or you change your mind about letting me just walk away. Do give my regards to the Bishop."

And then she quickly slipped from the library and left him behind.

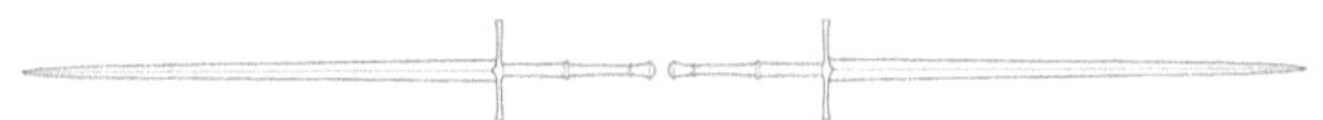

SO DID YOU DEFILE THE LIBRARY?" HIERONYMUS said when she caught up with him making his way south along the east range.

"Oh, do you really think so little of me?" she asked.

Hieronymus merely grunted. "So where to now?"

"Far from here, I think." She flashed him a smirk. "I have always wanted to visit Navarre."

He chuckled. "I am sure there are plenty of places for us to get in trouble in along the way."

"Doubtless, so at least the road will be entertaining. Come on, let us be off."

Presenting a special first look at

THE ADVENTURES OF ELSABETH SOESTEN

BAIT AND

SWITCH

THE BLUR OF SOMETHING RATHER LARGE and heavy flying towards her caught her eye, and in one fluid movement Elsabeth spun away from her horse, her sword flashed from its scabbard, and she cut the melon aimed at her head neatly in two. The halves spun harmlessly past her in a shower of juice and pulp that splattered a broad streak across her heart-shaped face.

She was not exactly certain from which direction the missile came, but judging from the chorus of curses raining down on her from the villagers approaching her, she needed no specifics. If her deft defense against the unexpected attack startled any of the crowd they did not show it, and if anything the failed assault only enraged them further. This was especially evident when a hasty shower of stones followed the melon and sent her scrambling to the far side of her old Lizarran jennet, Felis, who danced nervously and snorted at the commotion.

Hieronymus, his portly round face framed by his unruly mane of graying hair and beard, clutched his carved wooden staff and stepped between Elsabeth and the crowd, pleading for their attention. "Peace, sons and daughters, peace!" he said in his passable Navarrese, touched with a heavy Boehman accent. "Don't give in to wrath. Remember what the Son of the Baron would say of forgiveness!"

Neither the travel-and-ale-stained black woolen habit of his order, nor the sword and buckler hung at his hip, made an impression on the crowd. A hail of insults answered him, most directed at her to judge by the count of "whores" and "harlots" screamed by the women of the village. The men mostly kept to the rear and well out of the way, more than a few with looks of utter embarrassment on their faces. The village priest, a handsome man somewhat younger than her twenty-three summers and dressed in a brown woolen habit, stepped forward to join the fat friar's efforts to mediate the situation.

"I beg of you, my children," he said, "let justice prevail, not anger. If this woman has wronged you, then let the Baron of All cast his judgment and she will be punished accordingly."

He turned to Elsabeth. "My child, will you come forward?" he said, and Hieronymus looked askance at her as well, as if waiting for her response. She gave the slightest nod towards his horse, and Hieronymus slowly inched his way over to Josephus. The old Hackney took the excitement in stride, and disinterestedly browsed on the grasses on the village outskirts where they stabled. "There need not be any violence if you will consent to answer to their charges."

Elsabeth wiped the melon pulp from her face with one elbow and swept the tail of her brown leather coat back behind her hip to clear her scabbard. She rammed her sword home and flashed the priest a mischievous smirk.

"Oh, there is no need for that," she said, her own Navarrese was mostly clean with little in the way of an accent. She swept her black felt hat from her head and held it over her heart. "Bless me father, for I have indeed sinned, and lain with several men of the village. And if the women here are as skilled in their beds as they are at flinging stones, then 'tis small wonder I found them so willing to join me."

Hieronymus rolled his eyes when he reached his horse, and a fresh volley of stones, curses, insults, and oaths filled the village.

"Well that will certainly smooth things over," he said in Boehman as he hurried to ready Josephus for flight.

"We already got paid for the job," she replied in kind in a low voice, "so there is no need to come back again, anyway. Let us just go before they light the torches."

The priest managed to contain the crowd again with great effort, and turned back to her. "I beg of you, my child," he said. "For the good of your soul you must make amends to those whom you have wronged!"

Elsabeth tsked at him, and set her hat back atop her head at a rakish angle. The broad brim, pinned up at one side, shaded her eyes from the sun. "Oh Father, and I thought my soul was already in such good hands when I was on my knees before you last night. I would think all of Navarre heard your prayers with the way you were carrying on."

The priest's face turned a brilliant shade of crimson, and for a moment he sputtered and could not find the words for a rebuke. "Succubus!" he finally spat, and jabbed an accusing finger. "There for certain stands a servant of the Dark One himself! See how her tongue weaves salacious lies?"

"Well, now you did it, Tetty," Hieronymus muttered.

"Yes," she said, "I may have pushed this one a tad too far."

"In the name of the Lord, seize the witch so she might be hanged, and her corruption lifted from our village!" the priest said.

"Time to go?" Hieronymus said.

Elsabeth vaulted into the saddle. "Time to go!"

As the townsfolk surged forward, Elsabeth gave a cry and jammed her heels into Felis' flanks. Felis snorted and reared, and took off like a shot away from the village. Elsabeth's copper hair streamed behind her like a gleaming banner, with only a look over her shoulder to be sure Hieronymus was with her and to check for signs of pursuit. However the villagers had no riding horses to speak of, and had little hope to catch them.

They rode hard for several miles, and only when the village lay well behind them, hidden by a turn of the road as it passed through a small wooded area, did she pull up Felis and check her pace. Hieronymus rode up beside her and shook his head.

"Well, that was another fine mess you got us into," he said.

"Me?" she said in protest. "This whole adventure was another one of your schemes. I only tagged along to keep you out of trouble."

"Yes, you. God in heaven, girl! What has gotten into you lately? I have seen you leave a trail of broken hearts — and I suspect very angry wives — from one end of Boehm to the other, but this has been excessive even for you. Did you lay with every man there, or just the ones whose wives were throwing stones?"

"It was actually only two of them. Well, and the priest, but he was a strange one, and insisted only that I—"

He cut her off abruptly. "Enough, girl, enough! That is all I really can bear to hear."

She rolled her eyes. "You did bring it up."

"Only because you nearly got yourself hanged for it! And likely me with you. Now something has been bothering you ever since we crossed into Navarre. I am your priest, such as it is, am I not?"

Elsabeth eyed him incredulously. "Are you saying you want me to give confession now?"

"Who said anything about confession? I am merely offering you the comfort of my ear. And I rather hope you take advantage of it before the next village you scandalize sees fit to lock up our only means of escape before coming to hang you."

She sighed again. "If you must know, though 'tis rather none of your business, it has been nigh on six weeks since I have had satisfaction by means other than my own hands, and I am trying very hard not to think of Baron Cuncz and his magic wand. I am likely to get more enjoyment from bumping along in the bloody saddle. And now here I am telling you about it on top of it all."

"I happen to think 'tis a message. For too long you have willingly opened your body to any man with a pulse. The Lord of All does not wish to see you flitting from bed to bed like a common whore, 'tis unbecoming."

Elsabeth rolled her eyes at him. "And what about you? I am sure He thinks highly of the sort of 'indulgence' you offer the laywomen."

Hieronymus harrumphed and looked towards the sky. "Lord, grant me patience with your wayward daughter! I offer her advice and she responds by questioning my piety!"

"Your piety deserves questioning, and you well know it. Nor did I ask your advice. The sort of bed I make to lie in is none of your concern, so if you don't like it you can go and bugger yourself."

At that they rode in silence for some time, and after a mile or so they passed through the wooded area and broke out into open fields stretching out for some distance in all directions. No sign of pursuit followed them, and they passed no one else on the road, though at times they saw laborers at work in the fields. The road was a rutted and hard-packed dirt track that ran westwards across Navarre, and was at times crossed by little streams gurgling in stony beds passed by ford or bridges of crumbling and weathered stone. Here and there they saw the remains of old paving stones peeking through the dirt and turf like old bleached bones, a rare sign of the great empire that once stretched out of the Free City-States to the south, to cover much of Navarre and Coventry further to the northwest.

It was already midday by the time they set out from the village, and it promised to be well after twilight before they reached their destination, which Elsabeth noted Hieronymus had not been forthcoming about. Finally she could take no more of riding with only the singing of birds and the steady clatter of their horses' hooves to break the silence.

"Where are you taking us, anyway?" she said.

"Somewhere to get a drink, and maybe a bit of work to keep you occupied and out of trouble, though you seem to have a knack for drawing it wherever you go."

She rolled her eyes. "Any time you go looking for a drink and a bit of work I always end up having to get you out of trouble. Like that time you tried to hustle those gents in Aue and ended up hung by your ankles from the village church."

"That was not my fault! They were easy marks, and I would have had them if you would have just done as I asked."

"My sleeping habits are suddenly much less objectionable once you think you can use them to your advantage. Now, what are you planning this time?"

"My plan was to head for a place a bit up the road the priest back there—" he jerked his thumb over his shoulder, and motioned vaguely back towards the village "— mentioned before you were nearly hanged. He called it the Inn of the Four Ways."

Elsabeth let out a groan of exasperation. "Oh good God, not another inn. Why is it always a bloody inn?"

"Do you know of anywhere better to look for someone needing a sword arm or two? The Four Ways is right at a major crossroads so anyone on the road will be passing through. I am sure there will be no lack of merchants and travelers looking for protection."

"And 'tis also a good place for you to lose all our money on drink and dice. How long did it take before you had been through your share of the reward from Cuncz?"

Hieronymus glared at her. "As I recall you enjoyed your fair share of the libations along the road, Tetty. Every innkeeper between here and Leyen I am sure has been singing your praises after we passed through. Not to mention your name, among other things, has been on the lips of every bard and minstrel as well. Now, will you just trust me? I know what I am doing."

She sighed and shook her head. "It terrifies me every time you say that."

The rest of their ride was uneventful. Midday passed into afternoon, and soon the sun was sinking into the west, setting the sky alight with brilliant golds and reds as the pale blue ceiling overhead slowly deepened into indigo. The silver-white points of stars ignited in the gathering dark as the golden lights of their destination loomed up ahead of them.

The Inn of the Four Ways was a substantial structure nestled in the northwest corner of the joining of the two roads whence it took its name. The greater of the two ran north and south across Navarre, and was worn and deeply rutted by the passage of merchant wagons. The road Elsabeth and Hieronymus followed westward from Boehm was less well-traveled in these days, though once had been a major passage for goods moving overland. In summer months, the hard dirt surfaces were a sea of choking dust, making the Four Ways a welcome respite for travelers.

The Inn was virtually a town in and of itself, enclosed within a wooden gated palisade atop a low grassy rise overlooking the road, backed by a small wooded area with a clear bright pond beside it. A broad path branched off the westward road to run up to the main gate to the south, and bisected the grounds behind the wall before it exited another gate on the north face to rejoin the main highway. Brightly painted half-timbered homes and shops lined both sides of this path, creating a maze of crowded alleys with merchant stalls and several open squares dominated by the Inn itself at its heart.

The Inn straddled the path, with a long, two-leveled wing with peaked roofs and many windows on each side, connected by a central section, through which the road passed by means of an archway. Beneath the main wing were stalls for the sheltering of horses, and a doorway in each corner led inside.

Elsabeth left Hieronymus to arrange the stabling of their horses, and made her way inside.

She entered through the door in the southeast corner of the central wing, and found herself on a well-lit landing at the foot of a steep stairway. Golden light filled the room above, and there was music and the fragrance of cooking food along with the sour odor of beer in the air. Elsabeth started up the stairs and soon emerged in the inn's common room, a wide chamber that filled the entirety of the main wing above the stables below. Glass windows looked north and south out onto the road, and thick timber columns supported the ceiling above. A door on either end led to the east and west wings.

Trestle tables ringed an open space in the middle of the common room floor, where men and women danced to a jaunty tune played by musicians on pipes, drums, and lutes, while serving girls glided between tables and spun out of the reach of grasping hands. Elsabeth flashed one of the pipers a smile when he looked her way, then swept her eyes across the common room. She spied an empty table in the southwest corner, near another stairwell much like the one through which she entered. She sighed and made her way across the room, keeping to the wall and out of the way as she slipped past tables full of drinkers; some were stained and worn from the road, others were locals visiting the Inn to share news of the day and join in the revelry of the evening.

She reached the table, dropped heavily onto the bench with her back to the wall, and propped her sword against the table. Before long, a serving girl appeared bearing a platter of the evening's meal and a tankard of ale for her, which she set down with an uncertain eye on the sword leaning against the table. Elsabeth handed her a silver *pfennig*.

"I have a companion joining me shortly," she said. "Be a dear and have a plate and tankard brought for him as well. If 'tis not here before he is I'll be dealing with his grumbling all evening."

The serving girl inclined her head slightly and hurried off to the kitchens. Hieronymus arrived presently. He leaned his staff against the table and dropped heavily into the chair across from her. He frowned at the platter in front of her.

"Well, that is courteous of you; leaving me to contend with the horses and boarding, while you sit down to eat."

"Oh, don't start with me, the girl will be back in a moment, though God knows you could stand a fast. So are we just sitting around and hoping for someone to turn up?"

"More or less."

Elsabeth sighed and rolled her eyes. "Wonderful. We could just spend the night at ease and move on somewhere work was actually posted. Instead, we hang around just hoping for something to turn up on its own. Brilliant plan."

"Show some faith, my girl, and do keep your sword in view."

"Fine. But I wager our meal and board for the night that nothing turns up."

Hieronymus smirked over the rim of his tankard. "Wager accepted."

APPENDIX: READING BLAZONS

The coats of arms herein are presented in the form of the blazon. This is a particular heraldic language used to describe a coat of arms in a succinct manner that will automatically be understood.

The arms are always described in a specific order:

1. Any divisions of the shield which exist.

2. The field is described:

    a. In the case of a solid color, the tincture of the field (capitalized, even if the color is not the first word of the blazon) is given, followed by a comma.

    b. In a complex field, such as *chequy* (that is, checkered of two colors) the pattern is described, followed by a comma.

3. The principle ordinary or charge is given, followed by in order:

    a. Its attitude (IE the pose of a bird or beast)

    b. Its tincture

  c. Parts that might be colored differently

  d. A charge may have another charge placed on it.

4. Any additional charges placed around the primary charge described as above with their positions.

5. Any additional charges *on* the principle charge, again described as in the principle charge.

A blazon is always given from the *bearer's* perspective, not the viewer's. Thus dexter refers to the part of the shield on the bearer's right (viewer's left).

On a divided shield, the divisions are described beginning at the chief, (top) from dexter to sinister, then the base (bottom) in the same fashion, much like reading a book. Thus in a quartered shield, the top row would be quarters I and II, while the bottom row is III and IV.

For example, the blazon — *Quarterly 1st and 4th Azure, on a bend Or three bears statant erect Sable Quarterly 2nd and 3rd Gules, two longswords in saltire proper in chief a gauntlet Or* — would describe the following shield:

The bearer's upper right and lower left quarters are blue, each with a gold diagonal band from (bearer's) upper right to lower left. On this band are three black bears standing on their hind legs. The bearer's upper left and lower right quarters are red with two crossed swords with points angled upwards. The swords are colored naturally (silver blades and gold hilts). Above the swords is a gold gauntlet.

There are other elements of a coat of arms, including achievements, mantling, and supporters, but these do not appear on the shield itself.

GLOSSARY

ARCHITECTURE

Corbel
A wood, stone, or metal bracket jutting out from a surface and supporting a weight. Commonly used in fortifications to extend the battlement out from the wall. The gaps between corbels were often open to create machicolations.

Crenel
The gap between merlons on a battlement.

Garderobe
A Medieval and Renaissance term for the toilet in a castle or other similar dwelling. Also by extension the bathroom itself.

Machicolation
An opening in the floor of a battlement and between corbels, allowing defenders to drop stones, hot oil, or other defensive weapons on attackers gathered at the base of the wall.

Merlon
The raised portions of a battlement.

ARMS AND ARMOR

Arming Sword — A one-handed, double-edged sword, with a blade averaging about thirty inches. The classic "knightly sword" of the Middle Ages.

Brigandine — A form of lightweight armor consisting of many small oblong metal scales riveted to the inside of a garment, typically a doublet. This outer shell can be linen, canvas, wool, leather, or even richer materials such as velvet.

Buckler — A small round shield seldom more than a foot in diameter, typically made of metal, and held using a center grip. It was often paired with an arming sword.

Kriegsmesser — An oversized messer roughly the length of a longsword, and intended to be wielded in two hands.

Longsword — A two-handed, double-edged sword with a blade generally ranging from three to three and a half feet in length. Longswords are generally well-balanced between cutting and thrusting, and are quite fast and agile swords.

Messer — A sword with a single-edged blade that can be either straight or curved. The hilt is of knife-like construction, with a handle consisting of slabs of wood sandwiching the tang and held in place by pegs or rivets, which ends in either an end cap or hat-shaped pommel. The guard is typically straight, with a distinct projection on the right side called a *Nagel* to help protect the hand.

Rondel A dagger with a long, slender blade of lenticular, diamond, or triangular cross-section ending in a fine, needle-like point designed for punching through mail or penetrating the gaps in plate armor. The grip is cylindrical, with a disk or similarly-shaped guard and round pommel. One or both edges could be sharpened. It was particularly favored by knights, and often served as a sidearm or personal defense weapon.

Short edge The edge of a sword aligned with the back of the wielder's hand. As opposed to the long edge, which aligns with the knuckles.

ARTS OF DEFENSE

Alber "Fool." A principal guard of the longsword in German fencing traditions. The hilts are held in front of the hips, with the point angled towards the ground. Either foot can lead in this ward.

Ochs "Ox." A principal guard of the longsword in German fencing traditions. The hilts are held above the left or right shoulder, with the blade pointed forward towards the opponent and angled slightly inward. The lead foot is the opposite side from the sword (thus if the sword is on the right, the left foot is leading).

Pflug   "Plough." A principal guard of the longsword in German fencing traditions. The hilts are held at either the left or right hip, with the point angled up at the opponent's face. The lead foot is the opposite side from the sword (thus if the sword is on the right, the left foot is leading).

Vom Tag   "From the Day." A principal guard of the longsword in German fencing traditions, held either with the sword above the head, or with the hilts just below the left or right shoulder. The blade is held point-upward and angled back slightly. It is typically assumed with the sword on the fighter's strongest side, with the opposite foot leading (thus a right-handed fencer leads with his left foot, and the sword is held at his right shoulder).

CARDS AND GAMES

Devil   In the game of Karnöffel, the Seven card of the current trump suit for that hand. It beats everything but a Karnöffel but *only* if it leads the trick. Otherwise it is valued as a seven and has no other power. It cannot be played on the first trick of a hand.

Kaiser — In the game of Karnöffel, the Two card of the current trump suit for that hand. It beats all cards except a Karnöffel, Devil, or Pope.

Karnöffel — A form of trick-taking card game, notable for assigning unusual ranks to certain cards. Also in said game, the Unter of the current trump suit for that hand. It beats all other cards.

Ober — A playing card in German and Swiss decks. It is a face card corresponding to a Queen in the French deck.

Pope — In the game of Karnöffel, the Six of the current trump suit for that hand. It beats all cards except a Karnöffel and Devil.

Unter (Card) — A playing card in German and Swiss decks. It is a face card corresponding to a Jack in the French deck.

HERALDRY

Argent — One of the two recognized metals, either silver or white.

Azure — One of the five recognized tinctures, referring to blue.

Bend — An ordinary in the form of a diagonal line, from upper dexter (bearer's upper right) to lower sinister (bearer's lower left). A bend sinister is a diagonal line in the opposite direction (from bearer's upper left to lower right). In addition to an ordinary, multiple objects can be placed diagonally, described as "in bend." A charge described as "bendwise" is rotated to follow that angle. A bend can also describe a diagonal division of the shield, "per bend."

Chief   Referring generally to the top portion of the shield. A chief is also an ordinary across the top of the shield. A charge can also itself be placed "in chief," meaning that it is placed towards the top of the shield, rather than in the center.

Erased   When part of a charge is removed and the remainder is left with a jagged edge. Most commonly seen with heads or other body parts.

Erect   An animal depicted standing upright.

Escutcheon   Either the shield on which a coat of arms is painted, or a separate charge within the coat of arms. When used as a charge, the Escutcheon may have its own blazon.

Fess   An ordinary in the form of a horizontal band running across the shield. In addition to an ordinary, multiple objects can be positioned "in fess," meaning lined up across the shield. A fess can also be a line of division; "per fess" would mean the shield is divided in two along a horizontal line.

Gules One of the five recognized tinctures, referring to red.

Or One of the two recognized metals, referring to gold.

Ordinary A simple charge or device, generally in the form of a line, bar, cross, or other simple geometric pattern. An ordinary is considered a primary charge, and can have another charge placed on it, for example "on a fess."

Proper Indicating that the referenced object is in its "correct" or "natural" colors, as opposed to using conventional heraldic colors. Proper colors for many objects are officially defined in heraldic tradition. IE *a sword proper* always has an *argent* blade and *or* hilt.

Quarterly A shield divided into quarters. Each quarter is numbered 1st through 4th from dexter to sinister, and then chief to base. Each quarter of the shield can have its own blazon.

Rampant An animal (typically a predator, such as a lion) charge standing erect, with its forelimbs raised. Depending on the locality, it may stand on either both hind limbs, or on one with the other raised to strike.

Sable	One of the five recognized tinctures, referring to black.
Saltire	An ordinary in the form of a St. Andrew's cross. Two objects can also be described as "in saltire," meaning diagonally crossed (IE, *two rods in saltire*).
Statant	An animal charge standing with all four limbs on the ground.
Segreant	Similar to rampant, but reserved for winged quadrupeds. In this pose, the wings are always addorsed (spread open behind the animal. On the right wing only the top is visible) and elevated (wingtips angled upwards).

HORSES

Affrus	A roughly-bred and inexpensive type of draught horse used for harrowing or ploughing fields. Shorter than the typical cart-horse.
Courser	A light, strong, and swift warhorse. Though not as heavy, powerful, or expensive as the destrier, the courser was faster, and thus favored for the rigors of hard battle.
Jennet	A small, compact, and well-muscled riding horse of good disposition, noted for its

ambling gait. It is smaller and frequently less expensive than the palfrey. The modern Spanish Jennet is very similar in appearance and gait, though the historical jennet was not a specific breed.

Palfrey   A highly-valued riding horse with an ambling gait, that is larger than the jennet. It was popular both for general riding, as well as hunting and ceremonial use, and was particularly popular among the nobility. A well-bred palfrey could be just as expensive as a knight's destrier.

TITLES AND RANKS

Armarius   The director of a monastic scriptorium, who provided scribes with their materials. He also served as a librarian of sorts, and could deny access to particular books.

Freiherr   A German noble title, equivalent to the English Baron. Often used interchangeably, though Baron is less formal.

Gnädige Frau   A German honorific, meaning "Gracious Lady." Archaic and seldom used in modern German, but formerly used to address a woman when her name was not known, or not used.

Prior   One of three ecclesiastical positions. A Claustral prior is a superior of an abbey, and is the most senior officer below the abbot or abbess, and assists them with administration of the abbey. A Conventual prior is the head of an independent monastery that is not a full abbey. An Obedientiary prior is the superior of a satellite monastery of an abbey.

WEIGHTS AND MEASURES

Pfennig
A silver German coin roughly equivalent in value to a penny (about 1/240 of a pound).

Span
A unit of measure defined as the distance between the tips of the outstretched thumb and little finger. It equates roughly to nine inches.

OTHER

Nunnery
Ironic slang for a brothel.

Pattens
Raised wooden soles attached to shoes, often by lacing or straps, to lift the wearer out of the mud and protect the softer, thinner soles of the shoe itself while traveling.

Small beer
Beer with little or no alcohol, often drank with meals in place of water. *Why* it was drunk in place of water is the subject of myth and debate, ranging from providing extra calories for field workers, to being

safer to drink than water in pre-industrial societies because of the brewing process.

Town Privilege   Privileges granted to a town such as a degree of self-governance, trading rights, and the right to establish guilds. The exact rights could vary from town to town, and be either temporary or permanent.

ABOUT THE AUTHOR

D. E. Wyatt was born and lives in St. Louis, Missouri. When not writing he is an occasional gamer, a student of German swordsmanship, a saxophonist, and works in IT.

www.ingramcontent.com/pod-product-compliance
Lightning Source LLC
Chambersburg PA
CBHW030835110726
47900CB00006B/1892